THE RECKLESS

Also by David Putnam

The Innocents
The Vanquished
The Squandered
The Replacements
The Disposables

THE RECKLESS

A BRUNO JOHNSON NOVEL

DAVID PUTNAM

OCEANVIEW PUBLISHING
SARASOTA, FLORIDA

ISBN 978-1-60809-288-8

Cover Design by Christian Fuenfhausen

Published in the United States of America by Oceanview Publishing

Sarasota, Florida

www.oceanviewpub.com

10 9 8 7 6 5 4 3 2 1

PRINTED IN THE UNITED STATES OF AMERICA

This one's for my favorite brother, Van,
the bravest cop I know.

THE RECKLESS

CHAPTER ONE

SUMMER

I SAT ON the couch holding my four-year-old daughter, Olivia. As I often did, I caught myself staring at her, marveling at her beauty, her innocence, and her utter vulnerability. I held a love for her so pure that it rose in my chest and caused a little ache. She brought her perfect tiny hand up and playfully shoved my cheek. "Come on, Pop Pop, be ungry. Be ungry."

I closed my eyes: the start of the game. She squirmed in my arms trying to get me to put her down on the floor so she could flee the now sleeping beast.

"Oh no. Oh no. Let me go."

I set her down as she shrieked. Her legs pumped in the air. She took off as soon as her feet hit the carpet. I gave chase. She ran around and around the living room. I stopped. She waited, her eyes wide with excitement. I raised my hands as claws. She bent over, tucking her elbows into her tummy, and shrieked again.

In a much different, deeper voice, I said, "Suddenly, I'm feeling kinda hungry."

She screamed and ran for cover. She didn't make it. I scooped her up, swung her around once, and gently tossed her on the couch. She tried to back up, but I grabbed her leg and held her in place. "No. No monster."

I slowly moved up the sleeve of her arm. I moved quickly, put my mouth there, and blew, my lips blubbering against her skin. She laughed so hard she lost her voice.

Dad came in the room dressed in his US postal uniform. "Son, I wanted to tell you something last night, but you came home too late."

I stopped terrorizing my daughter and looked up. She patted my face. "Come on, monster, you're still ungry. Come on, monster?"

"Just a minute, baby girl. I know. I'm sorry, Dad. We were on a surveillance, and the target came home right as we were about to call it a night."

"Did you get him?"

A glimpse of last night's violence flashed before me. The open eyes of the man wanted for murder lying in the street, staring at nothing—no breath, no heartbeat, a trickle of blood at the corner of his mouth. The damaged grill of our car, inches away, steam and water hissing out as if the radiator were angry.

"What did you want to tell me?"

He knew I didn't like to bring my work home. I worked on a violent crimes team. Describing what happened, saying the words inside my home, my safe zone, would somehow corrupt what I held most dear. And last night hadn't gone well. We had to take the guy down hard—what Robby Wicks would call, "Blood and bone."

Dad held up his hand and waved. "That's okay, never mind. I forgot the rule."

I got up. "No, Dad, it's not that. It's—"

"No, Son, you're absolutely right. I . . . I just forgot."

The doorbell interrupted. I stepped over to the door. "That'll be Mrs. Espinoza." She watched Olivia on days Dad and I both worked.

"Son, wait?"

I opened the door and took a step back, startled.

"Ned? What the . . . What the hell? What are you doing here?"

Ned Kiefer stood on my porch holding a small child.

I hadn't seen Ned for years, not since the night I left him in St. Francis Hospital, beat to hell from the encounter with Willis Simpkins.

My mouth sagged open all on its own.

Ned stepped in. "Hey, Bruno, you're gonna catch a lot of flies with that mouth."

"Ned, geez it's good to see you. I mean geez . . ." I hugged him as best I could with the little blond girl in his arm. "What are you doing here?"

"That's what I was tryin' to tell you, Son. Ned came by last night and asked if he could use Mrs. Espinoza for a few days until he got settled with a new sitter. I told him you wouldn't mind."

Ned moved deeper into the living room where Olivia stood watching, entranced with the little blond girl. Ned said, "Hi there, Olivia, remember me from yesterday? This is Beth. I told you all about her and here she is." He set Beth down. The two children looked at each other. Olivia raised a hand to touch her, as if she didn't believe Beth was real.

Beth looked exactly opposite of Olivia, with light skin, blond hair, and hazel eyes.

Olivia took after me with dark skin and brown eyes, though not near as dark as me.

Olivia was half-black, half-Caucasian. Her mother, the woman I thought I was going to spend the rest of my life with, ran off without saying a word. She'd been my partner on patrol. That particular night came at us hard and heavy, bloody even for a hot summer night in the ghetto. *Blood and bone.* She'd resigned without a word to me, and I didn't see her again until seven months later when she knocked on my apartment door and handed me Olivia. She said, "I can't handle raising a girl in this kind of world." I hadn't seen her since. That was almost four years ago. Dad and I had been raising Olivia, loving every precious minute of it.

Ned straightened up and looked at me.

"So, you have a kid?" I said.

"Yep, and they're almost the same age."

"You and . . . a—"

"Hannah, that's right."

I was glad he'd said Hannah's name and I didn't have to. Although, I couldn't see how he could've gone back to her. Not after that night several years ago when he and I caught her with another man at an apartment in South Gate.

I moved over and shook his hand. "Congratulations, pal."

"You, too."

I said, "I guess we kind of lost track of each other."

"Yeah, I caught that midnight transfer to Lakewood station after South Gate PD ratted me out to the captain."

Back then, I'd called Ned after his abrupt departure and left messages. When he didn't answer them, I went to Lakewood station and hung around waiting to see him. He'd managed to dodge my every effort. I sort of understood what he was going through: guilt over breaking up our partnership and ultimately our friendship with his bonehead choices. When we found his wife, Hannah, with JB, Ned went a little berserk. At the time, JB was a deputy with us at Lynwood station, and a friend of Ned's, which made it all the more hurtful. The number one rule in law enforcement was that you didn't cuckhold your brother in arms.

He dodged my every effort back then to reconnect. Even though I understood it, I still felt a little angry to have been cast aside that easily. We'd been close friends, and friends didn't cut you adrift like that.

And here he stood, years later, as if nothing had happened.

CHAPTER TWO

WE WALKED OUT to our cars, parked at the curb in front of the house. Ned kept looking at me in a strange way. I stopped. "Okay, what's the matter?"

"What?"

"You're looking at me like I got leprosy and my nose is about to fall off."

"It's just that . . . no, never mind."

"Tell me."

"You, ah . . . look different, and I . . . can't figure out what it is."

I hadn't said anything to him, but Ned had aged ten years, with more wrinkles at the corners of his eyes and across his forehead. He'd also lost a small part of his youthful exuberance. Even so, Ned's eyes still held that mischievousness that reminded me so much of our old friendship.

Ned snapped his fingers. "I know what it is. You're all grown up."

I shook my head. "Thanks, partner."

"No, no. You look more confident now, more like Andy Taylor, the sheriff of Mayberry. Confident, assured, in charge."

"Again, thank you for that. I have to get to work." I got in my Ford Ranger pickup. Ned followed along and stood at the window. He said, "So I guess I'll see you tonight when I pick up Beth." He shot me that old Ned smile.

I couldn't help it—I still liked the hell outta him. "Maybe, but I don't know. I'm working the violent crimes team now, and my schedule is really crazy."

"Yeah, I heard that. How do you like working for the infamous Robby Wicks? Is he really as ruthless and quick on the trigger as everyone says he is?"

I didn't like that description, nor what people thought of Wicks, though I could easily see how they might think that way. Wicks did nothing to disassociate his image with the perception that he'd just as soon shoot you as handcuff you.

I started the truck. "Good and bad," I said. "There's always the good and the bad no matter where you work. Wicks is great to work for. Best job in the department."

"That's great," Ned said. "All you can do is hope that there's more good than bad, right, partner?"

"That's right," I said. "So maybe I'll see you tonight. Maybe we can go to dinner and catch up."

"Yeah, I'd like that."

I pulled away. I didn't want to ask him anything about his job. I'd heard the rumors that traveled around the department just like everyone did. Ned had finally worked his way out of his hole from patrol at Lakewood station and got promoted to detective on a street narco team, his life's dream. He made it a full year before he pissed off the team sergeant, and got bounced to the narco desk at headquarters. A real pogue's job, he answered the phone and handed out case file numbers to the narcs in the field doing real police work. I knew Ned. That job had to be dampening his soul from the inside out. Snuffing out his flame. If he stayed on the desk too long, he'd be broken, with no way to come back.

I stopped at the dry cleaners and picked up two sets of uniforms I kept on hand in my truck just in case. Next door to the cleaners, I grabbed a cup of coffee and an apple fritter. I got back in the truck and headed for work. The first bite of the fritter brought on a smile. Ned always ate snowball cupcakes, pink marshmallow-and-coconut-covered devil's food cake. He washed them down with a Yoo-hoo chocolate drink.

I'd been rude to him, by flaunting my assignment to the violent crimes team. I hadn't meant anything by it, but now it sounded elitist, especially given his desk job at narco.

* * *

Six months after the violent crimes team started up, Wicks called in a favor, and the team moved from Lennox station to an abandoned grocery store in Downey, one next to the Donut Dolly donut shop and a check-cashing place run by an ex-cop.

Wicks didn't come right out and say it, but the team had to move away from the Lennox sheriff's station because of me. In one of my first investigations as a detective on violent crimes, I went under-cover into the Lynwood narco team to ferret out a group of dirty cops—deputies taking money for contract killings. At the end of the investigation, I shot the leader, a fellow deputy sheriff whom I'd grown to like and, in a skewed kind of way, respected a great deal. My bullet took him in the stomach, in the parking lot, at the back of the station. As a deputy, the violent act against a brother is some-thing you didn't easily come back from, an act that forever tarnishes your reputation, your soul. A kind of stigma that follows you like a dog's tail infested with mange, making you never want to look back.

Wicks and the higher-up brass thought an off-site location would be better, easier to stay off the radar. Some of my peers didn't under-stand what had happened and blamed me. The guy I'd shot had been popular with the deputies. Now he was doing twenty-five to life in a wheelchair, in Chuckwalla state prison, a prison located in the butthole of California. The saying went that if California ever needed an enema, they'd shove it in Chuckwalla.

* * *

I parked next to the China Gate in the same strip center, a restaurant not yet open for the day. I opened the door to our office. Eight desks, all with phones, sat in an island amid a vast unimproved slab of concrete floor. The place echoed every little sound. Seven men turned to look when I came in—Wicks had yet to allow a woman on the team. I checked my watch. I wasn't late. I had five minutes left.

Up front, Wicks stood next to the group of six men clustered in chairs. Ned Kiefer turned around, smiled, and said, "Hey, Bruno, thanks for showin' up."

Everyone laughed.

Ned? Here?

What the hell was going on? He'd said nothing at my house when he dropped off his daughter, Beth. He'd not said anything on purpose, just to see the look on my face when I entered the office.

I wandered in, stunned at this sudden change of events. As I got closer, another deputy stood. It took a long moment for me to recognize him in street clothes: Levi's, a short-sleeve print shirt, and work boots. Sergeant Coffman.

He was an ex-Marine who'd fought on Iwo Jima. He still kept his gray hair high and tight like in the Corps. And when he wore his uniform, he kept it pressed and clean, his black shoes polished to a high sheen. The whole package made him look like a World War II drill sergeant caught in a time warp. An absolute cliché, but he couldn't be more genuine. He'd never retire. They'd have to take him out in a box. The guy looked around fiftyish, when he had to be in his sixties.

I smiled and stuck out my hand. "Well, I'll be damned."

The taciturn Coffman's smile changed the whole concept of his wooden expression. He came toward me and offered his hand. "Good to see you, Bruno."

We shook, his hand strong as ever. "Are you two really on our team now?"

"That's right," Coffman said. "Just transferred in. Today's our first day. Me and Ned both."

I couldn't help but remember the last night I'd seen Coffman in the ER of St. Francis, hollowed out, shell-shocked, and asking how many men we'd lost in a long-ago battle from World War II.

"Now that we're done with old home week," Wicks said, "you mind if I get back to the day's briefing?"

"Sorry, Lieutenant." I took my seat.

"As I was saying before Johnson interrupted, we have been asked to assist the FBI in solving one of their little problems. The FBI has heard about the effectiveness of our team and decided they need our help."

Johnny Gibbs, one of the original members of the violent crimes team, let out a low groan, and said under his breath, "Not those assholes."

No one liked the FBI.

"That's right, Gibbs," Wicks said. "Those assholes. This is a chance for some real good PR. Something we need."

Gibbs said, "Aren't we supposed to come up on Frank Duarte today? He's wanted for three murders, in three different cities. Now that's a threat to public safety if you ask me. I think the FBI can wait."

I watched Ned watch the exchange. He kept his mouth shut. This must be the new and improved Ned. That, or he wanted to bide his time, see where the cards fell, before he interjected what he really thought.

"With our two new transfers, we have enough to do both," Wicks said. "Gibbs, Johnson, Kiefer, and Sergeant Coffman will now be an independent team. Coffman will be the supervisor. The rest of you will stay with me, and we'll go up on Duarte within the hour. Questions?"

I liked Coffman and Ned but still couldn't help feeling that the boss had cast me aside. I wanted to be on the manhunt for Duarte, not babysitting the FBI.

Wicks said, "My team, you're dismissed. Get started on the work-up for Duarte. Call all the involved agencies and get their reports. Coffman's team, stay here a minute."

The others got up and left.

Wicks said, "Bruno, don't give me that hangdog look. This is a good gig I'm tossing you. You wait and see, you're going to be eating this up with a spoon." He stepped over to Coffman and handed him a piece of paper. "Report to this address in one hour, and don't be late."

"Yes, sir."

"It's downtown Los Angeles. That's the office of the district US Marshal. You four are going to be cross-sworn as deputy US Marshals."

I couldn't help it; I smiled.

CHAPTER THREE

COFFMAN PUT THE old team back together, making Ned my partner. We rode in silence, shaggin' ass for downtown Los Angeles. I drove, weaving in and out. I didn't think we could make it in an hour, with morning traffic. I lost Coffman minutes out of our parking lot. He and Gibbs could find their own way.

I kept my eyes on the road. "You going to tell me how this happened? How you two got transferred into the team?"

What I really wanted to know was how come I hadn't known ahead of time.

"If I didn't know better, partner," Ned said, "I'd think you were a little irritated."

"What? No. Not at all. I didn't mean to come off that way . . . Well, you could've told me this morning at the house."

"Yeah, I guess that was a little mean. But you should've seen the look on your face when you saw me and ol' Coffman sittin' there in your office."

I stole a second and looked over at him. "I thought they were trying to force Coffman out, make him take his retirement. That's why they sent him back to work Men's Central Jail."

"Exactly. You believe they pay back all his loyalty and years of dedication like that? Bunch a bullshit."

"Ned—"

I looked at the road, dodging more cars for better position in the other lane as we headed straight up Alameda Avenue. I almost told him about what I'd seen happen at St. Francis hospital over three years ago. Coffman had been old then *and* slightly demented. Now, years later, he's older, but is he more demented? Was he more of a hazard out in the field, in a high-profile job with a constant threat of violent confrontations? If he refused to retire, wasn't he better off in a controlled environment, like in MCJ?

"What?" Ned asked.

"Coffman's got to be pushing, what, sixty-six or sixty-eight this year? Don't you think—"

"Ah man, not you, too. Don't you worry about Coffman. I'd put him up against the best sergeants in the department. You wait and see—when the shit goes down, Coffman will be there, covering your back. In fact, he'll be climbing over us to get in the action. Loyalty, trust, and honor go a long way, and he's got it all in spades. He was a Marine on Iwo, man, for crying out loud."

I let it drop. I trusted Wicks. If he thought Coffman capable, I'd go along with his decision. "What happened with you? How'd you get on the team?"

"I didn't do anything. I was just minding my own business."

"Yeah, right. And?"

"Okay. A few weeks back, Wicks came into narco headquarters for a meeting and saw me working the desk. He said hi and then asked how long I'd been working the desk. I told him about a year. And that was it. That's all he said. I didn't even have a request in for his team. Next thing I know, I'm transferred. Believe me, I cannot be more surprised, or happier."

"That's great. It really is. I'm glad to have you back as a partner."

"Me, too."

"Did you meet Wicks before, when you worked the field?"

"Yeah, I did. I was working Lakewood in a traffic car. Of all things, me working TCs and handing out citations. One of the guys on Wicks' team, Gibbs, he was in there this morning. He came off the freeway in a marked patrol unit. He exited way too fast, came off faster than the terminal velocity of the curve, hit the guardrail and tore up the whole left side of his car. They were working a surveillance, looking for some guy wanted for a bombing of a synagogue, or some shit like that. And Gibbs drove the patrol car in case the team needed the suspect's car stopped, or if he ran."

"I remember that night," I said. "I wondered why Wicks and Gibbs fell out of the surveillance. We ended up losing the guy, and Wicks was really pissed about it. Gibbs isn't known for his driving skills, but he's a good man to have beside you when it goes to knuckles."

"Right, right. So that night I caught the call to take the paper on the crash. Wicks was there. He said this was Gibbs' sixth crash and, if reported, Gibbs would be bounced from the team. I told him that was too bad, because the damage wasn't as bad as it looked, and it would only take about four hours to fix. All you needed to do was pull the two quarter panels and the two doors, and replace them. Simple. You should've seen Wicks' eyes light up." Ned shook his head and smiled as he remembered the incident. "He asked me if I was an auto-body man. I told him, sure, I could do it. He tells me not to draw a case number for the crash. Told me not to do a damn thing until he got back. He went to a pay phone and came back a few minutes later. He cleared it with my watch commander, who he knew, and we drove the damaged unit to a tow yard where he also knew a guy, and I fixed it. Took a lot longer than I thought. I had to primer the used replacement doors before I repainted them. At the end of the night, the car actually looked better than when they checked it out. Wicks said he owed me."

I nodded. "Wicks always pays his debts."

"Bruno, that desk job was eating me up, tearing my heart out. Wicks saved my life. I owe him big."

"Yeah, that's the other thing he does. Everyone on the team will walk through fire for him."

"You know I will, with him on my back if he asks me to."

"Like I said, good to have you in the car again, partner."

CHAPTER FOUR

WE DROVE FOR a few more minutes. Ned said, "You ever catch that asshole Darkman?"

I looked over at him. "Who?"

Ned smiled. "Come on, man, you gotta know that's what they call him?"

"No, who're you talking about?" But I knew. And no, I'd never come close to catching him. I didn't even know his real name.

"You know, that family killer from the back alley, the night we entered ol' Willis Simpkins inta the Disney on Parade competition."

Ned had aired the words I didn't want to hear. The anger from my inability to bring down the Darkman—years of pent-up anger and guilt continued to fester, creating a grim monster of regret. I couldn't find him and knew I could if I only had a name to work with. I'd only seen his face for a brief moment that night all those years ago when he came out from behind the death house and into the alley. But I'd never forget those eyes, the mask of hate, how he looked at me. There was no doubt in my mind he'd been the one to shoot that family.

Ned said, "Yeah, guys around the department call him the Darkman because of the way you describe him: the long dark raincoat, the black night watchman's beanie, the dark alley. I can't believe you haven't heard that nickname. At least the whispers about how, whenever you get the chance, you go back out and shake the trees for the guy when you don't even know his name."

"No, I haven't heard anyone sayin' shit about it."

"I'm sure it's because everyone walks on eggshells around you when it comes to that little topic. You've been known to bite a head off here and there over it."

I didn't argue with him.

"Good thing you or the Compton coppers never did find out the name. I wouldn't want to be accused of being the shooter on that one."

"Why's that?"

"'Cause that dead woman was Joey Lugo's sister."

"Joey Lugo, as in Scab?"

"That's right."

"I never heard that. Are you sure? Compton didn't say anything. The victim, the woman's last name along with the two boys, was Humphreys."

"That's right, different last names, different fathers, same mother. And Compton PD ain't exactly burning down the world with their clearance rates."

"How do you know all of this?"

"I worked narco, remember? Scab had word on the street, on the down low that he'd pay a hundred K to anyone who gave him the shooter of his sister. Sorry, I thought you knew."

"I didn't—not that it would make a difference." I tried to think if contacting Lugo now would make a difference. But if he couldn't find a name—

Ned said, "You know, Lugo probably did find out who capped his sister and made the guy disappear. That's why you couldn't find the Darkman—'cause he no longer exists."

"Huh."

"Hey, you ever get Scab in your sights, don't hesitate to drop the hammer on that scumbag. He's responsible for untold mayhem in the streets—drive-byes, South American neckties, you name it. You'd be doing this world a great favor if you take him out. I was looking to take him down when they transferred me to the desk. Hey. Did you hear what I just said?"

"Huh? Oh, yeah, yeah, I got it."

Neither of us spoke again the rest of the way.

We made it in time to be sworn in by the US Marshal. Coffman and Gibbs rolled in fifteen minutes late, Coffman a little tweaked at how slow Gibbs drove. Once Wicks jumped your ass over a deficiency, you didn't let it happen again.

We followed Gibbs and Coffman over to the FBI office in Riverside to meet our partners in this new assignment.

But the FBI would never look at us as partners. If you weren't FBI, you weren't shit—their age-old doctrine. I'd learned that the hard way.

The drive took an hour. We weren't going to be assigned out of the LA office but out of what they considered their rural office.

The commercial building rose up taller than any other building in the area. The blue glass and steel reflected the sun and made the building look uncomfortably warm. Eleven o'clock, and the mercury already broke ninety degrees, a sign summer would continue with its unrelenting heat in this second year of severe drought.

We took the elevator up to the top. The FBI occupied all of the eighth floor. The doors opened to a small waiting area, empty of any humans. A large plaster cast of the FBI emblem adorned the all-blue wall on the right. Twenty Wanted posters covered the left wall: the LA FBI office's ten most wanted, and the national ten as well. The receptionist, a woman with gray hair streaked with black and without a sense of humor, sat behind thick Plexiglas that made her office a bulletproof bunker. She wore a nameplate on her subdued dark tan and beige dress that said, "Wilson."

Coffman took the lead, walked over, and pushed the intercom button. "LA County sheriff's deputies here to see the RAC—the resident agent in charge."

"Yes, you are expected. Have a seat, and he'll be right with you."

Ned said in a harsh whisper, "If we're expected, then why the hell are we waiting?"

Coffman stood at parade rest. I watched him closely trying to see signs of cracks. The memory of the last time I'd seen him was still all too fresh in my mind.

*   *   *

The night four years earlier when Willis Simpkins picked Ned up and threw him into a yard car—we'd ended up at St. Francis hospital getting Ned's ribs checked. The patrol shift had been over for three hours or better, and I stood in the ER, waiting for Ned to get back from X-ray. The ER doors whooshed open. In walked Sergeant Coffman.

He still wore his spit-shined boots and green uniform pants, but no shirt. He wore a white strap t-shirt that exposed his shoulders and arms. His tan skin obscured fading tattoos from his long-ago Marine Corps days.

He moved slow and deliberate as if drugged. His eyes glazed over, unable to focus on any one object. He looked shell-shocked and hollowed out.

I hurried over to him. "Sarge, what's going on? Why are you here?"

He grabbed my arm in a vice-like grip, his eyes going a little wild. "How many did we lose?"

"What?"

"How many men did we lose to those little yellow bastards?"

I whispered, to no one, "Ah shit."

* * *

Nobody sat. We stood there like four animals in a zoo enclosure staring through the Plexiglas at Wilson the lion tamer.

We waited. She ignored us and typed on.

And we waited some more.

Twenty-one minutes passed before the all-steel door masquerading as wood opened. A diminutive man in a brown suit, white shirt, and narrow tie smiled and held the door for us. "Come, come. Sorry to keep you waiting. I was on a conference call with DC. My name is Joshua Whitney, Special Agent in Charge of this office." He offered up his hand.

I went by him first and shook. I smelled heavy cologne, something dated like Old Spice. His hand came away a little dry and chalky. He stood a bit shorter, and under his thinning hair, eczema in the shape of Cuba snaked across his scalp, red with white flakes.

Once the door closed, he moved ahead of us. "This way, please."

Conference call to DC, my achin' ass. He was probably cleaning under his nails and giving them a final buff while he let us stew in his lobby.

He led the way into his expansive, wood-paneled office, with a floor-to-ceiling view of the mountains to the north. I crossed the threshold from the hall into the office and saw Chelsea Miller standing off to the right.

Her jaw dropped in shock.

She hadn't expected to see me, either.

CHAPTER FIVE

FOR THE LAST several years, I'd tried to forget Chelsea. I'd fallen hard for her, and her for me. At least that's what I'd thought at the time. Dad said, "That's a woman's main job, to stamp out one fool after another, like the Federal Reserve stamping out dimes. They make a sport out of it." He didn't say it out of anger. He said it to make his emotionally ailing son feel better. He'd liked Chelsea, too.

The way we'd met, the FBI and the Sheriff's Department's upper brass had also slid Chelsea in as an undercover to the Lynwood narco team to ferret out the same deputies I'd been assigned to take down. Only they'd never let me in on their little secret. I believed her cover story that she was a sheriff's deputy, transferred from public relations.

In the end, I screwed up big. I violated the cardinal rule of under-cover, and told another deputy, a sergeant, that I was undercover. That sergeant, whom I trusted implicitly, turned out to be one of the bad ones I was sent in to hunt down. I would've been killed had Chelsea not broken her cover to save my sorry ass. She drove a car through a wall to get to me and shot to death that same sergeant I'd trusted. A black letter day for sure.

The FBI didn't like their agents driving cars through walls, breaking cover without permission, and shooting sheriff sergeants.

It was bad publicity. They rolled her up and banished her to the rural office in North Dakota, investigating tribal crimes, drunks, and domestics on the Indian reservation: the absolute bottom of the barrel, a career killer. That's what she'd told me. She told me she'd never work her way out of a hole that deep.

And there she stood in the Riverside FBI office, looking more beautiful than ever. Her brown hair longer now, almost to her shoulders—a good look on her. But her brown eyes remained just as luscious and alive with excitement.

At that moment I needed to see her smile. The wattage from her smile could power the city of Los Angeles with enough left over to warm my heart.

Her shocked expression shifted. And she did it; she smiled. Her eyes confirming, she genuinely enjoyed seeing me. She came over, hand extended. She'd made the move first to let me know: no hugs or pecks on the cheek allowed. Not in the office, not in front of her supervisor.

Peck on the cheek—hell, I wanted to take her in my arms, dip her, and kiss her right on into the other side of forever.

"Deputy Johnson, so good to see you," she said.

I took her hand, cool and strong, my eyes locked on hers. "Deputy Johnson?" I said it as a question to tease her, to put her on the grill for one long interminable moment.

She shook her head, the movement barely perceptible.

I let her off the hook. "I'm sorry, have we met? Oh, that's right, that's right, I think we worked a fugitive case a few years back."

She let out a breath. "Yes, I think so. That must be it."

After that black letter day four years ago, for two glorious weeks, she'd moved in with me at Dad's house, while I recuperated from injuries sustained in taking Blue and his crew down. We hadn't slept much and stayed in bed naked for hours on end. Sometimes until Dad pounded on the door, yelled that I had to watch Olivia so he could go to work.

Then, at the end of those wondrous two weeks, and without any notice, she just up and moved to North Dakota, to the new assignment. She wouldn't take any calls and sent me a long and lovely "Dear Bruno" letter explaining how it just wouldn't work out between us. She wished me a happy life. Stamped out a newly minted dime.

On long, lonely nights I still took out her letter and read it. Pathetic, that I couldn't get over the woman, after how she'd treated me, the way she'd made it painfully clear, with no room for interpretation, that we were through.

And now she stood there, my hand in hers for the briefest of moments, as we shook.

Her simple touch set off a whole slew of hot, moist, breathless memories of being wrapped in damp sheets.

She let go, put her hand behind her back, and retreated two steps to stand beside her boss, Whitney.

Ned moved closer to me, leaned up, and whispered, "Va va voom, partner. Va . . . va . . . voom."

I elbowed him. He grunted and stepped away.

Whitney moved behind his huge desk, which only served to make him appear smaller. He remained standing and put both hands flat on his blotter. "Special Agent Miller, would you please brief these gentlemen?"

"Certainly, sir." Chelsea stepped over to a large map behind us on the wall, one that I'd missed when I came in. The map depicted Southern California, from Santa Barbara, south to San Diego. The cities bristled with a couple of thousand blue and red pushpins. She kept her hands behind her back when she spoke. "In Southern California, bank robbery has reached epidemic proportions.

Twenty-four hundred a year, for the last two years, with no sign of letup. This year we are on track to beat even that number."

Coffman took several steps closer for a better look. "You have got to be shittin' me."

"No, sir." Chelsea said. "Those are the numbers. We have over fifteen Special Agents working on the problem full-time, and we haven't even scratched the surface. Right now, all we can do is chase our tails, shuffling paperwork."

"Agent Miller."

Chelsea always told it like it was, never pulled punches.

She looked at Whitney. "Yes, sir. Sorry, sir." She turned back to us. "Your agency has offered to lend a hand."

I wanted to throttle the little puke for treating her that way.

Ned couldn't hold it in any longer, and said, "Four deputies divided by twenty-four hundred—that's quite a caseload even for us. But don't worry, we can handle it." He smiled and looked around to see if anyone would laugh. "One riot, one deputy." An old adage Ned had stolen from the Texas Rangers.

Everyone looked back at Chelsea.

"Ah, no," she said. "You are going to come up on some of these criminals, and take them down, in progress, in high-profile, newsworthy events. We hope this will have a deterrent effect."

Coffman shook his head. "Not a chance in hell."

Whitney, from behind his desk, said, "Excuse me?"

Coffman took a step toward him. "No offense, but you're trying to put your values onto these mutts. It's not like that. These criminals do not fear the system; they thrive in it. They don't care if they go to prison. Prison, for them, is like earning a merit badge. No, I think you're wrong in your thinking here."

"So, you're saying you don't want to participate in operation Burnt Eagle?"

"Not at all. This will be a real kick in the ass, chasin' these guys. I wouldn't miss it. I just don't think it'll have the overall desired effect you're hoping for. In fact, I know it won't. But we are here to do whatever you ask and do it to the best of our abilities. You want bank robbers taken down and mounted on the wall, no problem. Just turn us loose and stand back."

Whitney turned to Chelsea for her reaction.

Had I not witnessed Coffman's meltdown that night at St. Francis, I would have thought his comment nothing more than LA County Sheriff braggadocio. Now I wasn't so sure that after we took down the first bank robber, he wouldn't go looking for a good taxidermist.

CHAPTER SIX

WHITNEY CHECKED HIS watch. "Special Agent Miller, I have a call coming in with the LA office SAC. Would you escort these gentlemen to the bullpen investigative office and give them their first case assignment and caseload?"

"Yes, sir. This way."

Ned turned away from Whitney's desk, tilted his head back and forth, silently moving his lips mocking what Whitney had just said. I elbowed him again as we followed Chelsea to the door.

He whispered, "Hey, cut it out. You're not buying into all this pomp and circumstance, are you?" Then he spoke through his nose. "Excuse me, sir, might I place these lovely handcuffs on your wrists? Please? I said please."

I shook my head, trying to get him to shut up. I didn't want to engage him within hearing range of Chelsea or to let him continue to make an ass of himself. I slipped ahead so there'd be no one there to talk to, but he caught up and whispered, "Burnt Eagle? Are you friggin' kiddin' me? They gotta put a name to it, really? We're gonna be chasin' bank robbers, right? Not tossin' Molotov cocktails at low-flyin' eagles."

We moved down a long hall with multiple doors and little signs, chest height, on the wall next to them: white collar, political corruption unit, domestic terrorist unit, and many more with acronyms I'd never seen or heard of before.

Coffman walked side by side with Chelsea talking quietly with her—a place I wanted to be, and at the same time didn't.

We came to a door at the end of the hall. Next to it, the narrow blue nameplate simply read: *Robbery*. Chelsea punched in a code and entered. We followed. This room contained at least twenty desks, all out in the open, all with men and women dressed in business attire sitting behind their desks writing or talking on the phone.

Ned poked me in the back. "No wonder they got a problem. These birds aren't gonna catch any burnt eagles sitting on their asses in the office."

I waved an arm behind me. "Knock it off."

Coffman heard me, not Ned. "Bruno, you want to act like an adult, or do you want to wait outside?"

I didn't answer him.

Chelsea never slowed as she moved down the aisle of desks to an empty one with the title "Team Leader" on a plaque. "Okay, here's the deal," she said, turning to face us. "I'll be your liaison for this operation. We have signed an MOU—a memorandum of understanding—with your department and have made arrangements to pick up all your overtime."

Gibbs said, "Hallelujah, now we're talkin'."

Chelsea looked at him. "I'll be the one putting my name on the overtime slips. You start producing, and by that I mean you take down some of these offenders, and I won't care how much OT you rack up. You do the dick-around, and I'll cut it off."

Ned jabbed me and guffawed, but this time made no verbal comment.

Chelsea said, "We want to give you everything you need to be successful: vehicles, equipment, training, whatever you think you'll need."

Ned straightened up and started to listen more intently, as did Gibbs.

I said, "What about buy money? Our department holds the purse strings too tight, and it hinders our effectiveness. Money is what these crooks are all about. It's the only thing they understand."

Coffman, in a lowered tone, said, "Besides a bullet."

I continued. "You give 'em enough money, and they'll give up their mothers."

Chelsea held eye contact with me, eased down in her chair, opened a desk drawer, pulled out a gray metal cash box, opened it, and took out a wad of currency. "You chit out any expense and submit it with receipts, you can have all you want. Again, as long as you are producing. How much do you want for starters, Deputy Johnson?"

She'd caught me flat-footed. "I, ah . . . three hundred. Yeah, three hundred will work to . . . start off with."

She counted out three hundred in twenties, wrote it in a log, and had me sign for it. All of a sudden, I didn't like having a wad of fed money in my pocket. Too much responsibility.

The other three lined up behind me. She spoke while she counted. "Bruno, right there, that stack of files will be the team's caseload."

The stack stood about a foot tall, maybe twenty folders, some fatter than others. I picked up the top file and looked around. Every one of the other Special Agents at the twenty desks looked at us as if they'd never seen four deputies dressed in Levi's and polo shirts, with guns on their hips. Maybe they liked our gold badges clipped to our belts. Or maybe they didn't think we could read.

I looked at them until they looked away and went back to whatever kind of dick-around they were engaged in. Like Ned said, the crooks were not going to come knocking on their door to turn themselves in.

I opened the file: Dominic Johnson, white male, thirty-eight years old, and christened by the FBI as the Handsome Bandit. He'd

robbed eighteen banks in the Inland Empire Riverside and San
Bernardino counties, mostly Riverside. On the front work-up sheet
was a color booking photo, his features gaunt and drawn, with dark
circles under his eyes. The second photo, a black-and-white, depicted
Johnson walking through the bank, head down at an angle wearing
a ball cap, his right hand in his jacket pocket. A simulated weapon,
which meant he may or may not have been armed.

At the top of the sheet, large red font spelled out a ten-
thousand-dollar reward. I went deeper into the file and read a couple
of the summary sheets on robberies from the city police departments who took the reports. I understood this game too well. The
police departments took the report, did the preliminary investigation, and handed it over to their detective bureau. The PD investigation bureau then forwarded it to the FBI. The FBI took the report,
attached a scant FBI transmittal form, and filed the whole thing as
pending. If or when the originating agency made an arrest, the FBI
pulled the report from the file, attached a clearance transmittal, and
took the credit for the case with their agency. So why leave the office? All they had to do was wait. That's what Chelsea had referenced regarding the paperwork shuffle in the supervisor's office
when he'd chastised her.

I looked up when Chelsea finished the dole. "Hey," I said. "You
know this guy's name, you've identified him, and you haven't tracked
him down yet?"

Her smile faded and her eyes turned angry. "That's right. We
looked for him. He's a transient, couch surfing all over the place,
never staying any one place for more than a day or two."

Ned interrupted, "You said cars? You're going to assign us cars, so
we don't have to use our own? What kind of cars?"

She held my eyes a moment longer, then turned to look at him.
"That's right. Each of you will be assigned a car. They're down in the

parking structure." She looked back at me. "We'll go down in a minute, and you can decide who drives what."

Ned said, "We each get a car? We don't have to share?"

"That's right."

"Why this case?" I asked. "Why did you chose this one as the first to be worked? He's a known suspect. We don't need to follow him to take him down in progress. We just need to find him."

"Come here."

I followed her over to the big floor-to-ceiling window that spanned the length of the office. The blue tinted glass defused the brilliant sunlight outside, sunlight that heated the sidewalks and streets until heat waves radiated off the asphalt and concrete, making the world a convection oven. She pointed down. "See that bank?"

My mouth sagged open. "You're kidding me. This guy hit a bank right across the street from your office?"

Ned laughed. "Now that's embarrassing. I don't think I'd be spreadin' that little tidbit around too much."

Wilson, the clerk, hurried into the bullpen. "The Handsome Bandit just hit the Riverside County Credit Union, 1635 Mission Boulevard." She handed the slip of paper to Chelsea, who looked at all the agents in the room, looking at her. "Orange Team, you take this one. Blue team, you're on deck if another one comes in. Let's move."

Five agents came out of their trance, grabbed suit coats and war bags filled with their gear, and headed for the door.

I didn't know why, but my team didn't look at Coffman; they all looked at me.

Chelsea stopped grabbing her gear. Everyone in the room stopped and watched us. "Aren't you going to the bank?"

I didn't like her tone or the way all those agents looked at us, as if we'd just crapped the bed. "No. He's not going to be at the bank."

Chelsea's expression again turned into a scowl. "Then exactly what are you going to do, Deputy Johnson?"

I looked over at Coffman. He gazed out the window, as if unaware of what transpired around him.

"I'm hungry," I said. "I think we're going to lunch. We'll catch this guy after we get something to eat."

Chelsea shook her head and muttered, "Asshole." She grabbed the rest of her stuff and took off with her orange team, her five Special Agents in tow.

CHAPTER SEVEN

I GOT IN my truck with Ned. We drove around the block and then the next with Coffman and Gibbs following in their car until I came across the La Bufadora restaurant. "You up for some Mex?"

"You bet," Ned said. "I'm starving."

I pulled in, parked, and got out, carrying the Handsome Bandit file to go over while we ate. I already regretted the comment about catching this guy after lunch. What if we couldn't catch him at all? I'd let Anger and his pal Mr. Ego pick my foot up and shove it in my mouth.

Coffman caught up to us and took a firm hold of my arm. Too firm. I didn't like it. He said to Ned and Gibbs, "We'll see you two inside. I need to talk with Bruno."

They hesitated and then obeyed the sergeant.

I shrugged out of his grip. Sweat ran in my eyes and made me squint. Damn heat.

Coffman waited until they went inside. "I don't mind you taking the lead on these cases. I don't. You're one of the sharpest street cops I have ever seen. But I'm the sergeant. I'm the one responsible for what happens out here. You understand?"

He was right. I'd gotten a little ahead of myself. I'd forgotten what it was like to work with a team, with a sergeant supervisor. I'd been working too closely with Wicks, who treated me as an equal while we manhunted the lowest form of humans: serial rapists, murderers, and urban gangsters.

"No, you're absolutely right. I'm sorry, I won't let it happen again."

He didn't smile and patted me on the shoulder. "I know you won't, son." He started walking toward the restaurant door. I followed right next to him, the file sweaty in my hand. I brought my sleeve up and wiped the sweat from my eyes.

Coffman said, "I don't want to gig you twice in so many minutes, but that was also wrong the way you talked to those people back there. I understand that they don't see things the way we do. They come from a different culture than we do. We come from the street. They come from colleges. We need to get along, and if it takes eating a little shit, then we're going to belly up to the table. You understand what I'm saying here?"

"Yes, sir. I read you loud and clear. You won't ever have to worry about me again."

"Thanks, Bruno."

Inside, Gibbs and Ned sat in a large half-circle booth, the interior of the place all dark and cool and full of red vinyl. Ned said, "You two kiss and make up?"

Coffman sat down. "That's enough of that shit, Ned."

Ned whispered, "Yikes."

What Coffman said outside made me rethink the way I needed to operate. I slid in on the outside edge, next to Ned, opened the file intending to read every report from all eighteen agencies. I shouldn't have made that stupid-assed comment to all those FBI agents.

In the file, everyone—all the involved agencies—knew this guy, Dominic Johnson, and no one could put the grab on him.

In the back of my brain, I registered that the other three—Ned, Coffman, and Gibbs—ordered and that Ned flirted with the cute waitress. Coffman had shaken off his hollowed-out episode of staring out the window upstairs in the FBI office, enough to dress me down for the errors of my ways. Still, I fought over whether or not to talk to Wicks about it. Coffman just complicated matters. If I went to Wicks now, I'd come off sounding like sour grapes, retaliation for the scolding Coffman gave me.

I pulled out of my own trance long enough to order a couple of chicken tacos and an iced tea.

Ned reached over and closed the file. "Let it go, big man. Let's eat, relax, and have a good time, huh? We'll get back to it soon enough. All work and no play makes Bruno a dull boy."

I looked at him too long, something niggling at me about what I'd just read or just seen in the file. I closed my eyes and tried to let it bubble up.

Coffman said something to me that didn't get through. Then, said louder, "Bruno? Hey, Johnson, you hear me?"

Ned said to Coffman, "Hold it. Hold it. I've seen him do this before. Let him think."

I took in several deep breaths and let them out. I smiled and opened my eyes.

Ned slapped me on the back. "I'm liking what I see, partner. Come on, give."

I opened the file to the front page, with the two paper-clipped pictures. "What do you see?"

They all leaned in to look at the photos.

Gibbs said, "I see a white trash dude named Johnson. What happened, Bruno, you just realize he's a relative?"

Ned chuckled. "Wish I would've said that."

"Come on," I said, "quit foolin' around and look. Really look."

They all went silent and stared.

"I'm not gettin' it, partner," Ned said. "Just tell me."

I pointed to the color booking photo and stuck my finger right below his face. "What do you see?"

The minute stretched out, then Ned muttered, "Well, I'll be a son of a bitch." He shoved on me. "Let me out. Come on, let me out. Let me out."

"What?" Gibbs said. "What? I don't see it."

Ned all but shoved me out of the booth. I got up. He got out, reaching in his pocket for a quarter as he walked fast to the phone booth in the hall that led to Los Baños.

The waitress brought our food and set it on the table. I grabbed a taco. "You better eat. I have a feeling we're going to be rolling hot in about five minutes."

Coffman, his expression serious, stared at me. I'd just done it again—left him out of the loop, left him sitting there like a bewildered child.

I chewed the taco, pointed at the color booking photo, and spoke around the food. "The guy's a hype, a heroin addict. Look at his eyelids—they're droopy, and his pupils are constricted."

Ned hung up the phone too loud and ran out to the car.

Gibbs stopped, a forkload of beans and rice about to go into his mouth. "Now where's he going?"

I said, "To get a map out of the car."

CHAPTER EIGHT

I SAT ACROSS from Gibbs, his hands moving fast. Gibbs worked as a deputy long enough to know to eat when given the chance. He put an effort into scarfing down his lunch. He'd better be careful, or he'd lose a finger.

Coffman stirred his beans and rice around the burrito on his plate as he stared at my eyes. I slowly brought the taco up and took a bite. I didn't want him mad at me, but couldn't help thinking that this wasn't the Coffman I knew from our patrol days.

Ned came back in with a Thomas Guide map book, his expression like that of a kid at Christmas who just opened a present to find a Daisy Red Ryder BB gun. He sat down. "Okay, I called Riverside PD and got their narco division. I asked them, if I were a hype, where would I have the best chance to score some Mexican brown? He gave me three locations." He pointed them out on the map. "Here. Here. And here. About two- to three-block areas, each place. This shouldn't take us too long."

Coffman said, "What good's that going to do us? That's a lot of territory, and it doesn't mean he's going to be there. We're not gonna go door to door, and we don't have the manpower to set up a surveillance that big."

Ned eyed me.

I said, "We're not going to be looking for him."

"What?"

"We're going to be looking for someone to rat him out."

A rare smile crept across Coffman's face. "Excellent. Let's go do this."

I grabbed the second taco as I slid out. Gibbs shoveled faster, filling his mouth with the last of his food, his cheeks bulging. He picked up two tortillas as he slid out of the booth.

I yelled at Ned, "Get the bill."

He fumbled for his wallet as he juggled the Thomas Guide. "Ah, man, that ain't right."

Out at the cars, Ned put the map book on the hood. He made the assignments. "Gibbs, you and Coffman take this group of blocks right here. Jack-up any hypes you see, show 'em your cash and, ah . . . well, hey; I don't need to tell you how to do it. Then, after you work that area, move to this one over here. We'll work our area and meet you at that secondary location if we also come up dry."

He turned to look at Coffman. "You good with that, Sarge?"

He nodded. "We're too far out of our area for our regular radio frequencies to work. Go to CLEMARS so we can talk around. Also, our policy dictates that we notify the agency that covers the geographic area before we hit a house in their reporting district." He looked at me. "You let us know if you get something, you understand?"

I nodded.

"I mean it, Bruno."

"I got it."

He said, "Then let's hit it."

"Hey," Gibbs said. "How much money do we offer these dirtbags?"

Ned smiled. "How much you got?"

"Three hundred."

"It's not our money."

Gibbs smiled. "Got it."

We mounted our cars and headed out. I drove.

Ned watched the passing landscape and said, "You know, in narco we'd be lucky to get them to turn loose with twenty dollars for a street buy. Three hundred. Jesus. The feds got it all, and they don't know what they have when it comes to working the street. They still can't find their ass with both hands."

"That's not true. They know how to be there when you need them the most." Chelsea had broken her cover to save my ass. I shouldn't have treated her like that back in the office and needed to tell her I was sorry at the first opportunity.

Five minutes later, I turned off Olivewood onto Bandini. Ned said, "This is the start of our search area. Make another left here onto Osburn Place."

I did. The street looked like a dog rife with fleas. People walked on both sides of the sidewalks. None of them moved with any enthusiasm. They moved without any real destination. Some even demonstrated the more acute "high-step" symptom of a smacked-back hype.

The neighborhood probably once looked nice, ten years ago. Now all the houses needed paint or new roofs. An occasional house had a mowed lawn and trimmed shrubs. Almost all sported black wrought-iron bars on the windows and doors. I felt more comfortable in our own ghetto vs. this barrio.

"Pull over here," Ned said. "Let's jack that one, right there."

"We do that, all the rest are gonna run for cover."

"Then how do you propose we handle this, Mr. Ace Narcotic Investigator?"

I slowed the car's speed, rolled down the window, and pulled out the wad of twenties Chelsea had issued me. I opened the money and fanned the bills, like a poker hand. I held the money up in the window. The hot summer air blew in and made them flutter. "We're going to troll for a bank robber."

Ned chuckled. He pulled out his money, rolled down his window. "Maybe we'll get lucky and hook up a shark." He fanned the money and held it up.

"Maybe we'll get lucky and someone will try to rob us."

"We can only hope."

I pulled my handgun and stuck it half-under my right leg on the seat.

The first person we got close to, a skinny Hispanic gal with raggedy hair and greasy jeans, saw all the green fluttering in the car window. With the car traveling under five miles an hour, she ran up. I jerked the money back. She kept pace, her breath coming a little harder than normal. "What's up? Whatta need? You wanna cop some chiva?"

I said, "We're giving away three hundred dollars if you can help us."

"You Five-O?"

Ned leaned over close to me, to get a better look at her. "You want the money or not?"

"Whatta I gotta do?"

"Simple," I said. "Just tell us where this guy is?" I took the flyer off my lap and held it up.

She waved her hand. "You're Five-O, fuck ya all." She stopped, hesitated, and walked off.

Ned said, "She didn't know our man, or she woulda ratted on him in a heartbeat."

I continued down the street at the same speed, the tires rolling over grit and gravel that crunched and popped. Up ahead, the next pedestrian eyed us and stopped parallel to a tree in the parkway. He peeked around the trunk as we came by. I held up the money. He stepped from around the tree.

He looked more put together than the woman. He stayed out of the street and close to the sidewalk, moving faster now, pacing the car's speed. "What's goin' on?"

I kept the car moving to make us less of a threat. With our speed, we started getting too far away. He increased his pace, the money too big a draw.

"This is all yours if you do something for us."

"What, you want someone dead? For that kinda money you gotta want someone dead."

"Nope, I need to find this guy. That's all, just an address on one dude. Simple. And you get all of this."

He licked his lips. Heroin hypes did that a lot. He came our way. I slowed just a little, but kept rollin', barely. I held up the Wanted flyer.

He came even closer but stayed out of range in case we made a grab for him—the laws of the jungle.

"That there says ten grand. You bounty hunters or something?"

"No. You get this much for one address, no strings attached. It's easy. Just tell us how to find him."

He waved his hand. "No thanks." He backed to the curb, stepped up, turned and took off.

I again sped up to five to seven miles per hour and folded the top half of the flyer over to block out the ten grand in big red letters.

Ned said, "You know this is only going to work for about five or six hours, if that long. Then the jungle drums these shitbags use to communicate will start up, and your white brother, Dominic, will know we're out here shaking the trees for him. He'll be in the wind. Good-bye. He's gone."

"What happened to the old Ned? The Ned who never gave up, no matter what? What happened to the guy who Willis Simpkins picked up and threw across a yard into a car? The guy who got right up and grabbed a big rock. Huh? What happened to that guy?"

"I'm not giving up, partner, I'm just being a realist."

"Well, try and be a positive-thinking realist, would ya? All this negativity is working against us. I can feel it in my bones, like a vibration."

He put his fingers up to his temples, closed his eyes, and pressed. "Okay, I'm getting in tune with my criminal self. And wait. Wait. Oooh, it feels . . . it feels so nasty, and dirty, and oooh, sooo good."

The car caught up with another ped on the sidewalk. This one wore a long-sleeved green-and-black plaid shirt and a blue Dodger ball cap down low over his brow. His stringy hair hung from under the cap, covering his ears. He had to be baking, out in that heat, in that shirt. Anything to hide the needle marks on his arms. The jeans looked reasonably clean with most of his dirty knees showing through torn holes.

I slowed and held up the bait.

He stopped and looked from side to side for a trap. I kept driving at a fast idle, my foot on the brake to control the speed.

He ventured our way, the money pulling him like an invisible string. Three hundred in twenties would carry him—and the monkey on his back—several days before he started jonesin' again, and had to go back to boosting, and thieving and scamming the innocent and unsuspecting.

He followed along, his eyes on the money. I watched his hands, mine on the stock of my gun. A crook's gun didn't kill you. His hands did.

His voice croaked. "Whatta need?"

"I just need an address. Three hundred. Easiest money you'll ever make. Just tell me one address."

"Whose?"

He'd made us for cops and knew the game. I pulled down the money and lifted the Wanted sheet. He licked his lips and looked around again and again, his nerves strung wire-tight.

"I know that dude. I just saw him."

I stepped on the brake hard and stopped the car.

CHAPTER NINE

Ned popped his door, rolled out, and came around the back of the truck. I opened my door as I stuck my gun back in the holster on my hip. I held my hand out to him. "Take it easy. Don't get spooked now."

The guy continued to back up, getting ready to rabbit.

"You want this money?" I held it out—the only thing keeping him there.

Ned stopped. He didn't want to chase the guy in this heat.

"Where did you see him?" I asked, my tone lower, softer.

He stopped. "How do I know you're going to give me the money?"

"It's not my money. Here, you can have half until we get Johnson."

Ned said, "You can hold half. We get it back if we don't get Johnson."

"I don't know no Johnson." He pointed to the Wanted sheet in my other hand. "But I know that dude. He goes by Slick."

"That's fine. Here, take half and get in our truck and show us. That's all you have to do—show us the address. If he's there, you get the whole thing."

Ned said, "Don't worry. Slick won't see you. We're very good at this. You won't get burned."

The guy walked over to us and took the offered half, a hundred and sixty bucks in twenties. "I don't care if he does see me. A while back, he sold me some bunk shit. I paid good money for it. I was really sketchin', man. I really needed it. No, I owe him."

Ned held up his hand. "Hold it. Listen, we don't know you from Adam, and we don't know if your holdin' heavy, so I'm gonna pat you down for weapons, okay?"

He lifted his arms and put his hands on the back edge of the truck. Body odor wafted up. Ned and I made faces. Ned patted him down, quick and efficient, then said, "Hey, man, there's not enough room in the front of the truck—you're going to have to sit in the back."

"No problem." He vaulted in with an agility I would not have expected from someone opiate impaired.

"Where to?" I asked.

"Not far. Go up here, bang a right, go two blocks, take a left. It'll be the puke-green pad on the left, halfway down. You can't miss it."

Ned pointed a finger at him. "You run, I'm not going to chase you, not in this heat. I'm just going to shoot you in the back. You understand?"

He nodded. "Take it down a notch, bro. I'm good."

We got in. I drove, and Ned tried to raise Gibbs and Coffman on CLEMARS, California Law Enforcement Mutual Aid Radio System. They didn't answer.

He turned to me. "You don't think it's going to be this easy, do you?"

I didn't want to say anything and jinx it, so I only shrugged.

I made the first right. Ned slid the back window open. The dry heat poured in, overpowering the air-conditioning. "What if we can't raise them? Coffman's going to be madder than a hornet if we hit it without him."

"Try him again." I made the last turn and slowed. Ned worked the radio, trying two more times. Our snitch in the back turned around and sat with his back to the cab as we drew closer. He was right. Only one house matched the description of "puke-green." The guy in back scrunched down a little, pulled his ball cap down even further. He might not be afraid of Slick, but he was afraid of a snitch jacket he would never shake—the kind of jacket that would get him killed in the joint, if he ever went back. And he would go back, eventually. That was just part of the life he'd chosen.

I increased the speed. Ned stuck his face in the back window. "Point it out. I need you to point it out to me."

After a few seconds, Ned turned back around. "Okay, we're good. What do you want to do now?"

I pulled around the next corner and stopped at an alley. "ID our friend in the back. I'll keep trying on the radio."

Ned got out. The truck shook as the guy in back vaulted over the edge, to the ground. Ned talked to him, got his California ID card, and took notes. Coffman still didn't answer. I got out.

Ned handed the card back to him and said to me, "What do you wanna do, partner?"

"We can't wait. This guy Slick's a real transient, and we've already put it out on the street. He's going to hear about it soon. We're gonna have to hit it now."

"Okay, then let's go."

"Hold it. We need a uniform, in case this thing goes to guns, and at the same time notify Riverside PD, like Coffman said."

Ned stepped in close to me. "My partner lose his nuts since the last time we worked together?"

"We are out of our jurisdiction and—"

Ned smiled, held up his hand, reached in his back pocket, and pulled out his newly laminated US Marshal's temporary ID. He said, "Good for two years or until revoked," quoting from the small letters printed at the bottom of the nicely embossed ID.

"Sorry, partner. I still want a uniform to go in with us. If we have to shoot, I don't want to give him an excuse. I don't want him to say that he thought he was being robbed."

"All right. All right. How do you expect to make that happen? You see any cops close by?"

"When do I get the rest of my money?"

"Hold your horses, Rodney," Ned said. "I told you, not until we get this Slick in custody."

"Well, it's not going to happen with you two standin' here with your dicks in your hands. You want a black-and-white? Is that what you all are arguin' about?"

We both looked at him.

"Jus' go down this street about five blocks and bang a right, go two blocks, and you'll see a panaderia. There's a cute little chiquita in there with the sweetest little ass you've ever seen. And it's like honey to all them uniforms."

"You going to wait right here for us?" I asked.

"I'm not leavin' 'til I get the rest of my money."

"Let's roll."

Ned hesitated, then ran around and got in. I pulled a U-turn and took off. I watched the mirror. Rodney walked back toward the alley and into some overgrown shrubs at the edge of someone's yard.

We made the first turn and found a black-and-white on a traffic stop of a junker Ford Galaxy. They had the occupants out and sitting on the curb.

Ned hit me. "This is a good sign, partner. This is going to be our lucky day."

I pulled up and stopped behind the patrol car. The two cops on the sidewalk eyed us. The older one took a step back and put his hand on the stock of his gun.

We both got out, holding up our badges. The two cops came our way.

"LA County Sheriff's deputies," I said. "We're on a violent crimes team. We need an assist right now."

"What's up?" the older officer said. He wore an epaulet of a training officer on his shoulder, and a name plate that read, "Sinclair." His young-looking rookie remained silent, like all good rookies.

Ned said, "You just had a 211 of a credit union on Mission. You're looking for Dominic Johnson, and we just tracked him to a pad about five blocks from here."

"Well, shit. Let's go."

Ned laid the map book on the trunk of the car. "He's in a house right about here."

"Is it a light green shithole?"

"That's the one. You know it?"

"It's a slam pad. It's got an alley in the back they always split out of."

I said, "Then we're going to need one more unit to secure the back."

He pulled his radio off his belt and spoke into it. Then said to us, "Two minutes out."

"Okay," I said, "when your unit gets here, my partner and I will go in the front along with you. You can have your trainee do whatever you think you need him to do."

"Second week out, he stays with the car."

The excitement in the kid's face faded.

The backup unit pulled up. Sinclair briefed them. Then he grabbed his radio and spoke in answer to a question someone had asked. He turned to us. "Our supervisor wants us to wait for him."

Ned shook his head. "Naw. This guy's too slippery. He's gonna be gone if we don't move right now. The wait is not worth the risk. It's now or never. If you can't go, we'll do it ourselves. This was just a courtesy. He's robbing banks in your city, and we thought you might want a piece of him."

"Fuck it. We're going with you."

I said, "Let's move."

We ran for our vehicles.

CHAPTER TEN

NED SAT FORWARD in his seat, his eyes a little wider than normal. He was feeling the same thing I was over what was about to happen: a huge adrenaline dump, along with a little dopamine, caused a racing heart and a touch of euphoria. Didn't matter how many times I kicked in a door, it always felt the same.

The hot wind blew in and around us, drying out our eyes and lips. "Bruno, you go in first."

"No, this time I think I'll take the hot seat, in the second position."

Contrary to the popular myth portrayed in novels and movies, the first through the door wasn't the most dangerous position. The suspect inside sees and hears the first person coming through, and instantly reacts, but only fast enough to line up on the second one coming through the door: "the window of death." That is, if you hit the house fast enough like you're supposed to. The lead guy has to be quick to neutralize any threat to protect the second guy in. It's almost as if the second guy becomes a decoy.

"Let's not argue about it," Ned said. "You take first in this time. I do it next time."

"All right."

I made the last turn. In the rearview, the backup black-and-white made the turn into the alley. The second car, with Sinclair and his trainee, stayed with us. I gunned the truck. Opened it up.

"Here we go," I said.

I hit the brake hard and skidded up in front of the house. We got out and ran. As I entered the dirt front yard, I caught the faintest hint of teargas. I drew my gun. "This is it. He's here."

Sinclair from behind us yelled, "How do you know?"

No time to explain.

The front door stood ajar. I leaped the two steps to the porch, stutter-stepped, and kicked the door open.

I entered on the run. "Sheriff's Department! Sheriff's Department!"

The place, a shotgun shack, smelled of mildew mixed with shit. I stepped high over the floor, covered in every kind of trash ten inches deep. I continued through the living room, Ned right on my ass. We waded down a long hall toward the back of the house. I didn't stop at the first door, a bathroom. I didn't stop at the second door, a bedroom, and went right for the room at the back. Sinclair said they always fled out the back.

I entered the last room just as a white male struggled to his feet from a filthy mattress on the floor. I kicked him in the chest. He bounced off the wall and came back at me. I pistol-whipped him with my gun barrel. He went down, out cold.

I stood there, breathing hard, wanting to hit him again, but only if he moved.

Ned grabbed me. "Take it easy, partner. Take it easy."

I shrugged him off. "I'm good." I went down on one knee and handcuffed him.

Ned said, "Is it him?"

Slick lay facedown on the filthy mattress.

"Yeah. It's him. Can't you smell the teargas?"

Sinclair holstered his gun. "Yeah. I do. What's it from?"

"Dye pack from the bank," I said. "It goes off when you exit with the bait money, red dye smoke mixed with teargas." I rolled Slick over. Blood covered one side of his face from the laceration my gun barrel gave him on the top of his head. His right front pants pocket bulged with money. The faded blue denim over the pocket was burned bright reddish orange. That whole clump of bait money was no longer good. The intense heat fused all of it together.

Sinclair said, "Son of a bitch, that is him. You got him. We've been huntin' this bastard for the better part of a year."

I still tried to catch my breath. The excitement, the summer's heat, the reek from inside the house, and the short run all worked against me. "You want him?"

Sinclair looked shocked. "Hell, yes, I'll take him."

Ned grabbed my arm. "He's ours, we found him."

"It's their city and it's their banks he took down. He belongs to them. Take him, he's yours."

"I guess I owe you guys a beer." He pulled his radio and called in his trainee.

Discouraged, Ned holstered his gun, turned, and walked back toward the hall. "More like a case of beer."

"You got it, no problem," Sinclair said. "And thanks."

The trainee escorted the bloody Dominic Johnson outside and had him sit on the curb to wait for paramedics to patch him up. I followed along, the pure heat of the outdoors better to breathe than the still, fetid air inside. In the front yard, the sun bared down on my head until I felt like an ant under a kid's giant magnifying glass.

I held my hand up to block out at least some of the brightness and looked around for some shade. Two houses down on the sidewalk, Rodney stood watching, his ball cap still down low just above his brow, as he tried unsuccessfully at inconspicuous. I walked down to him. "Thanks, man, you did good."

"Where's my money?"

I folded the hundred and forty into a tight little square and shook his hand transferring the money as subtly as I could. He shoved it in his pocket without counting it, turned, and fled at a quick pace. I watched him go. I didn't know if I'd done him any favor. Three hundred dollars cash, all at once, could kill someone addicted to heroin.

Three Crown Victoria vehicles, white, black, and maroon, made the corner and roared up the street, headed our way. I turned and took the few steps back to the house where Dominic sat at the curb, hands cuffed behind his back, his head bleeding. He swiveled toward me. "Of all things, caught by a nigger. Thought I was having a nightmare when I saw your black ass comin' for me."

I'd learned, early in my career, not to engage the ignorant, and those besieged with bias. It benefited no one. I kept going, bracing for impact as the FBI came on the scene.

CHAPTER ELEVEN

I CAUGHT UP to Ned, who stood on the sidewalk by my truck. He said, "Incoming. The Wicked Witch of the West." He smiled. "Now you're gonna pay for not going to the bank with the suits and for that comment about catching this asshole after lunch. Man, that was a good one, though. I think I actually got some wood over it."

"Knock it off. She's not like that."

"Wanna bet? She does not look happy. You stomped all over her great and wondrous FBI pride. Did it right in front of everyone, back there in the office."

All three cars had stopped at the curb. No one inside moved for one long breath.

She got out on the passenger side of the lead car. All the other doors to the cars opened at the same time, dutiful little soldiers. She left her door open and stood there. "Bruno?"

She wanted me to come to her.

I didn't answer, didn't move.

She came over and stopped right in front of me, too close, violating my personal space. I didn't step back. Any other time, I would've enjoyed it, would've reveled in it. Her eyes alone had the ability to beguile me, to transport me back to another time, a place where I'd envisioned a different outcome for us entirely.

"Bruno, what the hell happened here?" She pointed at the bloodied prisoner. "Tell me that's not Dominic Johnson, with his head bashed in? What did you do?" She didn't wait for a reply. She hurried over to where Dominic sat on the curb. The RPD trainee did his job, intercepted her, held up his hands to fend her off. She held up her tiny gold fed badge. "FBI. Is this Dominic Johnson?"

"Yes, ma'am."

Dominic said, "Nice ass. How come it couldn't a been you that arrested me? Damn girl, you got it goin' on."

Ned whispered, "Good question."

She turned and stepped back over to us, as she pointed at Dominic. "What happened? How in the hell did you catch him that fast?"

Ned, with a straight face, said, "Ma'am, he just sort of jumped out at us as we were driving by. Said he wanted to turn himself in and go to jail. Said he was tired of runnin', all these months, from the FBI."

I fought hard not to smile.

Her face flushed even more in the heat. "Bruno?"

"We developed a confidential informant who gave us the location of a known fugitive, an armed and dangerous fugitive. We responded to this location and, fearing the suspect, a known transient, would flee at any moment, we forced entry and took him into custody, without incident."

"Without incident? What do you call that on his head?"

"Yeah, police brutality," Dominic said. "I was just mindin' my own business sleepin' up in my crib when that thug there clubbed me in my head. Damn nigger."

"You shut up," Chelsea said.

She turned back to me. "You can't go into a residence after a fugitive unless you have a third-party search warrant to search the premises for that person."

Ned stepped in closer, his smile gone. "You have got to be kidding me?"

"No, she's right," I said. "But the legal remedy has nothing to do with the criminal aspect of the arrest. The arrest stands."

She said, "That's right, smartass, but you just exposed yourself to a civil rights violation for illegal search and seizure."

"I've been there before."

Her face filled with rage. She raised her finger.

Before she could speak, Ned interrupted. "Hey, no problem. We can just let him go and catch him again."

Her mouth dropped open in stunned silence.

I grabbed Ned and tugged him away.

Coffman and Gibbs pulled up sometime during the exchange and now stood close by, listening. I didn't know how much they'd heard.

Chelsea pointed at me and spoke to Coffman. "Do you know what these two boneheads have done?"

I watched Coffman's expression. I cared about what Chelsea thought, cared that I'd angered her, but at that moment, I cared more about what Coffman thought.

His expression remained blank. "My men do what they gotta do."

"Is that the way it's going to be?"

Coffman said nothing and didn't move an eyebrow.

Chelsea called to him as she headed toward her car, "Can I speak to you over here, please?"

Coffman held my eyes a moment longer, long enough to make me feel two feet tall. "Sure." He followed her and stood close by while she ranted using her hands as she spoke, her volume low, so only he had the pleasure of her words. Unruffled, Coffman listened, casually took a fat black cigar from his pocket, unwrapped it, bit the end off, spit into the street, and took his time lighting the tip. Blue-gray smoke rose in the still summer air as he continued to nod, as if agreeing with everything she said.

The RPD cop, Sinclair, came up to me. "Sorry, looks like you're in the grease."

"Yeah, looks that way. Can you have your trainee go back in that pigsty and search for the gun and any more money Johnson could have secreted before we got in there? Your trainee can only search the room where we caught this guy."

"Sure, I understand." He moved off and spoke with his trainee.

Chelsea ended her conversation and came back over. "Just how did you develop this so-called confidential informant?"

"Found him on the street."

"Did you pay him?"

"Yes, three hundred dollars."

Ned said, "Three hundred dollars for a bank robber who has robbed eighteen banks, one of which was across from your office, is cheap at ten times the price."

"You're an idiot."

"You can't talk to him like that." I looked for Coffman to help out.

He took the cigar from his mouth, squinted in the smoke, and said nothing.

Chelsea said, "Did you get a chit signed by this so-called informant?"

"No. We didn't have time, under the circumstances."

She again turned and headed for her car. "Fine," she said, "that's coming out of your pocket." She got in and closed the door.

Coffman said, "Johnson, can I have a word?"

"Ah, shit."

CHAPTER TWELVE

THE MERCURY HOVERED around ninety degrees after the sun went down. I sat on the stoop in the front of our house on Nord and watched the twilight encroach. Inside, Dad moved about, finishing up the dishes from dinner, the domestic clatter a comforting distraction from a needlessly hectic day.

Ned came out with two sweating beer bottles and handed me one. He sat down next to me and took a long slug. "You sure it's okay to leave Beth here overnight?"

"Two kids are the same as one, and she's already asleep. Looks like they really played hard today with toys scattered all over the house."

"Sorry about the crayon mural on the wall."

"Don't worry about it. They're kids."

"Who do you think drew the dinosaur and who do you think drew the house and tree?"

"If you can make out a dinosaur and a tree with a house, then maybe you better go see a shrink, pal."

"It's great that they get along so well. Thanks, I owe you. I'm beat, I can really use the break, even if it's only one night."

"You don't owe me a thing. And if you want to make it a couple, three nights, it's not a problem. Olivia can use the social interaction."

"I might just take you up on that." He held up his bottle. "Didn't think that RPD copper would really pay off with that case of beer."

"Yeah, a three-hundred-dollar case of beer, enjoy it."

"I'm in for half of that. We're partners, remember?"

"Thanks, but I didn't slow down long enough today to ask you if you wanted to play in my game."

He started to take another drink and stopped. "Bruno, you can always count me in for any game you wanna play. You never have to ask."

I took a drink to hide the emotional lump that rose in my throat, then said, "Hey, don't sit so close. People will think we're a couple or something."

He chuckled. "It's good to be back working together. I thought it was a little weird at first, but as soon as we started rollin' hot, we fell right back into the groove. I gotta tell you that was the most fun I've had in at least a year."

"Yeah, it was all right, wasn't it?"

"How big a piece of your ass did Coffman chew off?"

I gave him a fake smile. "He wasn't happy. In fact, I can safely say he was the maddest I've ever seen him. He yelled and waved his arms, damn near bit through his cigar. Couldn't help thinking, though, that some of it was just for show to ease the FBI's damaged ego. Hoped some of it was for show, anyway. Man, he was mad. No way did I mean for it to turn out that way."

"He had no right to go at you like that."

"Yes, he did. We should've waited for him."

"In our place, under the exact same circumstances, do you think he would've done anything different than what we did?"

"No."

"There, you see. Did he at least say, 'Atta boy,' for puttin' the Habeousgrabous on this guy so quick?"

"Yeah, he did, right at the end when I was walking away. I'm worried about him, Ned."

"Give it a rest. I told you, you don't have to worry about Coffman. He's a solid dude."

I clinked my bottle to his. We drank some more.

I said, "You never told me what got you launched from the street narco team and banished to the desk."

"Eh." He waved his hand. "It was nothin'. Really. The brass, you know how they can be, how they think. They always make a big deal outta nothin'."

"Ned?"

"All right. All right, if you gotta know. I can't believe you haven't already heard this. The story shot around the entire county and beyond, like some kinda black plague that's chased my ass ever since."

"You're stalling."

"All right. Here it is. I was workin' street narco outta Lennox station. You knew that part, right?"

I nodded.

"Okay, so it was my turn in the barrel. I had to take all the cases for the team over to the court to get them filed with the filing DA. I was hung over and in kind of a foul mood."

"Oh, really. That's odd."

"You wanna hear this?"

"Go ahead."

He paused, as if reliving the event, or trying to sort out which way he really wanted to tell it.

I elbowed him. "Go on."

"I'm in the DA's office, you know, in that outer room, waiting my turn along with all the other coppers there to file cases. Took a couple of hours to get to me. My turn comes. I go in, sit down at this guy's desk, and hand him the cases for the whole team. This dude, you know the type—dress shirt, tie, no jacket—is sittin' there smiling like he's havin' the greatest day ever, like this is the best job in the world. And there's absolutely nothin' to be smilin' about, and I mean nothin'. He's sitting in an office without windows, doing the old paperwork shuffle for a long line of dirtbags waiting in jail for their turn at the revolving door. Anyway, I'm not paying much attention to him because of my hangover. He's jabbering away and the first words that get through is that he's not gonna file one of our cases. And it happens to be one of my cases. He said the PC was too thin, not enough probable cause. I opened my mouth to argue with him, and that's when I see it."

"Oh no, what? What did you see?"

"Get this: the dude was under the influence of a stimulant."

"Ah, crap. Don't tell me that, Ned. Don't tell me you busted the deputy DA right in his own office?"

CHAPTER THIRTEEN

"I DID. I also found a half-gram of coke in his desk drawer. Got him for possession."

I started to chuckle. "You've got to be kidding. And they rolled you up for that?"

"Well—"

"Ah, man, what else did you do?"

Ned's tone shifted to a little less confident and he squirmed. "If you'd still been my partner, you would've stopped me."

"Tell me."

"That deputy DA didn't want to go to jail, and he resisted arrest a little. I had to choke him out."

I started laughing and couldn't stop.

"It's not funny, Bruno." Ned tried to keep from laughing and failed. "It's not funny. The DA said that his deputies wouldn't ever file another one of my cases anywhere in the county. That meant that I couldn't do my job, not as a real street cop."

I laughed some more.

Ned shook his head, swallowed hard, and put his hand on my shoulder. "Okay, and . . . and here's the rest of it. When I did put the cuffs on, I might've told him that now he'd be able to file his own case."

I laughed even harder.

"Bruno? Bruno, it's funny but not that funny. You wanna know what's really funny? Let me tell you what's funny as hell, my friend. You know what I saw today in that little turd's office, that FBI supervisor's office with the pin map covering one entire wall? Let me tell you what I saw when we first walked in."

I powered down the laugh.

"Not so funny now, is it, big man?"

I stopped laughing altogether. "What did you see?" But I knew. We'd worked together in a patrol car too long for him not to be able to read my signs.

He smiled and shoved my shoulder. "I caught a teeny tiny glimpse of some heat between you and ol' Mrs. Wicked Witch of the West."

"You've been on that desk too long, pal. Your radar's all banged up."

"Naw, I saw it. You went all gooey-eyed there for a second. I caught it. I don't think anyone else did, but I did. Tell me. Give me all the juicy details. She's built like a—"

"Okay, that's enough. Change the subject."

"What?" He looked confused.

"She's a distinguished member of the FBI, and you don't need to objectify her in that way. You don't need to talk about her like she's a piece of meat."

"Really, it's going to be like that, huh?"

"Yeah, just like that."

"Then that just means I'm right. That I read it right."

"Means nothing of the sort. You're absolutely wrong."

We drank our beers and watched the night sneak in all around until the light from the partially closed front door sliced downward between us and into the yard.

I couldn't get Chelsea out of my mind. The way she looked. The way she smiled. Her eyes. Seeing her brought back all those emotions I thought I'd buried for good. Emotions I needed to have buried, for good.

I said, "Can I ask you something?"

Ned turned his head to look at me, but I couldn't see his eyes anymore, with the dark on either side. "Anything."

"With Hannah, when did you know?"

"What are you talkin' about? What do you mean?"

"When did you know? And by the way, it's great that you got back together and you're making it work."

"Yeah, right. No one said anything about it working."

"When did you know she was the one for you?"

"She makes me crazy, Bruno."

"Yeah, Dad says those are the ones you want to look for. The spice that makes life worth it."

"Different kind of crazy, believe me."

"You going to tell me?"

His tone changed, and even in the dark, I knew the old Ned had slipped back into place, knew that what came next might only contain a smidgen of truth.

"Okay, you really want to know? On our third date, we drove out to Palm Springs for a long weekend. We'd slept together, but just hit-and-run kind of stuff. You know what I mean? We were driving through White Water, the place with all those thousands and thousands of windmills up on the hills, spinning all the time, generating energy from the wind."

"Yeah, I know the place."

"So as soon as Hannah sees all these windmills, she turns to me while I'm drivin' and says, 'What are all those for?'"

"And I tell her, Palm Springs is full of rich people and when it gets too hot, they turn on all those fans."

"Come on, Ned, I'm not buyin' this." I stifled a laugh.

"No, really. You know what she says? She says, 'Oh.' Just like that, 'Oh.' Right then, that's the moment. That's when I knew I was going to marry her."

I laughed along with him. "That's not true—you made that shit up. I know Hannah. She's not like . . . she's not like that."

I'd almost said that she wasn't a stupid woman, but she had at one time thrown Ned over for the notorious JB.

A sleek, dark Crown Victoria slid to the curb out in front of our house and stopped. The headlights went off. The driver got out and stood by the open door.

Chelsea.

Ned said, "Bruno, my man, you can kiss my white ass. I gotta run."

CHAPTER FOURTEEN

NED GOT UP and went inside. When the door opened all the way, the light flashed from the living room, the brightness obscuring Chelsea as she stood by her car. Ned came back out with two more beers, handed me one, and stepped down into the front yard headed for his car. Chelsea met him halfway.

Ned handed her the other beer and shot her his best Ned smile. "Go easy on him, he's my partner." He winked.

He walked on, toward the street. Chelsea whispered loud enough for me to hear, "Idiot."

She came over and sat on the porch right where Ned had sat. She took a drink, and said, "Nice evening."

"Yes, it is."

Why was she here?

Silence. We sipped our beers. My heart thumped hard in my chest. She had to be able to hear it. She had to know how I still felt about her. I really wanted to believe her presence meant something related to our relationship, but knew it couldn't. How could it?

I said, "What's going on? Why are you here?"

"I thought I needed to apologize for what happened out there today. Things just got away from me, and I'm sorry."

"I understand."

"No. It was a good job you did, and I shouldn't have acted like a complete bitch."

"You weren't a . . . complete bitch."

She smiled and shoved my leg.

I loved that smile, would pay a great deal to see it more often—like every day, from now until the other side of forever.

We didn't need to say another thing. I was content to just sit there with her the whole night.

She broke the silence. "I was going to call you when I transferred back to LA. I really meant to."

I didn't reply. I wanted her to continue.

"I kept meaning to pick up the phone . . . and . . ."

"I know," I said. "How have you been?"

I'd let her off the hook. She smiled again. "Good. Really good."

"You going to tell me how you worked your way out of that deep hole and won a transfer out of North Dakota?"

She took a long slug of beer, brought the bottle down, and stared at it. "That, my friend, is a long and ugly story."

"Can't be too ugly since you made it out. You're now team leader for all of bank robbery. That's really a good crack."

"Maybe another time."

"Okay, sure." By her tone, I knew I wasn't likely to hear the story, not for a long while, if at all.

More silence. I wanted to reach out and touch her shoulder, her neck—the lobe of her ear, run my fingertips gently through her hair. The memory of our naked and sweaty skin moving together, touching, sliding, jumped out into the forefront of my thoughts. The way she returned a kiss was electrifying, like nothing I'd ever experienced.

"I also came here to talk," she said.

"I figured as much."

"The way things went down today . . . I mean . . . well, the RAC has pulled me as the liaison for the team."

"Ah, man. Did you tell him about us?"

"What? No. Nobody knows, and I intend to keep it that way. It's just that I'm running the entire robbery bureau, and he now thinks your team is going to need more . . . attention. More time devoted to it than I've got available."

I wasn't sure I believed her.

"So you're saying that we're loose cannons and need to be reined in. That's why you drove all the way out here tonight, to tell me to power it down."

"Yes, that and to discuss a couple of other things."

"Hey, you want to go inside and sit on the couch?" My heart skipped a beat waiting for the answer, the couch a big tell in her true reason for the visit and in how this meeting would end.

"No, it's kind of nice out here."

"Go on, then."

"This is a little sensitive, and I could get into trouble for telling you this."

"I understand."

"Your team was brought in for one specific problem: to chase one particular group of bank robbers. This crew mostly involves the Rollin' Sixties Crips. They're hitting us pretty hard, at least twice a week, and we can't get a handle on them. They're a unique and involved problem I won't go into right now. I was going to put you on them tomorrow."

"But?"

She took another drink of her beer, more of a dainty sip, to allow her a moment to muster her words, and then said, "Here's the sensitive part—"

"Wait, let me guess. I embarrassed the FBI today, and now they wanna get even, take us down a couple of notches first, before they give us the real case."

She froze and stared at me. I'd hit it right on the nose.

"I'm sorry," I said, "I didn't mean for this to happen this way. Seeing you in the office like that caught me off guard, and then, with all those agents watching me and my guys as if we were . . . Well, I just let my mouth overload my ass. I promise you, it won't happen again."

She waved her beer bottle. "I should've known you'd have figured it out. And it's done. We're going to have to live with it. It was partly my fault." She smiled again and nudged my leg. "I should've listened to you when you said you'd get him after lunch. My God, Bruno, that took a jumbo set of balls to say something like that."

"Yeah, I'm not normally like that. You know me."

She cut her eyes away, a little embarrassed by the comment.

She said, "You're going to be assigned a new liaison. His name's Jim Turner. He's really a great guy, so take it easy on him, okay?"

"Can do." I wanted to lean over and kiss her but didn't have the nerve. I didn't want to risk shoving her away emotionally. I could wait; go slow with her until she was ready.

She got up to leave. "One thing though, Bruno, you really need to get a handle on Ned. I know you don't want to hear this, but I think he might be a bad influence on you."

"No, that was all me today. Ned had nothing to do with it." I reached out a hand, held my breath to see if she'd take it.

She did. Her skin was warm and soft to the touch. She smiled and held on. "I'll see you tomorrow at the office."

"Thanks for coming by and for the heads-up. I promise, I won't let you down."

"I know you won't." She held my eyes a moment longer, turned, and slowly pulled her hand from mine, fingers extending to the tips, until they parted. She headed for her car. All I could do was watch her go. She hesitated at the car door, got in, started up, and headed off down the street leaving my chest hollowed out.

The door behind me opened with a flash of yellow light. Dad stepped out. He sat on the stoop next to me. He didn't say anything for a long time. He wanted me to say it and I couldn't.

"That Chelsea I saw out here?"

I nodded.

We both said nothing.

He patted my leg. "It's getting late, why don't you come on in?"

CHAPTER FIFTEEN

OUR TEAM MET in the parking lot in Riverside next to the tall blue-glass building that housed the FBI on the top floor. I didn't look up. I didn't want them to see me do it and think me jealous of their federal aerie.

Eight o'clock in the morning and the sun already beat down on all things not smart enough to hide out in the shade. I stood by my truck, arms folded, with Ned next to me. Sweat rolled down the side of my cheek. Coffman and Gibbs came up. Coffman took the unlit cigar carcass from his mouth. "Lieutenant Wicks wants a word, Bruno, tonight after shift. Meet him at the office."

Ned said, "I'll go with you."

"I didn't say Bruno and Kiefer, did I, jackass?" He turned and headed for the double glass doors of the building, obviously still smoldering over yesterday's caper.

Ned said, "I'm going. It's not right you taking the heat for this thing. We both did it."

"Let it go. You're new to the team. You'll have plenty of opportunities to get chewed out. Just don't try and arrest and choke out Wicks. He'll shoot your dumb ass."

Ned socked me in the shoulder. "And you wonder why I don't tell you shit."

"Come on, let's get in there."

"No, really," he said as he tried to keep up. "Coffman already chewed you out. With Wicks jumping on, it's the same as stepping on your neck when you're already down."

"Wicks isn't like that. He's not gonna work me over again. It's something else."

"You sure?"

"I'm sure." But I wasn't. Not entirely. We made it to the door and entered.

No one spoke in the elevator on the way up.

On the drive over to the FBI office, Ned didn't ask what happened the night before after he left me on the porch with Chelsea. He knew I wouldn't kiss and tell, even if it had gone the other way. In fact, he said little, if anything at all. He'd come in the house, talked with Dad, played with Beth, drank a cup of coffee, and we headed out.

Something was eating at him.

I welcomed the silence. I needed to think things through about Chelsea. I played the night before back in my mind over and over and couldn't be sure if she was interested in getting back together. She didn't go for sitting on the couch, but the way her hand lingered in mine when she walked away spoke volumes. Didn't it? I needed to work up the nerve and just ask her out. Take the big step and ask her to coffee. Just the thought of asking her made my heart race.

The elevator door opened. We disembarked into the empty and sterile FBI waiting area.

The same clerk sat on the other side of the bulletproof glass. She saw us, picked up the phone, dialed, said one sentence, and hung up.

Ned said, "You know, we need to get a key to get in this place. I don't wanna come here every day and feel like we're waiting to see the principal, the ugly gal with a big wart on her nose waiting with a big paddle."

Coffman spoke around the dead cigar in his mouth. "That statement tells me a lot about you, my friend. Just keep in mind that I don't have a wart, but I do carry a big paddle."

The door at the side opened. An athletically fit FBI agent in khaki utility pants and a red polo shirt said, "Right this way, gentlemen." We filed through.

He wore his sandy-brown hair with blond highlights, short on the sides and longer on top like a school kid. He looked like a So Cal resident, with tan skin and blue eyes, who took a day off when good surf conditions hit the coast. This time, he guided us right to the door at the end of the hall that led to the robbery bullpen.

Once inside, he led us straight through the rows of Special Agents, who all looked up and stared. He stopped at Chelsea's desk. Chelsea looked up, caught my eye, and restrained a smile.

Our guide and escort stuck out his hand to Coffman first. "My name is Jim Turner. From now on, I'll be your liaison agent. I'm taking over for Agent Miller here." He looked at Chelsea and smiled.

Just that quick, my heart sank to the bottom of my feet.

The smile wasn't the big reveal though. It was the way their eyes worked each other over, the intimate depth of knowledge that transferred in that briefest of instants. My God. He and Chelsea were a thing.

Ned moved a step closer and elbowed me. He'd seen it, too.

"Knock it off," I said too loud. Everyone turned to look. I didn't move or acknowledge them.

I wanted to sock Special Agent Turner right in his perfectly white teeth, make him eat those enamel chompers like Chiclets gum.

Coffman's pager went off, disrupting the violent, smoldering undertone. "Excuse me, is there a phone I can use?"

Chelsea looked disturbed. She'd seen my grimace and now knew that I knew her nasty little secret, knew that she'd played me for a fool last night. She said, "Please, use this one." She handed him the receiver. Coffman dialed. Just that quick, I shifted from lovesick to angry. What a fool I'd been.

The smug Special Agent Jim Turner asked Chelsea, "Can I please have the Bogart case?"

She still looked at me, her expression now one of concern. She worried that I'd make a scene, ruin it between her and her beau, tarnish her newly recovered FBI reputation. I guess she didn't know me as well as I thought she did.

I said, "I'll get it. It's in our stack, right?" I moved to the side of the desk and started to go through the pile assigned to us the day before.

"No," Chelsea said. "It's not there." She pulled open her drawer. "I have it right here." She took out the fattest file folder I'd ever seen, at least five inches thick. She handed it to me, reached in her drawer again, and came out with two more file folders at least three inches, each. "Raymond Desmond Deforest. We've named him 'The Bogart Bandit.'"

Turner said, "Bogart has robbed eighty-six banks, from San Francisco, down to San Diego. We've been looking for him for two years." He gave me a smug smile.

Ned opened his mouth to make a snarky comment. I shoved the two smaller files into his chest. He said, "Hey, take it easy, partner."

Coffman hung up the phone. "Sorry to piss in your Wheaties, boys and girls, but we've been pulled off. We have to go."

Chelsea stood. "Hold it. According to the MOU your department signed, you are to be supervised and scheduled by the FBI, unless prior approval has been arranged."

"Yeah," Coffman said. "My boss said you might say something like that. So he said I can leave two guys." He turned to us. "Bruno and Ned, you're it. Me and Gibbs have to go help run down Frank Duarte."

"Ah, shit," Ned said. "Gibbs, you wanna trade?"

"No chance, my brother."

"Oh," Chelsea said, "I saw on the news that Frank Duarte killed again last night."

"That's right, and the press are starting to crucify the department over it."

"In that case, I understand."

Coffman said, "Thanks."

Gibbs smiled and said, "Hey, Bruno, catch ya on the flip, huh, man? We're out of here."

Coffman gave me the stink eye, nonverbally telling me to play nice. He turned and left to catch up with Gibbs.

Turner said, "Not to worry. You two won't be going out in the field anytime soon. It's going to take you three days at least to read and digest this file."

Now angry enough to spit, I looked at Chelsea and said to Turner, "I don't think it'll take that long. I'm familiar with the Rollin' Sixties Crip gang."

He looked at Chelsea as he said to me, "What are you talking about? This has nothing to do with that gang." Then it sank in and his confusion shifted to anger as he figured out I'd referenced a case I wasn't supposed to know about, the special one Chelsea told me about the night before, as we sat together on my porch.

No sense me being angry all by myself.

CHAPTER SIXTEEN

Jim Turner said, "Let's lay down the ground rules and be very clear, shall we? I am to be notified of any action you take on this case. You understand?" He handed Ned and me his business card. "Here are my numbers. You can always call the OD—the officer of the day—and he will know how to reach me anytime, day or night. So there's no excuse. Or you can page me. The numbers are all on the card. Are we understood? No independent action. I'm to be kept in the loop on everything you do."

"We're not children," Ned said. "And I'll tell you right now, I don't work well with a boot on my neck."

I grabbed him by the arm and pulled him along. "Come on, let's go get some coffee and start reading."

He put up token resistance before he turned and came along.

Special Agent Turner said to our backs and in front of the entire bullpen, filled with agents working diligently, shuffling papers from one side of their desk to the other, "See you two in a few days after you finish reading. And after you finish evaluating the case, I want you to submit a typed game plan, about how you intend on going after this guy."

I didn't have to turn around to see his expression. His words came out dripping with smug arrogance. He'd said the last part with plenty of witnesses to our marching orders, witnesses who could testify in our disciplinary review if we screwed it up.

I didn't mind that as much as the thought of Turner ever touching Chelsea, kissing her neck, nibbling her earlobe and—

An involuntary shiver rippled through my body; I wanted—no, needed—to put a fist in that guy's smug smile.

At the door to go out, Ned spun to head back. "Hey, they didn't give us our cars."

I gave him a gentle nudge, opened the door, and moved out into the hall. "I don't think we're going to be working this gig much longer, so it's really not going to matter." I'd made up my mind, made the choice even though I knew it was wrong.

"You gonna talk to Wicks tonight about what's happening?"

"I'll brief him, but I don't think he'll pull us. He'll say suck it up, that this is too good a deal to screw up. The overtime, the cars, the resources."

"Then what's gonna sour the Feebies on us?"

"Oh." He smiled and then chuckled. "You're gonna pull a Bruno Johnson, aren't you? You're gonna stick this case right up their ass, aren't you? You're not going to take three days to read the case file, and submit some bullshit typewritten game plan? You're gonna go nuclear and kick in some doors starting right now."

"Something like that. If I can pull it off, anyway." We moved down the hall to the exit and entered the waiting area.

"Count me in, partner. It'll be worth it just to see the look on those Feebies' faces."

"Now," I said, "I just hope these college boys left me something in this file, something they missed, that I can get my fingers into and exploit."

Ned pushed the "down" button on the elevator. "You know they did. They've been chasin' a known suspect for two years and haven't been able to catch him. How hard is that? In the last two years, how many people have you run down while on the violent crimes team? Huh? How many times have you been onto someone that didn't end with you feeding your handcuffs or zipping up a body bag?"

"We've been real lucky that way."

"Quit with the modesty. Your team's reputation is the talk of the department. You're headed for legendary status, my pal. Wyatt-fucking-Earp. You and Wicks both."

I hefted the five-inch report in front of him. "By the size of this, they did a lot of legwork."

The elevator dinged and opened. We stepped in and took it to the ground floor.

Outside in the bright sunlight, we walked in silence to my Ford Ranger and got in. I drove right to the La Bufadora restaurant, where we'd eaten the day before. At nine o'clock the place didn't open for another hour and a half. People inside moved around, getting the place ready. We sat for a moment, parked right in front of the door, not knowing what to do next.

Ned had gone silent again. "What's up with you?" I asked.

"Nothing."

"Something's eating at you. Come on."

"I can't keep anything from you, can I?"

"You gonna tell me?"

"It's a personal thing." He checked his watch. "I really need to be someplace. I thought I could blow it off, but that would be a bad choice, and I'm trying to make better choices lately."

I smiled. "What? Who are you, and what did you do with my friend Ned?"

"Come on, knock it off."

"You going to tell me what it is?"

"Naw, not right now. Thanks though. I do appreciate the concern. Maybe in a few days over a beer."

"You're scarin' me here, pal."

"It's not a big deal. Nothing I can't handle."

"You want me to drop you back at your car?"

"I don't wanna leave you hangin', not with this thing looming big on the horizon."

"You're not. It's going to take me at least a few hours to wade through this monster of a case and try to develop a game plan, if there even is one." I backed up, put it in drive, and headed for the street. "Why don't you read the file to me while I drive you back?"

"You sure?"

"Read."

"Okay, but fair warning, I get carsick." He leaned over a bit and feigned throwing up in my lap. He smiled and opened the first file folder.

"Raymond Desmond Deforest, 'The Bogart Bandit.' On the street, they call him 'Teener,' like a teener of coke. He's Negro, male, twenty-four, and a little guy, five feet six, a buck forty-five. He's got a tattoo of, 'Grape Street,' on his left bicep. He has a woman with huge breasts tattooed on his chest." Ned held up the Polaroid photo of the tattooed woman. I took my eyes from the road for a second and snatched a look. A quality tattoo, and based on the writing on the Polaroid, it looked like it came from OSS—Operation Safe Streets—the sheriff's gang unit from before Deforest started robbing banks.

"Grape Street Crips?" I said. "That means he grew up in The Nickerson," an area close to the Corner Pocket where I grew up.

Ned flipped the page, ran his finger down. "Yep, you called it, on 114th, 1574. And get this, this fucker has a cap, a gold tooth right up front in his grill." Ned pointed to his own incisor. "And these Keystone Kopps couldn't catch him. What the hell?"

Ned went silent as he continued to read, flipping page after page. I got on the freeway. My mind wouldn't come off of Chelsea and her beau, Jim Turner, so I didn't care that he didn't read it out loud. We hit some stiff traffic, the stop-and-go kind. For the next two hours, Ned stayed buried in the reports. He only stopped a few times to check his watch.

I got off the freeway and took surface streets to our office. When I pulled into our parking lot, Ned said, "These guys did a helluva job on this one. They worked every last lead and really put this case to bed. I don't know, partner, I think we're really screwed on this one. I mean, they checked every known associate and the associates of the associates. They sat on his neighborhood for six months, waiting for him to show, and nothing. They spared no expense on manpower. They also put out a fifty-thousand-dollar reward; broadcast it on the radio and television. They twisted up two snitches who said they could produce him. And still nothin'. A big zero. Robbery dicks from San Francisco and San Diego also did everything they could think of. They even wiretapped his mom. His mom, you believe it? That's a new low, a desperate move. They really want this guy."

He put the file down on his lap. "I think they gave us this case just to humiliate us. They know there's nothing to sink our teeth into. Turner—that smug bastard—he's gonna let us spin our wheels for a few days, until we admit we failed. And then he'll probably have us say it out loud right in the middle of their overcrowded bullpen, the same as a public hanging. What do you think, partner?"

"Huh? What?"

"I said, what do you think? You think the Feebs are sticking this case up our ass to get even?"

"Doesn't really matter. I'll get him tonight or tomorrow, no later than day after tomorrow."

CHAPTER SEVENTEEN

I TURNED TO look at Ned. His mouth sagged open and gradually turned into a huge smile. "Man, the FBI's got nothin' on you when it comes to arrogance. You're drippin' with it. But I love it, my friend. I do."

"I'm joking. No way are we going to catch this guy. Maybe in a couple of months if we work it full-time. But that's not gonna happen."

"Thanks. You really had me going there. What a letdown."

I said, "You gonna get out and get in your own car? You got that thing, right?"

"Not a chance in hell. I'm sticking to you like glue. I'm not going to miss it, if you happen to get lucky. Do you have any idea at all where to look for this guy? Where to start?"

"Not a clue."

"Jesus, Bruno, what are you gonna do?"

"Nothing I can do but drop back and punt. You might as well take off, do your thing, whatever that is."

"No, no, come on. Let's go. Let's at least give this a try. We got nothing to lose. It's still going to be a kick in the ass to try."

"All right then, let's go inside. I gotta make a phone call." I opened the truck door.

"You think … I mean, you really don't have any idea where to look for this guy?"

"Nope. I told you, not a clue."

"Ah, man, Bruno, you're not just yankin' on my dick, are you? You went and got me all jacked up for nothin'?" He punched the dash.

"Hey, take it easy on the truck."

I got out and headed for the door to our office, the converted grocery store at the strip center. Ned followed along. The door was locked, and that meant no one was inside. I unlocked it, reached in to flip on the lights, entered, and made a beeline for my desk, my mind now locked onto the problem at hand. I sat on the edge of my desk, picked up the phone, and dialed. Ned sat in my chair, put both feet up on my blotter calendar. "So, come on, give. You're obviously thinking of something, now, right?"

The phone beeped. I typed in the phone number to my desk phone along with a "911" and hung up. I said, "Yeah, but it's a real long shot. We're not going to chase this guy Deforest. Not in a direct line, anyway."

"What are you talking about?"

"You said the FBI has covered all the bases chasing this guy, right? Going at him head-on."

"I did. They didn't leave so much as a bread crumb to pick up."

"Okay then, we won't go that route. We can't afford to. We can't match their resources. We'll go in a totally different direction. You still have your buy money the FBI gave you?"

"Bruno, this guy isn't some localized heroin hype. That trick from yesterday isn't gonna work. I'd like to think that caper yesterday was good police work, but I gotta tell ya, we threw the dice and came up with a seven on that one."

I snapped my fingers several times in front of him. He reached into his pocket, pulled out his money, and slapped it in my hand. I counted the twenties. "Hey, you're a couple short."

"Man's gotta eat."

"Not with fed money. Are you crazy?"

"Take a breath. I'll hit the ATM."

The phone rang. I picked it up. Ned jumped out of the chair and moved to his desk. He picked up his phone and punched in on the same line to listen.

"Hey," I said. "It's me."

"Well, if it ain't the infamous Bruno the Bad Boy Johnson. It's good to hear your voice, baby. Why haven't you called me?"

"Been busy."

"It hurts me, to my heart, that you only call if you want somethin'. You never call just ta talk ta me. That last time when we did in that ol' boy Jefferson Sampson over ta the Fox Hills Mall, you promised me a little somethin', and you never showed up ta pay me off."

"I never promised nothing like that, Ollie, come on now. That's what you said, but I never agreed."

I looked over at Ned, who raised his eyebrows at the woman on the phone talking smack. He put the phone to his shoulder and made a circle with his index finger and his thumb. He stuck his other index finger in the circle and moved it in and out in a vulgar gesture. I scowled at him and shook my head.

"Ollie, you know I never said that. Right now, I really need your help. I need to find somebody real fast and I'm willing to pay for it."

"Oh, you're gonna pay for it, my little jellyroll." She cackled into the phone. "How can ol' Ollie hep?"

"I need to find a girl, and I'm in a big hurry."

Ned looked at me confused and raised his hands in a questioning gesture. I waved him off.

"You're always in a hurry. What's her name?" Ollie asked.

"That's part of the problem. I don't know her name."

"What? How'm I gonna find a girl if I don't know her name? I mean, I'm good, darlin', but you gotta give me somethin' ta work with."

"She's got a boyfriend who's Grape Street."

"Now dat's somethin' I kin work with. I know all dem gangstas up in there."

Ned smiled.

"His name's Teener. You know a guy named Teener?"

"No, no, can't say dat I do."

"That's okay, I want to know where his girl is laying her head. This Teener's name is Raymond Desmond Deforest."

"What's Teener done?"

"Banks. Lots of them."

Silence on the phone. "This one's gonna cost, Bruno. I'm serious."

"I can give you three hundred cash."

"No, it's not gonna be money this time."

Ned raised his eyebrows and did the vulgar thing with his fingers again.

"What do you need, Ollie?"

"It's my nephew."

"He get pinched? What kind of case? I'm sure we can work something out if you help me get Teener."

"It's not like dat. He's a good kid. He jus' fell in with the wrong . . . Bruno, I need you to put a boot up his ass."

"I can do that, no problem, and I'll still give you the three hundred."

"Let me page up my homegirl on a Hunert and First. She know all dem ganstas up in there. I'll call you back."

"Thanks, Ollie."

"Bye, lover." She hung up.

Ned hung up. "Who's this Ollie?"

"Few years back, I took her down comin' out of a rock house with a big bag of money. I took her right back in to get the dope. We walked into a birdcage."

"No shit. I've heard of them, but I've never seen one."

"Yeah, we were trapped like a couple of rats and she kept her cool. Well, sort of anyway. Ever since then, she's been doin' things for me, here and there. I keep her in my back pocket, for special capers."

"She signed up?"

He wanted to know if I followed department policy and procedure, and had her signed up as a regular informant, with a snitch number.

I shook my head.

He nodded. He'd worked narco and knew that sometimes you had to keep your snitches off the books or they could be stolen and abused by a major's narco crew. Headquarters narcotics got all the status reports on signed snitches, and if one was doing an outstanding job, they'd grab up the snitch, work them hard, burn them out without compassion or empathy, and then discard them like yesterday's underwear. Then the major's crew just moves on to the next one. I wouldn't let that happen to Ollie.

"Will she come through?"

"She hasn't let me down yet, but this isn't like any of the other cases we worked together. This one's a tough nut to crack."

"What does she look like?"

"She's got a heart of gold."

"Oh, that means she's two tons of—"

"Sometimes, Ned, I just don't know about you."

He shrugged. "Goin' for the girlfriend of Teener. That's a good idea, but I didn't' see one listed in the case file. He might not have a regular girlfriend. He might just be a player."

"With all the banks he's taken down, this guy has to favor himself as a Bonnie and Clyde kind of gangster. No, he's gonna have a regular girl, maybe a couple a three—one in each area where he operates."

The door to the office opened. We turned to look. In walked Lieutenant Wicks.

CHAPTER EIGHTEEN

WICKS NEVER SLOWED down. "Kiefer, my office."

"Ah, shit," Ned said. "I knew this gig was too good to be true."

I grabbed his arm. "What's going on?"

He jerked away. "Nothing. This is all about nothing. That's the problem. And it's none of his damn business."

Ned followed Wicks into his office that used to belong to the grocery manager and closed the door. The muffled yelling started right away and reverberated off the glass-paneled walls. Not just Wicks either. Ned yelled back, used his arms in wild gestures and even pointed at Wicks in an accusatory manner. What the hell was Ned into? No way should he be yelling at Wicks. Wicks wouldn't put up with it.

The office door flew open and banged the wall as Ned stormed out.

Wicks exited his office. "Detective, don't you dare walk away from me. Get back here."

At the door that led outside, Ned turned and flipped Wicks the bird. He disappeared as the door eased closed in a flash of daylight.

Wicks came toward me, still breathing faster than normal.

"Boss, what's goin' on with Ned?"

No way did I want Ned launched from the team. He'd only just been assigned there and I'd missed him. Didn't know how much, until he showed up.

Wicks finally quit watching the door and looked at me. "What? Oh, I can't. I'd fill you in, but it's personal and not work-related, so I can't. If human resources found out, they'd come down on me with both feet. But if he doesn't pull his head out of his ass, it's going to turn into work-related. After he cools down, have a talk with him, would you?"

"Sure, but if I don't know what it's about, how am I going to talk to him?"

"Don't play games with me, Bruno. I'm not in the mood. He's the one who's going to have to tell you."

"Okay. You're not going to launch him from the team, are you?"

"No. Hell no. You're on my team, you're part of the family. He stays until the department says otherwise. And if he doesn't correct his behavior and his lack of respect, I'll just put him on the Wicks get-happy program. But if he doesn't pull his head out of his ass pronto, it won't be up to me. Come in my office. Let's talk."

"My turn in the barrel?"

"Quit your whining and take a seat."

I followed him in and sat down in the chair in front of his desk. He sat in his own chair, put his gray snakeskin cowboy boot up on the desk, and pulled a pint bottle of Old Granddad whiskey from a drawer. He unscrewed the top and offered the bottle. He knew I didn't drink the hard stuff. "No thanks."

He took a slug, screwed the cap back on, dropped the bottle in the drawer, and shoved it closed.

"How's the thing with Duarte going?" I asked.

It wasn't like Wicks to come off a manhunt, especially one with such a high-profile target.

He waved his hand. "We're about five hours behind that asshole. We just hit a house, and they said he was there five hours ago. We'd have him in pocket now, but everyone's scared to death of this prick, and won't volunteer any information. We gotta do a lot more squeezin' than we normally do. We could really use you on this one, Bruno. If you and I were runnin' and gunnin' on this one, we'd already have him on a slab. But I think we'll get him by morning, tomorrow night latest."

"About yesterday, boss."

"Damn good job, grappling up that guy like that. Keep doin' what you're doin'."

"Oh, that's not exactly what I thought you were going to say. I thought you called me in to talk about the poor relations with the FBI? I didn't mean to run my mouth like that."

He put on half a smile, got up, came around, and sat on the corner of the desk. "I just told you, grabbing that bank robber was great. That's exactly what I expect from you. And yesterday, I might've told you to maybe power it down a little, but not now, not today. I want you to stick it to 'em and do it with my blessings." He held up his hand. "But within reason. Don't go capping any of those Feebies with friendly fire." He smiled more broadly. "Unless you think you can get away with it."

I didn't return his smile. This sounded too ominous.

His expression shifted to grim. "I'm real sorry about this, Bruno. I am. I picked you special for this job, thinking it was something entirely different, when it's not even close. I'll owe you big once it's done."

He might've had more than one snort before the meeting. It's hard to tell with Wicks. He could hold his liquor and still shoot with a deadeye.

"I'm not following you. Just tell me what's going on."

"Ah, hell. I handed you a shit sandwich and I can't see any way around it. We're gonna have to see it through and take a big bite."

"Explain."

He nodded. "I thought this was going to be a great gig; all the overtime we wanted, money, resources, deputy US Marshal status. I mean, it was too good to be true, and I should've known right off that it wasn't any good. Not with the FBI involved."

That sinking feeling came on in earnest. "And?"

"They boxed us. And like some kind of dope, I let it happen."

I waited. He'd tell it at his own speed. Didn't matter how much I prodded. He looked back over his shoulder at the closed desk drawer, for his friend Old Granddad, who beckoned to him.

"I found out early this morning," he said, "what's really goin' down. What they really want our team to do. I tried to get us out of it, but the Deputy Chief said we signed an MOU and we'll look like shit if we try to back out of it now. He said we'll just have to go easy on this one."

"Robby, what's going on?" I never called him by his first name, and in the two years I'd worked with him, I'd never seen him this concerned over any other operation.

"This whole bank robbery team they put together with our violent crime team folded in is nothing more than a front, a way for them to cover their own asses. And, at the same time, hang us out to take the fall. They're going to give you a case that we never would have touched. They want us to handle it because it has too much potential to blow up in their faces, a real public relations nightmare. In fact, I don't see us walking away from it with anything less than a black eye and probably a lot worse."

"Does this have to do with the Rollin' Sixties Crip gang?"

"How in the hell did you figure that out?"

I shrugged. "That's all I know. If they want us to handle this case you're describing, then why did they give us that case yesterday and another real stinker today?"

"My guess is they wanted you to fail on both, so when they gave you this stinker with the Rollin' Sixties, they could say, 'See, those buffoons with the Sheriff's Department really don't know what the hell they're doing, and that's why they screwed the pooch on this one.'"

He chuckled. "And then yesterday, you take the guy down in a couple of hours. That couldn't have been a sweeter deal. You really rubbed their noses in it. Man, you have no idea how much that tickles me."

"So now they gave me a case that's impossible to solve, and you're telling me this is all part of the same plan?"

"They want you to roll over and play dead. They want you to knuckle under, and say it's impossible, just before they give you this other one, with the kids involved."

"Kids? No, no, no. Not kids. Ah, shit."

CHAPTER NINETEEN

TEN THIRTY AT night I sat at the kitchen table in our house on Nord, going over the Thomas Guide map book, plotting out the next day's action plan. All the houses we'd need to check, going door to door in the summer heat and in one of the most dangerous parts in South Central Los Angles. No way did I think I'd come up with the Bogart Bandit. Not going at it like this. Not with the information I had to work with. We had no other options left but to go door to door. We had to go back over the same territory the FBI already covered, hoping they missed something. They did not have a good reputation for talking to people of the street—my one and only advantage. A small one. And according to Wicks, the whole thing was nothing more than a study in futility. But I wanted to kick something. Maybe even an FBI agent named Jim Turner, kick a lung out of him. How could Chelsea—

Didn't matter.

This case was only a stall until they gave us the real one: the one that involved kids. That one I didn't want to think about until I had to.

The only illumination in the house, a low-watt hanging light over the dining room table, encapsulated my entire world. The front door stood open, to let in what little breeze the summer night would allow. Dad had gone to bed at nine. He got up early every day to work his postal route. He'd been a neighborhood postman for the last twenty years. He never missed a day calling in sick and rarely took vacation. I didn't see him ever retiring from the job. He thought it a great honor to serve the public. From my first memories as a child, he'd always been a postman.

Dad came down the hall and out of the darkness, carrying Olivia, who fussed a little. Dad wore sleep on his face like a mask. "I'm going to get her some warm milk, see if I can get her back to sleep."

"Here, give her to me. You go back to bed."

"No, I'm okay. I'm up now."

He handed me my daughter. She sat on my lap facing me, smiling. "Hi, Pop. You wanna play dance, dance?" She patted my face and my world shifted on its axis. All the problems melted away. What a blessing—daughters. I could only smile and bounce her. "Not right now, baby. Tomorrow for sure, okay? I promise."

But something niggled at my brain. What was it? I played back what had just happened, and realized what it was. The way Dad had held Olivia when he came in, one arm under her legs, the other under her shoulders. That and her being a vulnerable little girl had suddenly caused me to flash on an incident from the past. I'd suppressed it for the better part of thirteen or fourteen years. Instead, I sat back in the chair as the memory rolled back onto me, thick and heavy and uncontrolled. I couldn't figure out why I'd not thought of it until that moment. I wanted to think it was the fatigue, the mess of problems that swirled around in my head. But that wasn't it at all. The huge responsibility Olivia represented had brought on the ugly memory.

* * *

Angry people in the Watts riot of 1965 burned to the ground all the big grocery stores in South Central Los Angeles. Dad called it the Watts Rebellion. The stores never came back, and we had to make the trek out of our neighborhood to a large grocery to get whatever the corner markets didn't carry. We usually designated the Sunday after payday for the event. In the Mayfair parking lot, Dad stopped to wait where a man was loading his car with groceries by himself while he tried to supervise two little girls in frilly dresses, with socks and black patent leather shoes, five and six years old. I was only twelve at the time and couldn't really tell their ages, for sure. We waited for his parking spot. He closed the tailgate to the station wagon and ushered the two girls into the back seat. He got into the front seat and tinkered with something, maybe rectifying his checkbook, or who knew what. Then he started the car . . . just as the back door on the far side of the station wagon opened, and the little blond head of one of the little girls bobbed as she started to get out. Maybe she'd dropped her doll getting in. Who knew how a child's mind worked? Dad muttered, "Oh, dear Lord." He shoved our car into park and opened his door. "Hey. Hey. Wait," he yelled at the man in the station wagon.

I got out, too.

The man didn't hear and backed up.

A horrible scream came from the far side of the car. The man braked hard. The car lurched to a stop. The man looked around, frantic, and then pulled the car forward. He got out and ran, with us, to the far side of the car. I didn't want to look, but couldn't help myself. The man's daughter lay on the ground, in her pink frilly dress, with the rear tire resting on her bare legs. She slapped and clawed at the tire, as she gave a long low keen, a sound that chilled me to the bone. The man instantly turned hysterical. He yelled,

"Oh my God, what've I done? Baby. Baby. Hold on. Hold on." He wasn't thinking straight, and with every passing second, pure panic continued to rise within him and took control. He grabbed the fender above the wheel well and tried to lift the car off his child. He howled and lifted, and howled some more. This all happened in a second or two.

Dad grabbed the white man, swung him around, and slapped him, hard. "Get in your car and back up. You hear me? Back up your car." Dad shook him. The man's wild-eyed panic cooled, some. He nodded and ran around his car. The little girl had stopped her keening and had lain back, her eyes closed. Dad knelt down next to her, picked up her shoulders, and held her. "Easy now." Dad yelled at the man, then to the little girl in his arms, "It's going to be okay, sweetie. You're going to be okay."

The panicked man hit the gas, and the tire on the girl's legs spun before it drove off of them. Dad pulled the girl out from under the car, muttering, "The damn fool. It's okay, sweetie, I got you now. It's all over." He carried her with one arm under her damaged legs, his other behind her shoulders as he hurried away. I followed. He slowed and turned to hand her to me. I held up my hands. He said, "Okay, then you're driving. Get in our car, behind the wheel."

"But I—"

"Don't back-talk me. Not right now, Son. Just do what I say, please."

The man and his other daughter ran to catch up. Dad didn't slow. "She going into shock. We need to get her to the hospital, right now. There's one real close."

The man nodded, his face pale, his eyes not focused enough to do anything but follow orders. He and his other daughter got in the back seat and slammed the door. Dad got in the front seat, and I got in behind the wheel, scared to death. I'd never driven before except when I was a kid on Dad's lap.

Dad held the wounded little girl in his lap, her white legs deformed and black in places, from the tire spinning. Dad calmly said, "Bruno, move your seat up until you can reach the peddles."

I did.

"That's good. Now you've seen me drive many times. You can do this. We have to hurry, Son. Foot on the brake." He pulled the gearshift down into drive. "Now foot off the brake and on the accelerator."

In a trance, I did exactly what he said. "Good. Good, you're doing fine. Speed up a little and head over that way, toward the street. Come on, let's move it. Let's move."

Behind me, the sister leaned up to my ear. "Is my sister, Kelly, going to be okay?"

I couldn't answer. I was driving. I pulled out onto the street too soon, misjudging the speed of the approaching car. It swerved around us, and the driver laid on the horn.

"Faster, Son. You're going to have to go faster. You're doing fine. We only have ten blocks to go, that's all." He brought his foot over and put it on top of mine, and pushed down. The car lurched forward.

One block passed, then another.

"There. There's a police officer," Dad said. "Honk the horn. Honk."

Dad had always taught me to stay away from the police whenever possible, that sometimes the police did not treat blacks appropriately. That's all he'd say about it. My entire life, I'd dodged them, took the long way around, whenever I came upon them. Now, he wanted me to get their attention while I was committing a crime.

I did as he asked and pushed on the horn. Beep. Beep.

"No, lay on it, and don't let off." We zipped by the cop on his motorcycle going in the same direction, as I laid on the horn. "Now pull over," Dad said as he put his foot on the brake pedal. "That's it.

That's it, you're doing just fine." We came to a complete stop not even close to the curb. The cop put his kickstand down. He started to take off his black gloves, as he sauntered up, too slow, to the driver's side. He bent down in my window. Sweat ran in my eyes, and my hands shook on the wheel. I couldn't look right at him but did out of the corner of my eye.

Dad said, "We have an injured girl here. We're headed to the hospital. She's hurt real bad."

The cop lifted his sunglasses. He saw the unconscious white girl, with the injured legs, on Dad's lap. "Sweet baby Jesus."

Dad said, "We're not far from the hospital."

The cop looked perplexed, as if he couldn't decide on a course of action. Dad said, "She's in shock."

The cop's expression shifted back to professional. He pointed at me. "He's not old enough to drive."

Dad said, "He is today. We're wasting time."

"Follow me." He ran back, got on his motorcycle, fired it up, and zipped around us with the siren blaring. Dad put his foot down, on top of mine on the accelerator, and we took off.

* * *

Back in the kitchen with Dad warming some milk, the memory reminded me that I had to pay attention, all the time, to Olivia. I couldn't take my eyes off her for one second. That heavy responsibility piled on, with all the other problems that I had to push aside, or go crazy. I cooed to Olivia and bounced her on my lap.

Looking back on what he did that day, Dad rescuing that little girl, he'd really taken a big chance. That whole situation could've—and probably should've—turned out horribly different. Dad deserved a medal for it, and no one else even knew about it.

"Hey, Dad?"

He looked over at us. "Yes, Son?"

"You remember that day, in the grocery store parking lot, when that little girl got hurt?"

"Of course I do. What made you think of that right out of the blue?"

"I was just wondering if you knew what happened to her?"

"She's a doctor up at LCMC—Los Angeles County Medical Center."

"What? How? I mean, you never told me that."

He just shrugged, picked up a plastic cup, and poured the milk from the pan. He came over and handed it to me. Olivia took it and sipped.

"So you kept track of her?"

"Not really." He sat down on the chair at the table. "Days after it happened, might've been several weeks, Joe came and knocked at the door." He pointed over to the front door. "I recognized him right off. He looked different, though. More put together. He said he just wanted to shake my hand and thank you and me for what we did that day. You were in school."

"Huh."

Dad stood and stretched. "Here, give her to me."

I didn't want him to take her but let her go anyway, after I kissed her forehead.

Dad took the empty cup from her and set it on the counter. Her eyes were already at half-mast. Her head lolled and rested on his shoulder. "When Ned comes in, tell him I need to talk to him about Beth, okay?"

"Sure. But how—"

"Joe and Lucy and Kelly send us Christmas cards every year. You know that."

I let it sink in. "Oh, you mean Joseph and Annie and their two little—that was them? I thought you said they were friends from work."

"I never said that. I guess that's just what you assumed. Goodnight, Son, see you in the morning. Don't stay up too late."

CHAPTER TWENTY

AN HOUR OR so later I still worked over the Thomas Guide making notations right on the map book.

From outside, Ned said, "Coming in."

You never walked, unannounced, into someone's house. Not in the ghetto. His feet clumped on the wooden steps. He appeared in the doorway, his hair a little disheveled, and lacking the famous Ned smile.

"Sorry I'm late picking up Beth."

I put the pencil down next to my revolver on the table. "I told you she could stay as long as you needed her to. Come on in, have a seat."

He came in the rest of the way and sat across from me, automatically facing the open door. His eyes looked a little bloodshot, and an odor of beer followed him in, and filled the room removing the softness from the scent of warmed milk and Olivia.

I reached in my pocket, took out a wad of twenties, and slid it across the table to him. "I stopped at the ATM on the way home tonight. If you need more than that, I'll go to the bank in the morning. Just tell me how much you need."

"What's this for?" He picked up the money.

"Don't play me, Ned. Something's going on. You stormed out of the office this afternoon. And I gotta tell ya, I wouldn't talk to Wicks like that again. He's got a long fuse when it comes to his men, but when he goes off, he really goes off."

He tossed the money on the table. "You think this is all about money?"

"I don't know what it's about. You won't let me in, and I'm kinda gettin' angry about it."

His voice went up a little. "Oh, I see. This morning when you asked for my fed money, I'm shy forty bucks. So now it's that old warning they drilled into us at the academy, 'watch out for the deadly three Bs: booze, broads, and bills.' And you think it's the bills running me down. Keep your money, Bruno, my friend, and thanks for the offer."

"If it's not money, then what is it?"

He kind of stared off, his eyes going a little blank, in a semi-trance. I watched him.

He finally said, "You ever think about Olivia? I mean, who would take care of her if something happened to you?"

"Sure, all the time. What brought this on?"

"What? Oh, something that happened on patrol in Lakewood. I never used to let those old calls bother me, but they come back on me now, more and more, since I have Beth to think about."

"Sometimes it's better to talk about it instead of keeping it all bottled up."

He nodded, still not looking at me. "I don't think so."

"Try me."

He shrugged, still not fully engaged. "It was a call of a med aide, 'man down.' This guy, about thirty years old, a dumbshit, really, for not turning off the electricity in his emptied pool before he changed out the light. Electrocuted himself. He was dead. This left his five-year-old son there by himself. The poor kid didn't know what to do. He only knew that when someone was hurt you put a Band-Aid on it." Ned turned to look at me, his eyes vacant as if he relived it. "When I got there, the dead dad was laying in the bottom of the empty pool, with Band-Aids all over his face and arms."

I hadn't been present at the call Ned described, but it resounded deep inside me.

Dad wandered into the living room and broke the spell from the story. He stood in his pajamas, sleep heavy in his expression. "What's going on?" He rubbed his right eye with a fist.

"Nothing, Dad. Sorry, we didn't mean to wake you a second time." I looked at Ned. "Me and Ned are just reviewing what we're going to do tomorrow."

Dad said to Ned, "Hey, I wanted to talk to you about Beth."

Ned took a couple of steps closer to Dad. "Is something wrong with her?"

"Maybe it's nothing, but she seems more skittish than a little girl should be. She spooks real easy."

"I haven't noticed anything like that, but then I'm not real used to having a little girl around. You think it's something important? Should I do something?"

"Like I said, it might be nothing. We'll just keep an eye on her for now, okay?"

"Sure, you know better than I do, so I'll defer to your experience. And thanks again, Mr. Johnson, for helping me out with her."

He waved off the gratitude and came further into the kitchen. He looked at the map book on the table and saw my more recent notations. "That's our neighborhood. Son, who are you hunting this time? Is it someone we know?"

Ned said, "We're looking for a girlfriend of a bank robber." Ned turned to me. "Hey, did your informant come through with a name?"

"No, after you left, Ollie called me back. She only caught a whisper on the street. A big maybe is all she could get for us. She got a possible first name, that's it, and it's paper-thin at best. She gave me 'Bea,' as in Bea Arthur, like the actress, or bee, like the insect. Don't know which. Now we have to go door to door to find her, so we can get her real name. It's a long shot. She might not even be the girlfriend of the Bogart Bandit."

Dad leaned over and squinted. He put his finger on the map. "Bea lives right there just off of Mona, 1500 block of 115th."

My mouth sagged open in awe. Dad could do that to me, right out of the blue, step up and make my world just a little easier. He'd been doing that since I was a kid. Way back, I started calling it daddy magic.

"Son of a bitch," Ned said.

"Watch your language, Ned," Dad said, "we got children in the house."

"Sorry."

"Dad, you really know a Bea who lives in this area?"

"Just said I did, didn't I? Nice little gal, everyone calls her—"

"Honeybee?" I said.

"That's right, that's the one."

The skin on my back and neck prickled at the confirmation and the abrupt shift in the situation.

Dad said, "But she doesn't live there anymore. Her mama doesn't know where she got off to. Ran away with some street gangster. It's really sad. Her mama thinks she's pregnant. That's why she took off, ran away from family and friends who are just tryin' to help her.

Thinks she went somewhere south, maybe Moreno Valley or Hemet. Somewhere like that."

"Do you know her last name?"

With his knuckles, he knocked on my head. "'Course I do, Son. I'm a mailman, remember? They call her Honeybee Holcomb. Bea Holcomb."

CHAPTER TWENTY-ONE

NED STARTED LAUGHING. "If this isn't the shit. This is it, isn't it, Bruno? This is a lead the Feebs don't have. And all they had to do was ask the local mailman."

That wasn't exactly true. Ollie had a big hand in it, and I'd still owe her the money, and the favor with her nephew.

Dad shook his head at Ned's language.

"Yeah, I think we can work this," I said. "It's going to be a little easier to track her than the Bogart Bandit, but not by much. So don't get your hopes up."

Ned stood, wandered over to the couch. "I have faith in you, partner. Mind if I sleep here tonight? We're gonna want to get an early start tomorrow." He didn't wait for the perfunctory "yes," stretched out on the couch, and laid his arm over his eyes.

"Sure," Dad told him. "You're welcome anytime, Ned, my boy, as long as you come back with a brush and a bucket of high gloss white, to repaint our walls."

Ned chuckled. "Oh no, old man, my lovely and perfect little Beth doesn't know how to draw, especially on walls. That's all on Olivia."

My turn to chuckle. "You have any proof of that?"

He raised his right hand as if *testilieing* in court. "I don't want to be a rat, but I saw the whole thing, Your Honor."

Dad smiled and waved his hand. "Sure, you're right. See you all in the morning. I'm going back to bed."

I waited for him to get down the hall and his bedroom door to close. "You going to tell me what the problem is, the one Wicks knows about and I don't?"

"Naw, why ruin a good high. I mean, I can't believe you came up with a name like that, right outta the blue. Hey, after I left, did Wicks chew your ass like we thought? Over disrespecting the FBI?"

"Not at all. He said he thought it was great. In fact—" I stopped short. I didn't want to give Ned, of all people, the go-ahead to disparage the FBI at every opportunity. He already did that too often.

"Then what did he want?"

I pulled a chair over, closer to the couch where, at the same time, I could still see out the door, if unwanted guests tried to approach the house from the street. "I guess I should tell you what's going on."

He didn't look too concerned. He pulled his arm down, opened one eye to gaze at me. "Damn straight you better fill me in."

"The FBI is running a game on us."

"And you're surprised because why? I'm not. Go on, give it to me."

"They started up this whole bank robbery team for one reason. They want us to chase one particular crew that's causing them a problem."

"Okay . . . and?" He closed his eye, unconcerned.

"No, this is a real turd they handed us. This crew they want us to take down is made up of fourteen- fifteen- and sixteen-year-old kids."

Ned sat up. "You're shittin' me?"

"No, and it gets worse, a lot worse. A guy by the name of Amos Leroy Gadd recruits these kids off the basketball courts, right here in my neighborhood. Well, a little north of here anyway, Rollin' Sixties turf. Good kids from good families. He brainwashes them.

Then he offers them a thousand dollars each—more money than they've ever seen. He arms them with real guns and gives them a stolen van. He tells them no matter what happens they can't go to jail 'cause they're juvies. He follows them to the bank, watches from a car down the street, and follows them back here to the ghetto. They're doing two banks a week. He rotates the whole bunch of these kids, so they never work the same job together. This makes it harder to identify them, and to backtrack to Gadd."

Ned whistled and shook his head in amazement.

"The bad part," I said, "is that a couple of those kids have gone missing. Word on the street is, Gadd snuffed them to keep all the others from talking, and it's worked. No one is saying a word. No one. And we'd need a witness to arrest Gadd for conspiracy, or he's just going to keep on corrupting and endangering these children. The children will go to jail, and Gadd won't. If we don't flip one of the kids, there's no way we can touch Gadd. And even then, I don't think testimony alone will be enough to put Gadd away. We'll need some kind of corroborating evidence that isn't there."

Ned moved to the edge of the couch. "So, let me get this straight. We're supposed to follow some armed kids around until they rob a bank and then take them down in progress? What if they shoot at us? We can't fire back, not at a bunch of kids. And what if they flee in a van? We can't chase 'em. They might crash, and get hurt or killed."

"Exactly."

"FBI. Those bastards."

"No, but listen. I've been giving it a lot of thought, and this might be for the best."

"How in the hell do you figure that?"

"Another team on these kids might not give them the chance we would."

Ned looked away from me and out into the night through the front door. After a moment he said, "That means . . . I mean if it's what I think you're saying, they can shoot at us, and we can't shoot back at them. And we still have to try and take them into custody."

"Something like that . . ."

He didn't say anything for a moment, as he pondered that dilemma—the same one that continued to bang around in my head. Put in that situation—where it's the kid or me—could I pull the trigger? Not likely. Then what happens to Olivia?

Ned finally said, "Hey, I need to ask a big favor."

"You got it."

"If anything ever happens to me, will you take care of Beth?"

"Nothing's going to happen to you."

He looked back at me. "No, I'm serious, will you?"

"Of course I will. You didn't have to ask. That's a given."

The sad part was that I couldn't, in clear conscience, ask Ned to look after Olivia if something happened to me. I loved Ned like a brother, but I couldn't do it. He was a sharp street cop, but he tended to make the wrong decisions in his personal life.

Ned said, "Looks like we need to go after this Amos Gadd and light his ass up. That's the only way we can stop this violent scenario he's put in play. He called the game, so I won't feel bad about it one bit."

"Wicks left it up to me, but he said, if he were chasin' Gadd, it would be all about the blood and bone." A term Wicks used when he caught up to a crook who didn't want to go to prison, and the crook, weapon in hand, took a stand against Wicks.

CHAPTER TWENTY-TWO

I SHOULD NOT have gone to sleep thinking about the terrible confrontation: the one looking down the top of my gun at a kid running out of a bank with a bag of money in one hand and a gun in the other. The image remained vivid, alive, the expressions of fear and hate, the smell of despair and gun smoke, as I drifted off. It mixed with the other nightmare, one that I'd finally beaten back, and had not seen for at least three or four months.

The one set in the parking lot behind Lynwood sheriff's station.

* * *

Two aisles over in the main driveway, Blue came running in from the street, looking over at us as he ran on by.

Wicks stiffened. "Bruno, you wait right here." He took off his suit coat and let it drop to the ground. He walked with deliberation toward the trailer, his gun hand now free to draw his Colt .45.

Blue turned, running backward, slowed, and then stopped. He faced Wicks.

I followed along behind. "Wait. Wait." I didn't want Wicks to gun Blue. I got to within a half a step behind him when he stopped about thirty feet from Blue. I still wasn't thinking too clearly.

Wicks said, "Blue, I need to take you in, now."

"I don't think so. You okay, Bruno? You look like hell. You're bleeding. What happened?"

Wicks said, "Thibodeaux's dead."

The light in Blue's eyes shifted to that same look I saw that night in the alley behind the gas station on Mona; shifted to pure predator. "That's too bad. Dirt was a good friend, a good man to have in a pinch. He'll be missed. You have something to do with that, Wicks?"

"Of course I did. But if you're asking if I dropped the hammer, no, I didn't."

"You, Bruno?"

I shook my head. "Thibodeaux put Mo Mo down."

"Like I said, Dirt was a damn good man." Blue started walking closer.

"You don't seem too broke up over it," Wicks said.

Blue shrugged. "Such is life in the ghetto."

That's when I saw the sock over Blue's hand. Adrenaline dumped into my system, clearing my head and making every muscle in my body hum with tension, ready to act.

"Wicks?"

"Not now, Bruno."

"Wicks?"

"Bruno, I said—"

Blue raised his hand, the one with the sock. The one with the small .38 hidden inside.

In one motion, I shoved Wicks to the side and drew my gun, the stock slick and at the same time sticky in my hand.

Blue fired.

The bullet zipped by my ear, inches away from being a fatal shot.

I fired one time. The bullet caught Blue in the stomach. He went down hard.

Wicks fired from the ground, and hit the trailer behind where Blue stood, not a moment before.

"He's down," I yelled. "He's down." I moved into the line of fire so Wicks wouldn't have another shot. All the energy drained out of me.

The first time I ever shot my gun on duty, and I shot a cop, right behind the sheriff's station.

Wicks scrambled to his feet and over to us. "Jesus H. I didn't know he had a gun in his hand. I thought it was just a sock."

On my knees, I took the smoking sock, and gun, away from Blue, who said, "You shouldn't have stuck your nose into it. Wicks needs killin'. You'll regret it; believe me, you'll regret it."

"Yeah, yeah," Wicks said. "Look who's on the ground, gutshot, pal."

Wicks turned to me. "What did I tell you? Never leave it unfinished. If he's good for one, he's good for all six. You understand me? Always finish it."

*   *   *

The next morning, I woke early without the alarm, my body slick with sweat, shivering in a hot bedroom, the metallic taste of burnt gunpowder on my tongue. Not real, just a memory.

I showered and shaved and put on a comfortable pair of jeans and a khaki shirt, with the name patch "Karl" over one breast pocket and "Hammond Trucking" over the other. I now had eight of these kinds of shirts hanging in my closet. In the two years working with Wicks chasing murderers and violent degenerates, who lacked any sort of moral compass, I found I looked and acted too much like a cop. When I put on the Hammond Trucking shirt and donned a green John Deere ball cap, I could virtually blend in anywhere, as an innocuous truck driver.

I put my department issue four-inch model 66 .357 Magnum in a pancake holster on my hip and a second gun, a model 60 .38 caliber Chief, in my waistband, both of them under the shirt and out of view.

In the living room, Ned's arm hung off the couch as he continued to snore. I put the coffee on just as Mrs. Espinoza knocked at the door. Ned still hadn't stirred.

Dad came from the back of the house wearing his postal uniform, carrying Beth and Olivia, one under each arm. He set them down. Olivia ran right to Mrs. Espinoza and jumped up into her arms. Mrs. Espinoza said, "Hola, mija."

"Ola, Mamie."

I wished Olivia had run to me and jumped in my arms. I promised myself to cut back on my time on the job, to be home more often.

Beth saw her dad on the couch, let out a little yelp, and ran to him. She patted his face with both her hands. "Papa. Papa." He woke, sat up, and smiled hugely. "Well, hello there. How's my little girl?" He stood, scooped her up, swung her around, and gave her a big hug.

I poured two cups of coffee and handed him one. "You better get yourself a shower. We're going to be rollin' out soon."

"Why you dressed like that? You goin' trick-or-treatin'?"

I ignored him and kissed Olivia on the cheek. She stuck her arms out. It made me smile and warmed my heart. I took her from Mrs. Espinoza and bounced her a little. Ned handed Beth to Mrs. Espinoza. Olivia leaned out to her, so I handed my daughter back.

I walked to the phone and dialed a number from memory, a friend from school, who now worked at the county department of welfare.

Ned came over sipping his coffee. "Who are you calling at seven thirty in the morning?"

"Angie. She works . . . yes, hello, is Angie there? Yes, I'll hold, thank you." I put my hand over the phone. "You better jump in the shower."

He nodded and sipped his coffee, his hair in disarray, his face still heavy with sleep.

"Angie, it's me, Bruno. Can you run a name for me, please? Yeah, yeah, I'll owe you another dinner. Her name's Bea Holcomb. She's a BFA about twenty-three or twenty-four. She used to reside on 115th Street. Yes, I'll hold, thanks."

Ned hadn't moved. "Ned, get going."

Angie came back on the phone. I said, "Okay, thanks," and hung up.

"Well?" Ned asked.

"That was a no-go." I hadn't realized how much I wanted that to work.

Ned said, "You've used that before, going through welfare?"

"Yeah, they always have the most recent address because the social workers monitor the home and the people on the dole want their checks. Man, I really wanted that to come out differently."

"Was that LA welfare?"

"Yes it was." His question gave me an idea. Dad had said Bea might have moved to Moreno Valley or Hemet. I picked up the phone and dialed the same number. "Angie, it's me again. Hey, do you have a number for a contact who I can call to run that name through San Bernardino and Riverside Counties? Uh-huh. Yeah, that'd be great. Thank you." I hung up. "She's going to call them and then call me back. You better get in the shower. I'm not kidding here, Ned."

"We don't even know if this is the Bogart Bandit's girlfriend," he said. "Your snitch only told you it *might* be, right?"

"Her name's Ollie—don't call her a snitch."

The phone rang. I picked it up. "Hello?" I grabbed a pencil and started writing.

CHAPTER TWENTY-THREE

NED STOOD CLOSE enough to read what I wrote, and whispered, "I'll be a son of a bitch."

I elbowed him for his language in front of the children.

"Thank you," I said into the phone. "Yes, and if this works out, I'll owe you ten dinners. No, I'm absolutely serious. Thanks again, Angie."

I tore the paper off the pad. "Come on, let's roll."

"What about my shower?"

"Too bad. How many times did I warn you, huh? If you're going with me, we're rollin' right now." I went over and kissed Olivia good-bye. Ned kissed Beth and followed me to the door. I stopped. "Really? You're not going to shower?"

"You just said you weren't going to wait. I don't care if I smell me because it's just me. I can't tell the difference. You're the one who's going to suffer all day."

"Okay, hurry, go."

"You'll wait?"

"Yeah, I'll wait."

He rushed off to the bathroom, yelling over his shoulder. "You better be out here when I get done."

Twenty minutes later, we turned onto Century Boulevard, headed east to the freeway, Ned's hair still dripping.

"It's opposite traffic," I said, "so we should get there by ten or so."

Ned said, "Did you call that dickhead Jim Turner, our brave and wondrous liaison with the FBI?"

"No, did you?"

"No, I was in the shower. You call Chelsea, that sexy girlfriend of yours, to brief her?"

"No. And she's not my girlfriend, so knock it off. We'll call them if and when we get a viable lead."

Ned clapped his hands together. "Hot damn. This is going to be great."

"Don't jinx it. This is still a long shot."

"No it's not—not when I'm riding shotgun with the great Bruno the Bad Boy Johnson."

"There. You just went and did it. You jinxed this whole thing."

The drive to San Bernardino took an hour and a half. Ned had the Thomas Guide open on his lap navigating, feeding me directions. But I knew the way. In the past, the team had chased other violent offenders back to San Bernardino. The farther south we drove, the drier the environment became. Not much remained green. Shrubs and ground cover along the sides of the I-10 freeway burned brown when the state turned off the water, to conserve. The bright summer sun rose higher in the sky washing out most of the blue with blending variances of yellows and whites. Nine thirty in the morning and the air-conditioning was working hard to keep us cool.

I exited at Waterman and took it north. After a few miles, I set up to make a right turn onto Third Avenue.

"Hey, hey, wait. Not here," Ned said. "Keep going north, to Baseline, and turn left."

"We need to make notification that we're working in San Bernardino's area."

"Seriously?"

"Yes, seriously. What if we knock on the door of this apartment, and it goes to guns. We just violated our department policy for failure to notify the agency with jurisdiction. Then, when the cops respond to shots fired, they don't know we're out here capering. When they roll up, they won't know us from Adam, and they might shoot us."

"A white guy and a black guy in an all-black area. I think they'll figure it out."

"We're making notification."

"Okay, Dad."

"Yeah, you're right, someone has to be the adult in this relationship."

Two long blocks from Waterman on Third, I turned into the San Bernardino County Sheriff's Department parking lot and dumped the Ranger in a visitor's slot.

We went in and approached the front desk. Ned grabbed my arm and moved ahead a little as he reached into his back pocket. He pulled his ID and showed it to the young woman wearing a white blouse with sheriff's emblems. "Deputy US Marshals." Ned smiled and turned to me. "I always wanted to say that."

"Can I help you?" the clerk asked.

I showed her my sheriff's flat badge. "Yes, thank you. Don't mind him, he's a twit."

She smiled.

"Yes, can I please speak with your detective sergeant?"

"Just one moment, please." She dialed.

Ned whispered, "Man, that smile of hers made me want to—"

I elbowed him. He grunted. "Hey."

"We're guests."

"I was just gonna say, what a difference. Not like the reception we get at the FBI office."

"No you weren't. You were going to say something vulgar."

He smiled. "Okay, I was."

The cute clerk hung up. "He'll be right out."

The door to the side opened. Out stepped a man wearing a green polo shirt with a bright yellow sheriff's star embroidered over the breast, and black utility pants. He wore a gun in a black pancake holster on his hip. He extended his hand. "Sergeant Samuelson."

I shook. "Detective Bruno Johnson, and this is Detective Ned Kiefer. We're with LASD's violent crimes team."

"What can I do for you?"

"I just wanted to make notification that we're going to be in your area tracking a fugitive."

"Great. What can I do to help?"

"Nothing," Ned said. "We got this."

"Could you spare a couple of guys to go with us, for communications and backup?"

"We have our own operation going—a multiple jurisdiction, multiple search warrant service—and I'm kind of tight on manpower right this minute. Can this wait a couple of hours, maybe three?"

"No problem, we can handle this," Ned said again.

"This guy we're after," I said, "he's a pretty heavy dude, a bank robber, who's been evading law enforcement for two years."

Samuelson hesitated. "Right. I understand. I can give you two guys but—" He hesitated again, and looked from side to side. "Ah, they're really great guys, good street cops, but they're a little green. They're brand-new detectives."

"No problem, we can use them."

"Be right back."

The clerk buzzed the door. He went back the way he came.

"Bruno, I got a bad feeling about this."

"Why? You were green and new once."

"But like you said, this is a heavyweight we're going after."

"He said they were great street cops. I'll take a great street cop over a veteran detective any day."

"You got a point there."

The door opened and out stepped two deputies, both wearing green polo shirts and black utilities.

"You the detectives from LA? My name's Tony, and this is my partner, Mike."

We shook. "My name's Bruno, and this is Ned. Do you two have street clothes you can change into? We don't want this guy to see us coming."

"Sure, no problem."

"Great. We'll meet you out front in the parking lot."

Ten minutes later, a white Toyota Camry drove around the side and stopped. Tony and Mike got out wearing denim and long-sleeve work shirts. They looked like construction workers.

I put the Thomas Guide on the hood of their car. "We're going to an address right here looking for a girl named Bea Holcomb."

Tony said, "Sergeant told us you were looking for a badass bank robber. Is this girl a bank robber?"

"No. We think it might be the bank robber's girlfriend."

"Oh, I gotcha. Good idea."

Ned put the Bogart Bandit file on the hood and opened it. "We're looking for this guy. He's listed as armed and dangerous and has a no-bail warrant out for him for multiple bank robberies."

Tony said, "Now we're talking." He picked up the file and looked closer at the photo. Tony looked younger than Mike by almost ten years. Mike didn't say much.

Mike said, "What do you want from us?"

"You guys have radios?" I asked.

"Yep."

"Then because of the communication issue, we're going to split up. Tony will come with me."

Ned shot me the stink-eye.

"And, Ned, you ride with Mike in their car." I pointed to the map. "We'll pull up and park right here and walk in."

Tony said, "Sound's great, let's roll."

I smiled at Ned, who gave back a forced grin.

CHAPTER TWENTY-FOUR

TONY SAT IN the passenger seat, his body humming with excitement. "Your department issues you guys trucks to drive?"

"No, this is my truck." I didn't want to tell him how cheap the SO was when it came to cars. His question also made me decide to pick up the cars the FBI had offered us, as soon as we finished out the day. There wasn't any reason to drive our own vehicles.

Tony said, "That getup you got on is really cool. I bet you can go anywhere wearing that. I'm going to ask my sergeant if I can do the same thing."

I didn't want to tell him to wait until he had some time under his belt as a detective. If you penetrated too far, too fast undercover and didn't know how to handle yourself when you got there, it was usually too late, and the street ate you.

I only nodded and looked up in the rearview. In the car right behind us, Ned and Mike sat in the white Camry, neither of them speaking. Mike stayed right on my butt, giving me the Blue Angel treatment: a patrolman kind of move. I turned right onto Waterman, still headed north. I asked, "So how long have you been with the Sheriff's Department?"

"Five years."

"You made detective pretty quick, then."

"Little better than average for time in grade. How about you?"

"Been with the department about five years, two with the violent crimes team."

"Very nice. I'd give my left nut to work a team like that." He pointed. "Your turn's coming up right here, make a left."

I knew the route having memorized it from the map.

Tony said, "I know this area, and if it's the apartment complex I'm thinking of, it's a derelict, with no one living in it."

"Ah man, you could've said something earlier ... no, sorry, I'm wrong. We need to check it either way."

"Couple of months back, might've been three or four, I went there on a call for service, a 415 domestic. The guy there said most of the apartments were vacant. The owner just didn't rent them out again after somebody moved out. He wants to renovate so he can charge more. Like I said, though, that was months back. Here. Take a left right here, on Wall. That's it, about halfway down there, on the right, that big white and light blue two-story apartment."

I pulled to the curb. "We'll walk in from here."

"All right by me."

We got out. Ned and Mike parked behind us. Mike reached back in and pulled out a shotgun. He racked one in the chamber and held it down by his leg to be less conspicuous. On the sidewalk, I said to Mike, "That's the target location, and it's a two-story. The apartment we're looking for is number 213. It'll be one of those on that top row. Since you have the gauge, you stay outside and watch the windows, in case our boy, if he's in there, decides to jump."

Mike nodded, and with his free hand, took his aviator sunglasses from his shirt pocket and put them on as we continued to move.

A few pedestrians walked on the sidewalks on both sides of the street, and watched us. A couple of cars drove by and slowed to peep the intruders in their neighborhood.

Two houses away, a machinelike noise echoed off the neighbor-hood house fronts, and a white chalky powder billowed into the air over our target apartment building.

We left the sidewalk and stayed on the cracked concrete walk leading to the complex. Without a word, I looked at Mike and pointed to the long row of apartments on the second story. He nodded and took cover by a tree in the parkway.

We had to move fast now. People would be talking and passing the word. A white guy—Mike, standing by a tree on the street with a blower—couldn't be mistaken for anything other than the law come-a-knockin'.

The noise grew louder as we entered the quad area of the semi-defunct Sycamore Arms Apartments. Three painters, dressed in white and wearing industrial-grade breathing masks, used a sand-blaster to take the paint off the stucco walls inside the quad. The dust obscured everything, the same as a light fog. Chain-link fencing surrounded a pool now filled with dirt and weeds tangled around an overturned kid's tricycle. The grit and dust immediately invaded my nose and mouth and lungs. I suppressed a cough and headed for the exterior steps that led up to the cantilevered walkway on the second floor. A door opened next to us and out stepped a black gang member tattooed and dressed in blue, representing the Crips. He didn't look surprised. He looked angry.

Ned automatically grabbed him, put him on the wall, and patted him down. We couldn't leave anyone on our flank. Ned knew that and hung back. Tony stayed with me as we ascended the stairs. Two more gang members came out of the apartment. Ned took a step back, hand on his gun in his holster, and pointed for them to grab the wall. He waved for us to keep going.

Halfway up the steps, I leaned out to look at the cantilevered walkway above us. A short male, black with a white slingshot tee

shirt, black pants, and bare feet, stood outside an apartment farther down the long row of doors. The cord from an electric shaver
snaked inside, and he continued shaving his gleaming and semi-
bald pate.

His stature matched the Bogart Bandit's description. Sort of.
The same height anyway, but if it was him, he'd put on a few
pounds, maybe twenty or thirty. He looked a lot rounder, fleshier
than in his photo. His whole body was chubby, including his
face. I wished I could see his chest, to confirm the tattoo of a woman's naked breasts. My heart rate accelerated until it pulsed in
my throat. I continued to move toward him, concealing my excitement, as I fought the urge to reach under my shirt, draw my
weapon, and start yelling.

We made it up the stairs. I slowed and whispered to Tony, "Let
me take the lead, you just back my play."

"You got it, chief."

The guy shaving his head kept his back to us, unaware of our presence. I hoped he stayed that way until we got right up on him. Ten
apartments to go.

Seven.

Five.

He must've sensed something. His shoulders stiffened, and he
stopped shaving. If this really was Deforest, he'd been hunted
hard and heavy for two years, and his instincts had to be honed
to a fine edge. He slowly turned, saw us, and smiled. He looked
back to see how far he stood from the open apartment door, where,
if he was the Bogart Bandit, he'd have his gun stashed, probably
several.

I kept walking at the same speed, unperturbed, and nodded to
him.

Three apartments to go.

He held my eyes trying to get a read on me and didn't nod back. A bad sign.

Two.

We came up on him, and I said loud over the noise of the sandblaster, "Hey!"

"Can I hep you?"

When he said it, his gold-cap glinted in the top row of his teeth. Confirmation.

This was the Bogart Bandit.

I looked at Tony to see if he'd caught on to this sudden change in our status, how the threat level increased from a casual contact to just short of going to guns against a violent felon. He hadn't noticed.

I said to Raymond Desmond Deforest, "I'm with welfare and child protective services." I pulled out my sheriff's flat badge, flipped it open fast, and pulled it back so he didn't have time to read it. "We need to count how many children you have in your apartment to verify entitlement."

I didn't want to fight him on the cantilevered walkway if he resisted. Someone might end up going over the rail. It happened once before when I worked with Wicks. A big biker named Shackleford went over—broke both arms and cracked his skull. He died four days later of a swollen brain. *Blood and bone.*

Deforest looked us up and down one more time, deciding whether a black guy dressed like a truck driver might actually work with CPS. He'd played it smart for two years. He'd been able to evade every effort to capture him. I didn't think he'd fall for my ruse.

"A'ight, den, come on in." He turned and took the two steps back to his open door, and entered.

I moved quickly to stay with him, Tony right on my butt.

Inside, as soon as our eyes adjusted, I found we'd made an awful mistake. Four more gang members sat in chairs and on the couch, all of them much bigger than Deforest. We were outnumbered and outgunned. That's why Deforest had agreed to go in. He knew the odds would change in his favor.

A fifth gang member, behind us, closed the door, trapping us like a couple of rats.

CHAPTER TWENTY-FIVE

TONY DIDN'T LOOK scared at all, too much of a new guy to be scared. His trumped-up bravado let him falsely believe he could take on the world and win. He stared Deforest down and finally tore his eyes away to look at me to call the play. I'd caught his look out of the corner of my eye.

There was nothing for it. We'd run out of options when we crossed the threshold. I pulled both guns at once, my hands moving at lightning speed, and yet still not fast enough. I moved right up on Deforest, the Bogart Bandit, as I pointed my gun at his nose yelling, "Everyone down! Everyone down on the floor. Now. Get down. Get down. On the floor. Sheriff's Department. Sheriff's Department. Get down. Get down."

Tony drew his gun and grabbed a hold of the gang member behind us, the sharpest move he could've made. I reached out and swung my arm around Deforest's throat, yanked him toward me. Now they'd have to shoot through him if they wanted me.

The other four didn't react as fast as we did. They'd just started going for their guns, reaching while I'd grappled up Deforest.

"Don't," I yelled. "Don't do it. I'll shoot him."

Everyone froze for one interminable moment.

"I said, everyone get on the floor. Do it now."

The moment broke, and the four moved to the floor and went prone.

Behind me, Tony whispered, "What now?"

"Get on your radio and call for backup."

"I don't have a radio."

I broke eye contact with the ones on the floor, the ones I held my gun on, and looked at Tony. "What do you mean you don't have a radio?"

"We didn't bring handhelds; they needed all of them for the operation. We only have the one in our car."

Deforest, his chin in the crook of my arm, said, "What are you going to do now, Mr. Pooleeseman?"

"Shut up." Then I said to Tony, "Cuff that guy you got and then you're going to step out the door and yell to my partner." Outside with all the noise from the sandblasting, Ned didn't know what we'd stepped into.

Deforest said to his friends on the floor, "They cain't shoot you—you don't have any guns in your hands. Dey can't shoot an unarmed nigga. You kin take 'em. Ten thousand for the homeboy who—"

I tightened my grip on his neck with my arm choking off his words, and whispered, "Try me. You'll be the first one, fat boy. I'll pump one right in your melon."

This time, with his face bloating, his lungs struggling for air, he rasped out, "Twenty thousand."

Three of the gang members on the floor started to get up.

The apartment door kicked open. Ned rushed in following his drawn gun, his voice calm and controlled. "Peekaboo, assholes."

Mike, with his aviator sunglasses, swung the shotgun into the room and leveled it on the three getting up from the floor. They saw the gauge and eased back down.

We cuffed three more and ran out of cuffs. Tony went to Deforest's phone and called in an additional sheriff patrol unit for transportation.

I said to Ned, "Let's toss this place." We started a methodical search and immediately turned up six handguns, a sawed-off shotgun, and a cheap TEC-9—a poor man's machine pistol.

Deforest asked, "How'd you all find me? The FBI's been all over my ass for three years now, goin' on four, and they couldn't do it. No, sir, dey didn't even come close."

Ned stopped pulling up the carpet and looked at him. "Don't try and flatter yourself, little man. It was only two years and the way we found you, we got a tip that some Oompa Loompa with a gold tooth had moved in here and we knew it had to be you."

Mike with the shotgun and sunglasses smiled. Ned laughed too hard at his own joke.

The crooks on the floor laughed, too, and one said, "Man, dat's harsh, but I kin see it. I can. Bogart, man, you could be in dat movie with Charlie and his Chocolate Factory."

They'd heard the name "Bogart" the FBI gave Deforest, probably from the television when they put out the reward.

"Shut up, all of you all, or when I get out, I'll come for ya all. I will. I don't look like no got-damn Oompa Loompa. Shee-it."

Ned moved closer. "Really? I bet if you put on ten more pounds I could even get you a job in the wax museum as one of them Oompa Loompas."

Now everyone laughed. I suppressed a smile. "All right, knock it off."

I went to the phone, took out the business card Jim Turner gave me, and dialed the direct number to his desk. He answered on the first ring. "FBI, Special Agent Jim Turner, bank robbery."

Ned hurried over and put his ear right up next to mine.

"Special Agent Jim Turner, this is Deputy Johnson and—"

"Yes, Deputy Johnson, how is all that reading coming along? I forgot to tell you that I'd prefer you read the file at a desk in this office. Would you return to this office, now please?"

Ned let out a little giggle.

I said, "Aah, I don't think it's necessary to read that file anymore."

He paused, his next words cautious. "Why is that, Deputy Johnson?"

"We got the Bogart Bandit."

Another long pause. I tried to imagine him sitting at his desk among all his peers, and next to his boss Chelsea Miller, as his face started to bloat and turn red, his hand turning white holding the phone. "Fuck you." The words came out in a harsh whisper.

He'd broken character. I never imagined some uptight admin pogue like him saying something like that, not an up-and-coming Special Agent with eyes on a plum assignment in D.C., and especially not in his office in front of all his peers.

Ned howled with laughter. I stepped away from him. He followed along. Turner had to be able to hear him.

I said into the phone, "Where do you want me to take Deforest? He's a federal fugitive, and I think I'm supposed to take him forthwith to appear before a federal magistrate, right?"

Silence.

Jim Turner must've been trying to get himself under control. He came back on, his words spoken through clenched teeth. "If you have him? If you really have him, bring him to me. I want to see him."

"Sure thing, Jim. To your office?"

"No. Where are you?"

"San Bernardino." He didn't want to make matters worse by me parading the Bogart Bandit in front of all his peers in the FBI bank robbery bullpen.

"Bring him to the front parking lot at San Bernardino County Sheriff's Department. I'll see you there in twenty minutes." He slammed the phone down when he hung up.

I said, "Okay, good-bye," to nobody and hung up. It was small-minded of me but I couldn't believe how good that felt.

CHAPTER TWENTY-SIX

TEN MINUTES LATER we drove the Ford Ranger with the Bogart Bandit, Raymond Desmond Deforest, wedged between us. The huge bulge of his fat body made it difficult to shift the truck and work the clutch.

Deforest looked at Ned. "Who do you two donut-eaters work for? I have a right to know who finally caught me. FBI? I heard you all talkin' ta the FBI on the phone."

"Shut up," Ned said. "Hey, Bruno, can you stop at that drive-thru right there. I'm starvin', and my large intestine is about to eat the small one and you know what that means—it'll probably give me a lot of gas." He put one hand on his stomach and moved his butt around on the seat. He pursed his lips as if trying to hold something in.

"Yeah, yeah." I almost checked the time. It didn't matter. I decided Special Agent Jim Turner could wait. Let him sit there in the parking lot festering in this heat while he tried to decide if I was yanking on his leg about the capture of Deforest. It also gave me time to savor the short-lived victory. Tomorrow they'd give us the case involving Amos Gadd and the children.

I wheeled into the Sonic Burger on Waterman and pulled into one of the service slots. A girl on skates wheeled over.

Deforest said to me, "I'll take a double cheeseburger with extra grilled onions, large fries, and a chocolate malted."

The nice blond skated up to Ned's window and gave Ned a big smile. "What'll you have, boys?"

"Damn," Ned said to her, "I haven't had dinner, and I'm already thinking about dessert."

The girl blushed.

Deforest laughed. "Nigga, you don't have a chance with dat fine piece a—"

Ned elbowed him.

"Ow—hey!"

"Give us two cheeseburgers, two orders of fries, and two chocolate malts. That good for you, Bruno?"

"Sure."

"Two?" Deforest said. "Did you order something for me? You didn't order anything for me."

Ned didn't turn around and kept looking at the girl in his window. "Do you have something light like a tuna fish sandwich and an ice tea?"

"Hey. Hey. No way, man. I don't want any kinda shit like that."

She continued to smile. "Yes, we do."

"We'll take that, too." He turned to Deforest. "You don't exactly have a say in this. You're lucky you're getting anything. Besides, you don't want to be an Oompa Loompa all your life, do you?" Ned reached over, patted him down, found some folding money in Deforest's shirt pocket. "And you're buyin'."

"Hey, dat ain't right."

The girl let out a little snicker until her eyes fell to Deforest's handcuffed hands, then she turned scared, her eyes went large, and her mouth formed into a small "O."

"It's cool." Ned pulled out his wallet and flipped it open. "We're Deputy US Marshals."

"Really?" the girl said.

"Yep, that's us, Deputy US Marshals."

"Really?" Deforest said. "I got caught by the federal pooleese. Man, I can't wait to tell Lil Marv about this. He's gonna shit. He's jus' gonna shit. And this whole time I thought you were a couple a donut-eatin' County Mounties. I woulda swore on my mama's eyes that you were. Damn."

"Hey," Ned said. "Watch it, there's a lady present."

"I'll be right back." The girl skated off. Ned watched her go in the side mirror mounted on the door. "Man, oh man, that girl's got legs that go all the way to the top."

I twisted, turning my back to the door as best I could to put a little distance between me and Deforest. "What did you do with all that money you stole from all those banks?"

"Damn, I get asked dat all the time. Every damn-body wants ta know dat. People think I got all kinds of money stashed away somewheres, that I got money comin' outta my ass. It ain't like dat. I get maybe fifteen to twenty from each bank job. Which is nothin' really. I got too many expenses. I gots three womens with chillrens ta support. Can't ever stay in one place more'n a couple a nights. Take's some real money ta do dat. And my homeboys, dey can eat, I'm tellin' yeah, dey kin put down the waffles and chicken."

"Fifteen to twenty thousand?" Ned said.

"Dat's what I said, funny man. You got saw dust in your ears?"

Ned said, "Times eighty-six banks, that's a million three on the low end and a million seven on the top end."

"Get the fuck outta here."

"No, it is, do the math."

"Are you shittin' me? Eighty-six banks, that's the number dey said I did? A million seven? Can't be that much. Can't be." His eyes defused as he tried to remember all the robberies he'd committed, all the pissed-away money he'd blown.

"Hey," I said. "What's it like to rob a bank? What's it feel like?" I never wanted information of that sort until I'd started constantly thinking about those children, enticed and lured from the basketball court, brainwashed and talked into robbing and scaring the living hell out of people. Putting a gun in someone's face, seeing the fear from the threat of death, and then taking something that didn't belong to them by force. The victims would be emotionally traumatized for the rest of their lives.

Ned said to Deforest, "What are you, some kind of degenerate gambler?"

"No, wait," I said. "Let him answer my question first."

"What?" He came out of his mini-trance.

"What's it feel like to rob a bank?"

He turned slowly to look at me. "It's like nothin' you've ever experienced. It's a rush, man, like you wouldn't believe. I'm tellin' ya, you cain't get that high even off the glass pipe, no sir. I shit you not. I love it. The power it gives me. The feeling dat I am somebody and everyone has ta stop and listen to me. For those few seconds, I'm it. I'm the shit. I'm God with the power. I'd be robbin' them banks even if I didn't get any money, dat's how good dat shit feels."

"Huh," Ned said. "Hope you enjoyed it. Now you're probably going away forever. Even if it's only one year for every bank, that's more time than you got left in this world, you chubby little Oompa Loompa. That's the kind of power the judge is going to inflict on your ass. Was it worth it?"

He turned to look at Ned. "Worth every year in the joint."

That was not what I thought he'd say. Every crook I'd ever arrested, each and every one of them, showed a deep resounding regret when I snapped on the cuffs. Not for doing the crime or for harming their victims, physically, and emotionally, but because they'd been caught and now had to pay the price with weeks and months and years subtracted from their lives. Lives now restricted to dimly lit little concrete caves sealed with bars that reeked of body odor and unwashed ass. But that wasn't the worst of it. The worst was the overpowering despair that filled every crack and crevasse and forced out every bit of fresh air.

The girl brought the food and hooked the tray on Ned's window. She gave him a big smile and skated off. Ned handed me a burger and fries. He set the tuna fish sandwich in Deforest's lap. I swapped it out with my burger and fries.

He looked at me. "Thanks, man, you all right."

Ned took a big bite out of his burger and talked around his food. "You're a soft touch, partner." He pointed his burger at me. "One day it'll get you in trouble, mark my words if it don't."

"You'd deprive a guy of his last cheeseburger and fries he's ever going to eat?"

Deforest was about to take a bite of his burger. "Aw, man, you had ta go and ruin it. Now I don't feel like eatin' nothin'."

"Good, I'll take it." Ned reached for the greasy burger.

Deforest pulled it way. "I said I wasn't hungry. I didn't say I was crazy." He took a bite and chewed. "You two are all right. Well, you are anyway." He pointed at me and said, "I guess I'd rather be arrested by a couple a US Marshals than some of those chickenshit sheriff's deputies."

"Really, you don't like deputies?" Ned asked.

"Hell, no. Dey the worst. I'm tellin' ya. And them damn LA County deputies, well; you kin jus shoot all dem assholes. They never give you one chance in hell. They jus' as soon shoot your black ass as look at ya. I'm not kiddin', dey bad. Trust me on dis. They'd never stop and buy you a last cheeseburger like dis. No way." He took another bite. "No, sir, they wouldn't."

We finished and drove the last couple of miles to San Bernardino Sheriff's headquarters—fifteen minutes late—and pulled into the parking lot.

Special Agent Jim Turner stood at the back of his Crown Victoria leaning against it, his arms crossed and his jaw locked tight.

I parked next to his car just as the door on the passenger side of his car opened. Out stepped Chelsea in a black pantsuit and low heels. She wasn't happy. Turner hurried over to Ned's open window and looked in. "Son of a bitch." He kicked the side of my truck.

"Hey, hey, don't kick my truck. What's the matter with you?"

Turner looked over at Chelsea. "It is him. They got Raymond Desmond Deforest, son of a bitch."

The Bogart Bandit turned to me. "Tell me I don't have to go along with this punk."

Ned chuckled. "I feel for ya, brotha, I do."

CHAPTER TWENTY-SEVEN

Two DAYS LATER all four in our team met in the Riverside parking lot of the FBI office, all of us driving separate FBI-issued cars. We came together walking toward the front door to the building, no one saying a word. Now the whole team knew the game and what was expected of us: follow some kids around, watch them take a bank down, then we take them down without firing a shot. The last couple of days I imagined a hundred different scenarios—none of them ended well for the kids. Vile and morally bankrupt men have taken advantage of vulnerable children for decades . . . for centuries. I never thought I'd see it to this horrible degree so close to home.

On the way to the top floor, Gibbs looked up to the corners of the elevator car. "You think they have this thing wired with video?"

Coffman took the dead cigar out of his mouth. "You can bet on it."

Ned unbuckled his pants, turned around, and started to take them down.

"Kiefer."

Ned stopped. "All right, Sarge, I gotcha."

I said, "Subtle. Real subtle and oh so professional."

The car stopped, the doors opened, and we spilled out into the vacant waiting area. The same clerk saw us through the ballistic glass, picked up the phone, and dialed. Eight forty-five—we were fifteen minutes late. Coffman said, "All right, let's everyone make the best of this and smile. Ned, you keep your pants on and your smart mouth to yourself, you hear me? Let Bruno do all the talking for us."

Ned put his hand up to his chest. "Why, Sergeant Coffman, what you must think of me. I declare."

"Can it."

"Yes, sir."

The door opened with Jim Turner holding it. We shuffled past, no one saying a word this time. We'd won the first volley. The first part of their plan to humiliate us with the initial two cases hadn't gone the way they intended. We'd won, and yet I still felt used and dirty. I wanted to get this next part over with and move on.

Two days earlier in the San Bernardino County Sheriff's parking lot when we turned over the Bogart Bandit, I cringed when Chelsea came up to me. She didn't smile, nor rail at me. She came up close and in a lowered tone that only I could hear, simply said, "I asked you to go easy on him. I'm ashamed of you, Bruno."

Go easy on him? All we did was capture a serial bank robber, and she was giving me a problem over it? After the game they'd tossed us into, how could she have the nerve to talk to me that way? I was angry, but said nothing in response.

For the next two days I did a slow burn. Her words continued to echo in my brain, along with her neutral expression, the look in her eyes. Today I felt differently. I wanted to see Chelsea again, but at the same time, I didn't. Foolish. I shouldn't be ashamed, not with what they'd planned for us right from the start.

Turner escorted us to a door in that long hall of doors, the one marked "Operations One." He opened it and went in. A large white-board on wheels filled one side of the small room. Our team moved in and sat in four of the ten chairs at the two tables. A huge blown-up photo of a BMA, a black male adult, covered one entire corner of the whiteboard.

Ned leaned over to me. "I guess the more important you are, the bigger head they give you, huh?"

I ignored him and continued to read and memorize the information: Locations Frequented. Types of Cars. Known Associates. A list of banks—a long list of banks, a hundred and twenty-three of them. I kept coming back to the blown-up photo. The man wore a beard interrupted on the right side of his face by a slash-like scar from his high cheekbone down to his chin. Someone went at this guy with a sharp knife. Too bad they didn't hit him lower, in the throat. The beard did a good job covering, but you could still see the scar plain enough. He couldn't rob banks himself. With an identifier like that, he'd get caught right away. Scratch that—the Bogart Bandit had a gold tooth right up front, and for a couple of years no one caught him.

In the blown-up booking photo, this new suspect had dark eyes, almost black—angry eyes. Down below the description read: "Amos Leroy Gadd, BMA 47yrs. 6'-6", 270 pounds."

Ned gave a low whistle and whispered, "Look at that big son of a bitch. It's going to take a buffalo rifle to put his ass down."

I came out of my trance and smiled. "Or a BFR."

"BFR?"

"A big fuckin' rock."

He laughed at the reference to the rock he used on Willis Simpkins that night years ago when Simpkins danced and sparked blue balls of electricity in a front yard sprinkler from the Taser.

Ned smiled, and his eyes warmed as he whispered, "Hey, Bruno, thanks for showin' up."

Turner handed out the operation packages—a thick sheaf of papers held together by a clasp at the top. "Okay, I'm told you already know the M.O. of our target that we call The Pied Piper, Amos Gadd, so I won't go into it. I won't even make any suggestions in how to approach this investigation because it wouldn't do any good anyway. Right? You're going to do exactly what you want no matter what I say."

Ned said, "You got that right."

Turner scowled at Ned and said, "Go ahead and flip back to the mauve tab."

Ned said, "Mauve? Really?"

Turner ignored him.

I looked for Coffman to yank Ned's chain, but Coffman was too angry over the box the FBI put us in—this bad dude Gadd that we couldn't go at head-on—so he let Ned do his worst.

I flipped the mauve tab and found color Xerox copies of US currency smudged with red dye—twenties, fifties, and hundreds.

Turner said, "We first got onto this crew from a tip from Caesar's Palace in Vegas. Casino security tumbled to this guy passing dye pack bank money."

Gibbs said, "All right, we're goin' ta Vegas."

I kept checking the side door waiting for Chelsea to join the briefing. Didn't happen and wasn't going to. For the last two days, she hadn't returned any of my calls.

Turner continued, "The background investigation shows that Gadd is a degenerate gambler and needs the bank jobs to fuel his disease."

"Disease?" Ned said. "Then isn't he going to be protected under The American Disabilities Act? Can we legally arrest him? I don't think we can." He smiled and tried to keep from laughing at his own joke and couldn't; a little snicker eked out.

"In this packet," Turner said, "you'll find all the names of the co-conspirators. To date, we have arrested three after the fact, and the cases were dismissed in juvenile court for lack of evidence. As you know, juvenile court is an entirely different animal—they overly favor the suspect. The rest of the names and photos are principals we've identified and have not yet made a case on."

I said, "You mean the children?"

He paused, glaring at me. "That's right, Detective Johnson. They are all under the age of eighteen, some of them just barely, but make no mistake, they are armed and they are extremely dangerous." He smiled as his words closed in and sealed the door to our trap, ensnared by the FBI's shady dealings and their total lack of fair play.

His smugness made me angry. The entire setup made me angry. I stood and started for the door. The rest of the team followed.

"I'm not done with the briefing."

I held the packet up over my head without turning around and kept walking. "Yes you are. We got all we need. You'll have Amos Gadd in your federal lockup by the end of the week."

Turner raised his voice. "I'm going to enjoy watching you work this one, Johnson. By the end of the week, you're talking out of the left side of your ass."

Ned stopped, turned around. "I got three hundred that says he does it."

Turner said nothing.

Ned said, "Didn't think so. No balls."

CHAPTER TWENTY-EIGHT

WE SAT ON our butts in our cars for two full days before we finally caught sight of Gadd coming out of one of the houses listed in the operational packet, a house assigned to Gibbs to watch. Gibbs came up on the countywide frequency at ten thirty in the morning and told us. We hustled over to his location in Baldwin Hills as he moved in and out of traffic trying not to lose Gadd in a delicate one-man mobile surveillance. We caught up and eased back off Gadd so he wouldn't hink up. You can do that with four cars, back off enough so the target doesn't have a chance to make you. We followed him to an apartment in Cerritos on Lilac. He went in and came right back out with a tall, slim white girl on his arm who wore a feline dress that hugged and moved with her curves displaying a total absence of imperfections. He drove her in his sleek black Lincoln Continental to Gardenia, the Gardenia Card Club. He got out, hurried around, and opened the door for his girl. She swung her long, long legs out and stood on tall high heels that helped her come up as high as Gadd's chin. She took his arm, and they headed for the card club door. In the brilliant sunlight, her white skin glowed bright against his chalky blackness.

Ned, in his own car, came up on the radio, said, "I got this, I'll go in and peep him." Across the parking lot from me, Ned got out of his car just as Coffman said on the radio, "No, Ned, stand down. Let Bruno go in."

Ned closed his car door, pretending he hadn't heard, and followed along at a good distance. Coffman must've forgot to un-key the mike, and said, "Goddamnit, Ned."

Coffman had a special place in his heart for Ned. How long could that last before Coffman took a large bite out of Ned's ass?

We waited out in the sweltering heat for three hours. Coffman came up on the radio. "One at a time, you two make a head call and get something to eat and drink. I'll go after you two get back."

Gibbs said, "Sorry, Bruno, I gotta go first, I'm about to burst. I won't be long, I promise." His car, a new FBI-issued Ford Thunderbird, started up and he eased his way out of the parking lot.

Four more hours passed. At six thirty, the sun started to drop toward the west behind the building, casting long shadows. The heat eased up a tad. Ned hustled out of the front doors headed for his car. Two minutes later, out popped Gadd and his girl, only this time, the girl walked behind him, trying to keep up, doing a shuffle-step in high heels, and not making a go of it. She tripped and almost fell. She hopped and pulled her shoes off—a big mistake, the asphalt hot as a frying pan. She ran faster.

Coffman said on the radio, "Trouble in River City—looks like our boy was the big loser."

Ned got in his car and leaned over out of sight. He spoke into his radio, "Gadd's pissed. He dropped his whole wad on Texas Hold 'Em, lost it all, maybe fifteen, twenty grand. At one point he was up almost thirty, then some punk Asian kid cleaned him. Made Gadd look like a real fool. I thought Gadd was going to rip his head off right there in the casino."

Gadd got in his car, started it, one foot on the accelerator, the other on the brake. He waited for his girl to catch up as the car surged in place again and again. This time, both shoes in one hand, she opened her own door and got in. Her door hadn't closed before Gadd took off smoking the rear tires.

We tailed him back toward Cerritos. Stopped at a red signal, I was two cars behind him. I could see that Gadd and the girl were arguing, using their hands to demonstrate their point. Their windows were open, but their unintelligible, muffled exchange barely made it back to me. When the signal turned green, Gadd leaned all the way across his girl's lap, opened her door, and shoved her out. She fought to stay inside the car, but he brought his leg around and kicked her hard. She tumbled to the street, and he gunned the car. Forward momentum slammed the passenger door shut as the girl rolled onto the street's grimy asphalt. The back tire just missed crushing her head.

Ned came up on the radio. "I'll see if the girl's all right." His car pulled out of the line of traffic as we continued on.

Coffman came up: "No. Let her go. She's okay. Ned? Ned? Stay with the surveillance. We can radio for paramedics."

I watched in my rearview as Ned blocked traffic with his car, got out, went up to the girl, and helped her to her feet. I lost sight of him. I tried to stay with Gadd as he raced his big Lincoln in and out of traffic. He still hadn't made us. Anger alone fueled Gadd's flight. We followed in and out of residential streets as he gradually slowed to the speed limit.

Forty-five minutes later I picked up the radio mike. "Hey, look alive. This is the neighborhood where he solicits the kids to do his bank jobs."

Coffman said, "Yeah, I figured as much. Give him a lot of room here, boys."

Gadd turned off Alameda onto 101st Street westbound and then turned north into the Jordon Downs Housing Project. I said, "You two stay back and let me go in. You'll be made in a second in there."

Coffman said, "Roger."

Gibbs just clicked his mike twice—the sign of acknowledgment.

Gadd toured around looking for likely victims and settled on a group of boys playing hoops—none of them looked over sixteen. I found a spot and set up a decent distance away. Gadd parked next to the court, got out, took his shirt off, and jogged into the game holding up his hands, his lips moving asking them to throw him the ball. The kid with the ball froze and looked to his friends. A couple of them shrugged, so he tossed Gadd the ball. Gadd smiled big, drove to the basket, nimble on his feet, and executed a beautiful reverse slam dunk. The kids looked impressed. The maneuver impressed me, and I hated the dude even more. I couldn't do that shot, and Gadd was twelve years older.

The sun slowly drooped below the horizon turning the sky blood orange. People who lived in Jordan Downs recognized an intruder amongst them and came by close enough to clock the occupant in the white Toyota Camry, my FBI car. I could pull it off okay during the day, but after dark it would be an entirely different proposition. After dark, gang members came out in force and would take my presence as a personal affront. They'd come right up to my car, ask me once where I was from, and if I didn't give the right answer, four or five of them would throw down and open up on me, riddle my car with bullets. I wouldn't stand a chance.

As expected in the ghetto, the gang members had torn down the street signs inside Jordan Downs and knocked out the streetlights. They'd arranged derelict cars in a tight formation to barricade the street should they want to detain anyone who ventured inside their territory. LAPD didn't go in the projects after dark with anything less than eleven units, half their shift.

Two hours later, Gadd, followed by all five boys, walked to his Lincoln. They all climbed in. Night had settled in by now, and Gadd drove them to Church's Chicken on Century and bought them all dinner. This association, the smile, an arm around the shoulder, a pat on the back—friendly familiarity for the purpose of exploitation—made me sick to my stomach.

He drove them home, making only two stops to drop off all five. We continued to follow Gadd over to a pad on 117th Street off Alabama, a two-story house red-tagged for demolition for the new 105 Freeway due to start construction. It had been *due to start construction* for the last twenty years. We sat on the house for another two hours. Every fifteen minutes Coffman tried to raise Ned—total lack of response. I started to worry about him and could only hope he didn't fraternize with Gadd's woman. *Fraternize*, that's what the department called it. But he wouldn't do that.

At the end of two hours, Coffman came up on the radio and called it for the night. "Pick him up early right here, let's say zero five thirty hours so we don't miss him. Bruno, get with Ned and let him know."

"Yes, sir."

CHAPTER TWENTY-NINE

JORDAN DOWNS WASN'T far from home, a few miles. I made it by nine thirty. I'd hoped I'd find Ned's car parked out front. It wasn't. My concern intensified. I headed for the door just as a Crown Victoria pulled to the curb behind my truck. My heart sped up. Chelsea maybe? Not Jim Turner. Please don't let it be Jim Turner.

The driver turned off the headlights and sat in the dark, hidden behind the window tint. I lifted my hands and shrugged. The driver's door opened. The interior dome light illuminated Chelsea. My heart leapt into my throat. I knew I was a fool for feeling that way after the fix she'd purposely put us in. The way she was using us—using *me*.

She eased her door closed, took two steps away from the car, and stopped. She had on a tee shirt with a country singer on the front, worn denim pants, and scuffed cowboy boots that clunked on the asphalt when she walked. She came around the front of the Crown Vic to the side, stepped back, leaned up against her car, and crossed her arms facing me.

For a long a moment, we just stood there looking at each other. Then I moved toward her. I stopped inches away. Her scent rose off her hair, tropical shampoo, coconut, with a hint of pineapple. I slowly raised my hands, put them on her shoulders. She leaned in, put her head on my chest, but kept her folded arms between us. We stood there a long time. I didn't know what she had in mind. I'd wait for her to give me a sign.

I wanted to close my eyes and revel in her presence, but couldn't, not in that neighborhood. I needed to keep a constant vigilance so no one could come up on me, on us. Still breathing her scent, I transported myself back through the years, to a time when we lay in my bed, hot and sweaty, content, everything right with the world. A time before everything got so damn complicated.

I waited.

She slowly moved her arms down and put them around me, her breasts now pressed against my chest. I pulled her in tighter. She raised her face to look up at me. I kissed her long and deep. I reached down, put my arm under her legs, and picked her up. She didn't take her eyes from mine. I turned and carried her to the house.

Once inside, I continued carrying her down the hall to my room, left the light off, and closed the door. The darkness enveloped us as I kissed her again, this time the kiss turning ravenous. I let her legs swing down. Her boots touched the floor. She tugged at my truck driver work shirt, couldn't wait, pulled hard. The buttons popped and skittered around the room. She yanked it down from my shoulders and free from my arms. I lifted her tee shirt over her head and tossed it aside. She went up on tiptoes and kissed me again as she worked my belt buckle, her fingers getting in the way of each other. I moved her hands to do it myself. She reached back, unhooked her bra, let it drop to the floor. She undid her pants, shoved them down, and stepped out of them. I picked her up and tossed her on the bed. She let out a little yelp. I took a deep breath and crawled in on top of her.

We continued to kiss. Her hand reached down between us. I groaned. She broke the kiss and in a harsh whisper said, "My panties, Bruno, get my panties."

I pulled back just far enough, reached down, and tore away her panties. Her hips rose with the abrupt movement. In a smoky voice she uttered, "Jesus."

I moved in fast and then checked my speed, hesitated. She reached up, took hold of my shoulders, her nails digging in as she pulled me down on top of her.

*　*　*

I woke with a start. Chelsea had moved, readjusted, draping her leg over mine. She snuggled her cheek deeper into the crook of my arm. "Sorry, I didn't mean to wake you," she said.

"That's okay." The first real words we'd spoken to each other. I didn't want to say anything more for fear of ruining it, and at the same time, I wanted to know her intentions. I knew mine. If she only asked, I'd gladly tell her. I also feared that she'd bring up the investigation, try to apologize for the disrespectful and despicable way her agency was using our team. Only she'd obviously not seen it that way. She thought that I had disrespected her and her agency by capturing two fugitives that they couldn't.

"So?" I said.

She reached up and put one finger across my lips. "Shhh. Just a couple more minutes, okay? Let's keep the rest of the world out for a few minutes more."

I nodded and waited. I didn't mind waiting, not with her resting in the crook of my arm, the feel of her warm breath on my skin, the beat of her heart next to mine.

But I guess I did mind waiting and said, "What's going on?"

She sighed, taking my hand in hers, hers so much smaller.

Another minute passed as she caressed my hand with her fingers. "I ah . . . I broke up with Jim."

"I'm sorry to hear that." The words sounded wooden even to me.

"No, you're not." She shoved the side of my chest with the palm of her other hand.

"No, I'm not."

More silence. I looked at my watch. The luminous dial read 2:30 a.m. I had two more hours before I had to get moving and that would be cutting it close. Coffman wanted us out there set up on Gadd at five thirty.

"What's going on with the case? You guys doing any good?"

I could understand why she didn't want to talk about Turner, but there was much more going on between us that I needed to know. "Just surveillance for now till we get the lay of the land. You want to tell me how you made it out of the North Dakota field office? Last I talked to you, you said that it was a career killer, getting transferred out there. What happened? How'd you score this plum job out of the LA office?"

"That's it, just surveillance? Really?"

"Don't try and dodge the question. Come on, tell me."

"I told you what happened in North Dakota was real ugly."

"I didn't see anything on the news. So it couldn't have been too ugly."

She let go of my hand and she started to get up. I gently took her arm and pulled her back down on me, her naked body tense and hot. "If you don't want to tell me, it's cool. Just know that I would like to find out so I can understand what happened to you, to help me understand what happened to us."

That last part was a lie. I wanted to know what lay in store for our future together and what happened in Dakota might hold the key.

She nodded and snuggled back down into my arm. "Can I tell you another time?"

"No."

"You're harsh."

"I've been called worse."

She swung her leg over, slid on top, and laid her head on my chest, not looking up at me. Her words came out small and hesitant. "It's a no-nothing office, four agents and a soup. Crummy little cases, mostly tribal related, with alcohol thrown in the mix, felony spousal abuses, burglaries, stolen cars, that kind of thing."

I didn't reply and waited.

"No one wanted to be there—every one of us a screwup, including the supervisor."

More silence.

"What happened?"

"Screwups are screwups. I found out about something this other agent did. I didn't want to rat him out and tried to fix it." She looked up at me. "I did, Bruno. You have to believe me."

I moved her head back to my chest and stroked her hair. "I do."

She hesitated then nodded. "One day I was working as the OD—officer of the day—and took a phone call from Detroit. This dope dealer named Beals wanted to talk to Mac—John MacDonald. I told Beals Agent MacDonald wasn't in and was on his RDOs—regular days off. Beals says that if Mac doesn't call him within fifteen minutes, he was going to call the IRS and 'spill it.' At first he wouldn't tell me what was going on, but after about ten minutes, I was able to talk him into it. I got it all out of him. I didn't know what MacDonald did in Detroit that got him launched to North Dakota because none of us talked about our indiscretions."

Indiscretions? The only thing Chelsea had done to ruin an up-and-coming career was to rescue *me* from a fortified apartment, drive right through the wall to do it, and once inside, shoot and kill someone about to shoot me. Not her fault. The FBI saw it differently. I not only loved her, I owed her everything.

She continued, "But according to this guy on the phone, before Mac left the Detroit field office, he had committed a major violation, not just of policy, but a criminal felony no one yet knew about."

"What was it?"

She hesitated. She didn't want to tell. "Mac, he'd been working narcotics and paid this doper Beals a million-dollar finder's fee on a ten-million-dollar asset forfeiture. That's SOP with FBI and DEA, ten percent. Only Mac held back two hundred thousand, skimmed it for himself. Beals only got eight hundred thousand. So when Beals got his 1099 from the Department of Justice and found that he had to pay taxes on the two hundred thousand Mac skimmed, he was pissed."

She stopped talking.

I asked, "What'd you do?"

"I went to Mac instead of following procedure by immediately reporting it, thinking maybe Mac could give the money back before it all came out."

I stifled a groan, already sensing the end of her story.

"I know. I know. But if he gave the money back, he might at least avoid some jail time. He'd still lose his job." She shrugged. "And what could they do to me—send me to North Dakota?"

"What happened?"

"I went to his apartment in Fargo and found him drunk—I mean stinking drunk. I got some coffee in him and walked him around a bit before I told him. When I did, he sobered up quick. He thanked me, said he knew exactly what he needed to do. I left him in his apartment and . . . and . . ."

I hugged her tighter.

". . . and I made it down to my car before I realized I'd just made a huge mistake, leaving him alone like that. I . . . I . . . ran back and just as I made it to his door . . . I . . . heard the gunshot."

Her tears soaked my chest as I continued to stroke her hair. I wished I could take the pain from her.

"Bruno, I didn't make it out of that hole by doing something great. They gave me a plum assignment so I wouldn't say anything that would give the FBI a black eye. I took the assignment like a good little girl and kept my mouth shut. The press never found out about it."

As she quietly sobbed, her tears brought on an ache to my chest. I'd hurt her by asking a painful question, forcing her to confront a painful issue, reopen old wounds.

I'd only just reconnected with her but I found myself loving her more than I had before—and that hadn't worked out so well.

CHAPTER THIRTY

I AWOKE WITH a start. In the dim light, Chelsea stood naked at the edge of the bed wiggling into her denim pants. "My panties are in shreds, thank you very much. Now I have to go commando style." She smiled, reached out to touch my arm. "Thank you," she said.

"Thank me for what?"

"Just for being you." Still braless and without a top, she grabbed up her boots and sat on the edge of the bed to put them on.

I reached over and placed my hand on her back, her skin warm to the touch. I didn't want her to leave. Not ever again. But I needed to get up and get moving.

I realized I needed to watch her, to burn these new memories into my brain—the way she looked, the way she moved, the way she smelled. I couldn't help thinking that we wouldn't survive, that the time we had last night might be the last I'd ever see of her—at least as lovers.

"Am I going to see you again?"

She got up and found her shirt, put it on over her head, picked up her bra and stuffed most of it in her back pants pocket. A red lacy loop and cup hung down. "Silly, why wouldn't you?" She leaned over the bed and kissed me. "Insecurity doesn't become you. It's not who you are."

"Tonight then?"

She'd gotten up to leave and hesitated. "Sure, of course, but it might be late. I've got a lot going on right now, and you're doing that surveillance, right?"

Her back was facing me so I couldn't see her eyes, but I detected something in her tone. Maybe I'd been a cop too long and deceit had crept into every aspect of my life, whether actual, or falsely perceived. This feeling now wrapped around her words and became so powerful I could almost taste its bitterness on the tip of my tongue. I forced myself to discount it, push it aside as pure paranoia. I had to trust someone—who better than Chelsea? She'd saved my life years ago, to the detriment of her career.

I jumped up, turned her around, and hugged her. She tried to wiggle away and patted my chest. "Come on, baby, I gotta go."

When I released her, she leaned up and kissed me on the cheek. "See you tonight."

"I'll be here waiting."

She opened the bedroom door and walked out. Her cowboy boots clunked quietly on the carpet runner over the wood floor. I waited, holding my breath, hoping she'd come back and we'd crawl back into bed, pull the covers over our heads, and pretend nothing else existed outside my childhood bedroom.

The front door opened and eased closed. A moment later someone popped into my room and scared the hell out of me. I startled and pulled a fist back to slug the intruder.

"Hey, hey. Take it easy, big fella. Remember me? It's Ned, your best friend."

I slumped back onto the bed still in my underwear. "Jesus, Ned, I almost knocked your block off." I took a deep breath. "And you might be a little presumptuous on the best friend thing."

"Ah, man, come on. I mean, not to be rude, but who else you got? Huh? Tell me, who?"

"Dad. I got Dad."

"I can't argue with you on that one, my friend."

He sat next to me. "Who was that who just walked through my bedroom and snuck out the front door?"

"By your bedroom? You mean my living room? You're sleeping on my couch? What time did you come in?"

"Don't try and dodge the question, buddy boy. And I think this is your father's house and his couch, too, not yours." He leaned over and sniffed me. I shoved his face away.

He smiled and raised his finger, shook it. "Ah, Bruno, my man, you got some last night, and I think that beautiful vixen who just snuck out had to be the wily and intrepid, wicked witch from the Riverside FBI office, am I right?" He shook his hand as if he'd touched something hot. "Va va voom, partner."

"No, you're not right—in any case, it's none of your business. And I told you, don't call her that." I did a surreptitious scan of the room for any evidence, and spotted a red silken swatch of torn panty. With my foot, I carefully nudged it under the bed without Ned noticing. At the same time, I asked, "Where did you get off to yesterday? Coffman's pissed."

"I was working."

"What, rescuing a damsel in distress?" As soon as I said it I knew exactly what he'd been up to. He wasn't rescuing, he was recruiting. "You worked her, didn't you? You signed her up, didn't you? What'd she tell you? She had to be fed up with Gadd for shoving her out of the car and leaving her in the street all skinned up." Gadd had literally "tossed her to the curb."

Before he could answer, a loud knock at the front door interrupted.

Chelsea must have changed her mind.

I jumped up and made it to the hall as Dad came out of his bedroom dressed in his pajamas, a ball bat in hand. "Bruno? What the hell, Son? This isn't Grand Central Station."

"I know, Dad. I'm sorry, this won't happen again. I promise to keep the noise down."

His concerned expression shifted to a smile. "Was that Chelsea last night?"

I glanced over my shoulder at Ned, who stood in the doorway to my bedroom with a huge smile, finger raised. "Ott, ott?"

"Later, Dad. Let's talk about it later, huh?" The knock came again, saving me.

"Bruno?"

"Please, later, Dad, okay?"

"Son, you better put some pants on before you go to the door."

"Oh. Yeah." I hurried back in my room, found my pants, and jumped into them. I hesitated at the bedroom door, looking back at the rumpled bed, the image of Chelsea sneaking out, her red lace bra hanging from her back pocket, Dennis the Menace kind of cute with his slingshot, and realized I hadn't been so happy in a very long while.

In the living room, Ned opened the front door to let in the beginning—an insidious kind of trouble that would eventually eat us all.

CHAPTER THIRTY-ONE

NED STEPPED AWAY from the door, a gun in his hand held behind his back, and let Ollie's huge bulk enter my living room. A few days earlier, over the phone, Ollie had given me the clue I needed to look for Honeybee Holcomb, which led to the capture of the Bogart Bandit. I owed her a big favor in addition to three hundred dollars. I'd forgotten all about the three hundred dollars. That had to be the reason for the unannounced visit. But at four thirty-five in the morning?

I liked Ollie as a person, but she still represented a part of my professional life I'd insisted on keeping separate from my personal life. No way did I want to blur those lines by her being in my house and, more to the point, putting in jeopardy the place where Olivia lived. How did Ollie even know where I resided? People on the street must have told her. She knew everyone, and those she didn't know opened up to her as if old friends, a unique phenomenon for the ghetto.

My anger dissipated entirely when she stepped in wringing her hands and displaying an expression of fear and concern I'd not known her to possess. Ollie had always been happy-go-lucky with a huge smile and bright eyes for everyone she met. She wore custom-made black slacks tailored to downplay her bulk and a voluminous teal green satin blouse. Multiple bracelets on both wrists rattled when she moved.

I hurried toward her. "What's going on, Ollie? What's happened?"

"It's my nephew. I tolt you about my nephew. You said you'd do somethin' about it. You promised me you do somethin' about it."

I caught up to her and put a hand on her shoulder. "I did say that and I will. What's going on, what's changed?"

"It's—" She froze mid-sentence. "Who's this fool?"

Ned had closed the door and walked in his stocking feet back to the couch covered in bedsheets, his gun hanging in his hand.

"He's my partner. He's okay. Go on with what you were about to say."

"A whitebread? You got yourself a whitebread as a partner? Mmm, mmm. But if you say he's okay, he's okay." She looked back at me. "Devon, my sister's boy, he done robbed hisself a bank."

"What?" I said

Ned came back from the couch. "What'd you just say?"

"I said my nephew Devon D'Arcy has been robbin' banks. Bruno, you have to help him. He's a good kid, really he is. He jus' fell in wit' the wrong group. You said you could help him. Now I need you real bad to help him."

Ned asked, "How many banks has he robbed?"

She looked from me to Ned, glared at him, and pointed a hand bejeweled with rhinestones mounted in gaudy gold-plated rings. "I don't like him."

"Yeah," I said, "I've been gettin' that a lot lately. But I promise, he's okay."

"Come on, man, I'm standing right here."

"Make us some coffee, Ned, would you please? Ollie, come over here and sit down. Tell me what happened."

She came over to the dining room table, but didn't sit. Her body vibrated with too much nervous anxiety. "My sister . . . she doesn't deserve dis, I swear ta God she doesn't. She works two jobs to feed dem kids—six, seven days a week, and Devon goes and does this. I wanna kick his ass up 'tween his shoulders my own self."

"How does your sister know he robbed a bank?"

"She fount some money in his room and ax him about it. And den you know what he done? He stuck his head up in the air all proud like he was king shit and said he'd taken down a bank in Monnaclair."

Ned moved in closer and said to me, "You think this is Gadd?"

"Yeah, who else could it be? It's too much of a coincidence for it to be anything else."

"Gadd?" Ollie said, her eyes going wide. "Who's this Gadd?"

"No, now you let me handle this," I said. "Where can I find your nephew? I want to talk to him."

"You ain't gonna arrest him, are you?"

Ned said, "Naw, he's just a kid, but he'll still have to answer for what he did in juvenile court."

"Really? You promise you ain't gonna arrest him?"

"You know me. You know I'll do the best I can. You know I won't lie to you, and I'm not going to promise you something now that I can't do. I can only promise to do the best I can."

"But he said—"

"I know what Ned just said. Here, look at me. You want me to be honest with you or do you want me to lie to you?"

"No, no, I trust you."

"Okay, if Devon cooperates and helps us, I'll do everything I can go get him probation. He ever been in trouble before?"

Her hand wringing shifted into high gear. Her numerous bracelets rattled at a higher pitch. "Well, he went in ta juvie once . . . maybe twice."

"Ah, shit," Ned said.

"No, no, it wasn't a big deal. He was only defendin' hisself, dat's all. And dat other time it wasn't his gun; it was—"

"Is he on probation?" I asked.

She nodded.

"Where can I find him and what's his probation officer's name?"

"Dat's jus' it, he gone. He up and took off when his mama fount dat money and took it from him. You got to find him, Bruno."

"Yeah," Ned said, "I think we know where to look for him."

"You do? Wait. Is it this Gadd fella? If he's corruptin' my nephew, you jus' point him out ta me, and I'll have the gangstas in the hood take care a his ass."

"No," I said. "You stay out of it. Let me handle it. Get me the addresses of the friends he hangs out with and the name of his PO. You understand? Drop it off here. And you stay out of it."

"You sure?"

"Yes. You have to trust me on this, okay?"

Ned asked, "Does your cousin play basketball?"

"He's my nephew, and yes he plays wit' his friends—"

"Over in Jordan Downs?"

"Dat's right. How'd you know?"

I said, "We'll take care of it, I promise."

She hesitated, staring at me. "I know you won't let me down, Bruno."

I guided her over to the front door and ushered her out. The wooden stoop creaked under her weight. "You goin' out directly ta handle dis?"

"I'm going out directly, yes."

She went down the two steps and headed off across the front yard. She hit the sidewalk and headed west. I stepped outside to see if she had a car. She kept walking westbound. I followed out to the sidewalk and watched. She kept walking, not headed to any car.

"What the hell?" I whispered to no one.

I came back in to find Ned folding up his bedding. "She's not going to be happy if we arrest her nephew."

"Yeah, I know," I said, with more anger than I should have. "This operation just got a lot more complicated."

"We gonna go after this kid Devon?"

"No, until she gets us that information, I think our best bet right now is to stay with Gadd. We don't want him corrupting any more children and putting them in harm's way if we can help it. Gadd's gotta be our priority. Besides, we stay on Gadd, he'll eventually take us to Devon D'Arcy. Come on, let's get outta here or we're gonna be late."

CHAPTER THIRTY-TWO

WE TOOK SEPARATE cars over to 117th Street and found no one there, not Gadd's car or Coffman or Gibbs. We'd somehow missed them all. I found it difficult to concentrate on the problem at hand. Chelsea's image, her walking out of my bedroom dressed in denim pants, cowboy boots, a worn tee shirt that hugged her curves, and her bra hanging from her back pocket, remained emblazoned forever on my memory. The heat of her kiss. The—

Ned came up on the FBI radio in his FBI-issued black Nissan Pathfinder and asked Coffman for his location. Coffman came back and asked for a meet at Stops, a hot link joint not too far away on Imperial Highway across from Nickerson Garden's housing project.

We found Gibbs and Coffman in the parking lot of Stops eating hot link sandwiches and chili fries at six o'clock in the morning. Stops never closed. They both stood at the back of Coffman's FBI Ford Taurus eating off the back deck of the trunk.

Ned walked by them, said over his shoulder, "Bruno, what do you want me to get you?"

"Whatever, it doesn't matter."

Coffman spoke around a mouthful of hot link sandwich. "What the hell happened to you? You look ridden hard and put away wet. You get any sleep at all?"

"No, not much. What happened to Gadd?"

"Gadd got up and out before me and Gibbs here set up on him this mornin'. That big Lincoln of his was gone. You're wearing the same shirt as yesterday." He took another bite.

I ignored the shirt comment. The shirt was the same kind as the one I wore the day before, khaki material with the same truck driver patch and fake name. I had six or eight of them in my closet. The one I wore yesterday, Chelsea tore the buttons off. I wasn't going to tell him that part. He'd go ballistic.

He pointed with his sandwich. "You talk to Ned? Did he stay at your place last night?"

I squirmed a little. "I really think you should ask Ned about his personal life. I don't want to get involved."

He glared at me a second.

I asked, "What are we going to do about Gadd?"

Coffman pointed his sandwich at me again. "You and Ned are late. I don't like that, Bruno. When I give you a time to meet, I expect you to damn well be there."

"I know, I deserve the ass chewing, but something came up."

"I don't give a damn what happened. You get to where you're supposed to be at the designated time." He took a step closer, his face going pale instead of red like it should've. Gibbs stepped in between us and held out his paper tray of chili fries. "You want some, Bruno, until yours gets here?"

I took one. When Gibbs offered his food as a diversion, his shirt sleeve pulled up a little revealing a partial tattoo, a fresh one still angry and red and slightly raised. I stuck the greasy ort in my mouth and pointed to Gibbs' arm. "What's that?"

Gibbs smiled proudly and pulled up his right sleeve. On his upper arm in bold black ink were the letters: "BMF." "Hey, you need to get one, too."

Ned returned before I could reply and put our food on the trunk deck.

Gibbs continued, "It's the violent crime team's logo."

"Really? What does it stand for?"

Ned said, "Brutal Mother Fuckers."

I stepped over to Ned and pulled up his right sleeve. He had the same fresh tattoo. I looked at Coffman, who took a bite of his sandwich and shrugged.

Ned said to me, "You gotta get one too, Bruno."

"Are you kidding me? Gang members get tattoos to identify themselves as gang members. We're not a gang. We don't need the public to make that correlation, or we're gonna look like a bunch of jack-booted thugs."

Ned had lost his smile as I spoke. "You don't need to be an asshole about it."

I waved my hand. "I'm sorry. I guess I'm just a little sketchy." I picked up my sandwich and took a bite. I needed something in my stomach. I also needed Coffman to get off my back.

I asked Coffman, "You got a tattoo?"

He pulled up his sleeve to display the faded tattoo of the Marine Corp emblem, the eagle perched on top of a globe with an anchor behind it. With the faded colors and his wrinkles, the globe looked more like a deflated basketball the bird had crapped out. "Got this when I was no more than a kid."

I wanted to ask him if he thought the BMF tattoo was a good idea but instead ate my sandwich in silence.

Gibbs said, "Well, what are we going to do? We going to split up and sit on his other pads until we pick Gadd up again? Doin' it that way is a major pain in the ass."

Ned gave us a smug smile. "I talked with Emma Wells yesterday, and she gave me his main pad."

Coffman lit up with excitement. "That the girlfriend of Gadd's he tossed out of the car yesterday?"

Ned smiled and nodded without guile.

Coffman should have chastised Ned for going against orders. Yesterday, Coffman on the radio had told Ned to stay with the surveillance when the girl got tossed out, and Ned did exactly what Ned always did—which was whatever suited Ned best at the time.

Instead, Coffman started gathering up his food. "Good job, Ned. Damn good job. Where is this place?"

I tossed my food into a barrel in between our cars. You can't eat a hot link and chili fries while driving, not without ruining your clothes.

* * *

We found Gadd's Lincoln in the parking lot of some upscale condos in Marina Del Rey. I remembered the condos from an incident a few years earlier.

After we took up positions to watch, Ned came up on the radio. "Bruno, you remember this place?"

"I do."

He chuckled. "Those people had no right at all to kick us out of that party. I mean, I was just mindin' my own business out there on the terrace. You know what I'm sayin'?"

I smiled. "No, you're right. They had no business kicking you out."

The radio went silent for a minute, then, "Hey, partner, it'd mean a lot if you got the BMF."

"I'll think about it." But I wouldn't, and there was no way he or anyone else would change my mind, not ever.

Coffman came up on the radio, "Watch your ten-thirty traffic."

He meant for us to keep the on-air conversation strictly business.

At noon I got out of the car, left the door open, and did some push-ups on the hot asphalt, my palms burning. I needed a nice long run to clear my head, but the pushups would have to do.

Crooks, physically, always held the advantage. They didn't have schedules to follow or any responsibilities whatsoever. They could work out any time they pleased. Cops, especially cops chasing violent felons, sometimes tracked them for forty hours without letup and had little time to work at staying physically fit.

At two o'clock, Coffman sent Gibbs to get us some food, boxes of fried chicken with biscuits and brown gravy. Not my first choice.

At five thirty Gadd came out, got in his Lincoln, and we took off following him. He headed through Torrance and into Hawthorne. He pulled into a rent-by-the-week motel with a sleazy bar on the same property, the Harbor Town Pub.

This time, before Ned could jump out of his car, Coffman came up on the radio. "Bruno, go in and see what he's up to. Ned, goddamnit, you sit tight."

I parked three cars down from Gadd's Lincoln, got out, stretched, and walked to the door. Before I went in, I double-checked to be sure my shirt covered the gun on my hip.

Inside, the kind of darkness only found in a cave made it difficult to see anything except the patrons at the bar. An eclectic bunch with barflies, after-work groupies, and a couple of women of questionable employment who drank cheap beer and watered-down cocktails in highball glasses.

Gadd sat next to one of the women talking quietly to her, his hand resting on her bare knee. I slid onto the empty stool right next to him, his back to me, and ordered a beer from the male bartender. The thought of the beer made my dry mouth even drier. I'd been sweating in that hot car all day with only one large Coke at lunchtime. The new relief bartender, a woman with red hair and who wore black pants, a white blouse, and black vest, set a tall draft in front of me. At the same time, she flashed a huge smile. I guess she liked truck drivers. She outclassed the joint by a lot and didn't belong there. I took a long pull on the beer; the cool liquid and carbonation tasted heavenly.

I leaned in a little, trying to hear the line of bullshit Gadd had to be feeding the woman next to him in his attempt to woo her into sex. He smelled of too much cologne and soap and something else I couldn't place. He wore black denim pants, a blue chambray shirt, and a brown sports coat tight in the arms, the fabric pushed out with his overly developed biceps.

His back suddenly went rigid, a primeval instinct warning him of something amiss. He looked up. He saw me in the mirror over the back of the bar. Stunned, I didn't look away, couldn't if I wanted to.

The beer glass, slick with condensation, slipped from my hand and clunked down on the bar. Foam slopped everywhere as I flashed back to the alley four years before. In the photo from the FBI case file, his heavy black beard had thrown me off. But now I got a close look at his eyes. I'd never forget those eyes.

I'd just sat down next to the Darkman.

CHAPTER THIRTY-THREE

I STARED IN the mirror at Leroy Gadd and him at me. His lips moved. His words like water cut around me, as if I were a big rock in a small stream. He repeated something. "Long haul or short haul? Hey, you okay, buddy? Ah, ah, Karl?"

"Huh? What? Oh, I, ah, haul produce up from Calexico, mostly lettuce and melons. Seasonal kinda stuff. I half-starve in the winter."

"You deadhead back down there?"

"Huh? Ah, yeah, not much call for produce trailers goin' back."

I didn't know what to do, how to react.

The redheaded bartender worked a white towel on the bar sopping up the spilt draft beer, smiling at me. Gadd said to her, "Go ahead and get my man here another and put it on my tab." He put his hand on my back.

I flinched. "No!"

Gadd startled at the abrupt objection to his kind offer. So did the bartender. The others down the way stopped drinking and looked. I couldn't accept a beer from a cold stone killer, a man who killed two kids and their mother, snuffed out their lives in the most brutal way, with a gun to the back of their heads while they waited in agony, each in their turn waiting for it to happen.

Four years of looking for him and here he sat right beside me. That same man who'd murdered now engaged in enticing more children to rob banks. My right hand shook as I fought the over-whelming desire to pull my gun and pistol-whip him across the head. Knock him to the floor and put the boot to him again and again and again, do it in the most wicked and violent way imaginable.

This wasn't me. I'd never fostered such thoughts before—going outside the law.

But I had.

A few years ago, on a hot summer night in the ghetto, I'd tracked a hit-and-run driver who'd run a small girl down in the crosswalk, killing her instantly. That night the law protected the offender as he stood in a safe zone on the other side of his threshold, the entry to his house. I couldn't arrest him while he stood inside. So, in a fit of rage, I reached in through his screen door and yanked him out onto public ground. Robby Wicks had pulled me off the man, or no doubt, I would've kicked him to death.

"Hey, pal," Gadd said, "you feeling okay? You look like you've just seen a ghost or maybe an ex-wife." He laughed and looked to the redheaded bartender to join him in his joke. She didn't. Instead, she shot him a fake smile.

"No, it's cool," I said. "I think I just ate a bad taco or something."

"I know how that is, believe me." He smirked, taking the inter-pretation of my comment down into the gutter, to the vulgar and the profane.

He spun further on his barstool to face me. He offered his hand to shake, his smile large and genuine, his eyes bright with a phony offer of friendship. "Jonathon Crum—spelled C-R-U-M, not the kind that you get when you eat a dry cookie." He spoke his lie about his name with the confidence of a true grifter. I couldn't take his hand. I couldn't touch him, not without pulling back and smashing his face to pulp with my fist.

But I had to, the job called for it. I gritted my teeth and took his hand. Oddly, it didn't feel like crocodile skin or slimy like a wet snake, something you'd expect from a character of his ilk. He squeezed with a strength that reminded me that I needed to pay more attention or fall prey as an unsuspecting victim lulled into a false sense of security.

At the same time, my mind spun a thousand miles an hour. Could I arrest him for the murder of that family four years back? I was a witness and could place him at the murder scene. Well, not exactly at the scene, but in the alley to the rear.

Of course, that wasn't enough. Not yet. The DA would never take a case to trial with one statement and no corroboration.

But at least now I had a name I could take to Compton PD, and they could compare his fingerprints to those at the scene. They could insert his name into their equation, look for a motive, look for opportunity. If they got lucky, they could make Leroy Gadd for those murders and put him away forever. They'd just need a little more time to do it.

Or maybe Gadd had been smart enough to cover his tracks, and even with this new information, this revelation, Compton PD might not be able to put the triple homicide on him.

Would this information affect our operation? No, not if Compton was serious about the murders. They'd quietly go to work on it and not tip their hand until ready. All agencies became deadly serious when it came to murder, and this one was a triple. And if nothing else, clearing three murders with one suspect really softened up the stats. They'd be highly motivated. The smart play for them would be to let our violent crime team continue to follow him until they got the warrant for his arrest, maybe a few days, a week at the most. That was—if the evidence was even there for them to find?

What if Compton tipped their hand and Gadd tumbled to the play? He'd go underground to wait it out. Or he'd flee the country, and there'd be nothing we could do about it but watch as he boarded a plane or drove across the border into Mexico.

The redheaded bartender set another beer down in front of me, just as evil in its purest form slithered into my brain whispering with a superheated breath describing a morally corrupt option: I could tell no one. I could keep this new information to myself and when the time came, which it inevitably would—an opportunity would present itself. If we did our job following around a notorious bank robber, he would eventually take up a gun and then a shoot-don't-shoot scenario would occur. If I didn't hesitate, didn't offer him the opportunity to drop his gun and just—

No. No. That would be wrong on so many levels. Dad had taught me better. To do it that way would make me no better than the morally bankrupt criminal who now sat next to me.

The beer roiled in my stomach and threatened to come up. No. No. I'd sworn an oath to uphold the law. I couldn't do that, not in cold blood. The opportunity would have to come naturally, a gun in his hand with a warning to drop it—making it my life or his.

He'd lose.

CHAPTER THIRTY-FOUR

I FINISHED MY beer, now bitter and sour, while Gadd went back to wooing the woman on the other side of him. I put ten dollars on the bar and walked stiff-legged out into the parking lot, my mind in a world of confusion.

Once in the car, I came up on the radio. "He's sitting at the bar with a woman he just met. I think we're going to be here awhile." I stopped short of telling them that I'd just recognized Gadd as the Darkman. I needed to think some more about it. What would it gain by telling them now? We were already up on him for too many felonies to count. None that we could prove until the case broke.

I sat in the parking lot of the Harbor Town Pub with the others and watched the black Lincoln and the front door of the bar. Gadd stayed in there another two hours. He came out with the woman on his arm and drove with great deliberation to an apartment complex on 213th and Avalon in the city of Carson, a cheap, run-down apartment probably belonging to the woman. Did we owe an obligation to warn her, to advise her of her possible ruinous choice in men? A tough decision nobody spoke of as we let the situation play out all on its own.

We stayed on watch until midnight when Coffman came up on the radio. "Bruno, you and Gibbs go get some shut-eye, four hours, then come back and relieve me and Ned. We're not gonna lose this guy again."

I didn't acknowledge on the radio; I started up and let the headlights of my car coming on let him know I heard the orders. I drove home by rote, my mind struggling with the decision not to notify Compton and to let Gadd fall prey to our surveillance and eventual takedown.

I pulled up, stopped in front of my house, and remembered about Chelsea. I slugged the steering wheel. I'd forgotten all about her. I should've found a pay phone and paged her with a code that said I wouldn't be able to make it. She'd probably come and gone after waiting too long. But how long would she have waited? The longer she'd waited, the more she cared. Only a kid with a high school crush would want to know that kind of information to further assuage a wounded ego.

I hadn't slept a lot the night before, just a scant few hours. Not a complaint at all. I wouldn't have missed the time being with Chelsea for anything in the world. But now fatigue hung off me like a warm, wet blanket beckoning me to lie down anywhere. Right there in the front yard would be fine. Curl up and sleep for two days straight.

Before leaving the street and walking into my front yard, I checked the street one more time for dangerous interlopers and spotted a car that didn't belong parked four houses down. I turned to face it, stared into the darkness as I stepped backward into the front yard, out from under the streetlight and deeper into the shadows.

The headlights came on. The car started. The tires chirped as it sped right toward me. I pulled my shirt back from over the gun on my hip and put my hand on the stock, ready to draw and fire.

The car, a nice silver BMW four-door—out of place for the neighborhood—pulled up and stopped on the wrong side of the street, nose to nose to my FBI car. I couldn't see inside, the window tint too dark.

I shifted my footing, drew my gun, and held it along the side of my leg. The driver's door opened to a woolly looking male, with big hair, and a full beard. He wore a black leather jacket, also out of place in this kind of summer heat. He wore a dress shirt and slacks, and the foot emerging from the car sported the in-vogue penny loafer. I watched his hands—empty—or I'd have pointed my gun at him. He climbed the rest of the way out. "Bruno—hey, man, take it easy, it's me."

"I don't know who the hell you are so don't make any quick moves. Step back by the car and into the light."

"Come on, you know me. We worked the street together. It's me, JB."

"Ah, shit." I reholstered my gun. I didn't like JB. He'd cuckolded Ned. Ned caught JB in flagrante delicto with Hannah four years ago. I'd been there, seen it for myself. Ned had since reconciled with Hannah. No way did I want anything to do with JB.

"Get back in your car, JB, you're not welcome here."

"Come on, don't be that way. Can we just talk? I need to talk to you for just a minute."

I turned to go in the house. "You got nothing I need to hear."

He raised his voice as if he wanted witnesses to come closer and listen, a real punk's move. "I wanted to do this friend to friend, but if you force me, I can call the cops, and you'll be arrested as an accessory."

I turned back and walked quickly up to him. "You can't have me arrested if I've done nothing wrong. Now get the hell off my property before I take you to the ground and arrest you for trespassing."

The other door to the BMW opened. Hannah's head popped up looking across the roof of the car. "Hey, Bruno."

"Ah, shit."

Behind me, the front door to the house opened a crack, Dad peeking out. The porch light went off so he could see better. Or maybe he knew about backlighting and did it to protect me.

Hannah closed the car door and came around. As she did, JB asked, "Have you seen Ned?"

I hesitated, trying to catch up with what was happening and didn't like the way the puzzle started to go together.

Ned had never reconciled with Hannah—or had Hannah recently gone back to JB?

Hannah walked over. She wore a dynamite pair of black leather pants that looked like someone designed them just for her body. She wore a tight pearl-colored satin blouse unbuttoned down almost to the bottom of her ample cleavage. Her leather jacket didn't have the zippers on the sleeves like JB's. Her long blond hair fell loose on her shoulders. She was nothing short of stunning.

I swallowed hard. "What's going on, Hannah?" But I thought I knew; I just couldn't believe Ned would put me in this situation. It all flooded back at once, Ned suddenly showing up after all those years, needing a babysitter for Beth. Wicks not wanting to tell me what was going on with Ned, that it was personal. And that it could become a problem for the department. All of it made sense now.

Hannah reached out and took my hand, her bright blue eyes burning right through me. "I think you know, Bruno. Ned's kidnapped my baby. He's taken Beth."

"Ah, shit."

CHAPTER THIRTY-FIVE

"I THINK KIDNAP is a strong word."

JB reached into his coat. I jumped past Hannah and grabbed his wrist. "Don't."

"Easy, big fella," JB said. "I'm just going for some court papers. You're a little paranoid, aren't you?" His breath smelled of spicy pork rinds and Dr. Pepper. You could take the deputy out of the ghetto, but you couldn't take the ghetto out of the deputy.

"Just because I'm paranoid doesn't mean someone's not following me. You two are staking out my house. You accuse me of accessory after the fact, aiding and abetting a kidnapper. How do you expect me to react?"

Hannah put her hand on mine and gave me the eyes again, full power this time. "Why don't we all just dial this down a little, huh? I don't want it to go down this way. I really don't. Why don't we go inside and discuss this in a civilized manner?"

My mind, all on its own, skipped back to that night in her apartment when Ned caught them naked. I'd stood right behind him. That image of her nudity, the smooth freckled skin, the curves and her wonderful breasts, made me flush with embarrassment. What the hell was this woman doing with the likes of JB? Ned was ten times the man JB ever thought of being.

I let go and stepped back. "We'll talk right here. What can I do for you tonight, Hannah?"

Tears welled in her eyes. "I just want my baby back. You can understand that, can't you, Bruno? You have a little girl." She took a step toward me and raised her hand to place it on my chest. I took another step back, took her warm hand and let it drop.

"I . . . I don't have your baby. You know me. I would never . . ." The lie clogged in my throat and wouldn't come out. I turned to look back at the front door that stood ajar and the darkness that filled in the crack. Dad had always taught me to tell the truth, and now he stood there listening to the conversation. I couldn't do it. I couldn't lie to Hannah. Not blatantly. "I haven't committed any crime. You'll have to talk to Ned about Beth. That's all I'm going to say." I held up my hand to end any further conversation and headed for the front door.

JB said, "Bruno, have Ned and Beth been staying here?"

Part of the crime of kidnapping, the aiding and abetting part, I had to have knowledge to fulfill the elements, to make me culpable. They'd just informed me Ned had taken the child, and now if I answered in the negative, they had me for the accessory charge. I stopped and turned back around. "If the child belongs to both you and Ned, then it's not kidnapping. It could only be a violation of a court order, if you have one. You're trying to bluff me with that kidnapping bullshit, and I don't like being taken for a fool."

Hannah took a step toward me. I raised the flat of my hand. She stopped.

"Bruno," she said. "What if I told you Beth was JB's child?"

"Ah, damnit, Hannah, don't play mind games with me. I know better."

She kept looking at me and stuck her hand out toward JB. JB pulled the papers from his inside jacket pocket and placed them in her outstretched hand. She handed them toward me.

I didn't take them.

She said, "We had blood tests done. This is a judge's court order declaring Beth as JB's child until there can be a hearing on the matter. That makes it kidnap."

"Does Ned know about this . . . these papers, I mean?"

I caught it in her eyes as she quickly tried to decide whether or not to submit the lie in her attempt to get Beth back. "Aaah, no. We haven't been able to find him to have him served."

She'd chosen to tell the truth.

Ned had been hiding out at my house to avoid the service on the court order. I hadn't seen or talked to him in years, and that made our house the perfect place to lie low.

I smiled. "Then, when and if I see Ned, I'll tell him. That's the best I can do for you tonight, Hannah. Now excuse me. I'm tired, and I only have three hours to sleep before I have to be back out on a surveillance."

"Just let us look in your house," Hannah said. "That's not asking a lot, is it?"

"Yes, it is. It's saying you don't take me at my word. It's also a violation of my right to privacy, and I won't subject Olivia to this kind of disturbance on a lark."

She said, "We can call the police—they'll let us look."

"Not without a warrant they won't. Will they, JB?"

She looked to JB. He shook his head, agreeing with me.

"Now, please, get off my property. I have to get some rest." I turned and walked away.

Hannah said, "You don't want to get in the middle of this, Bruno. It'll go down bad for you."

"Ned's my best friend. You seem to have forgotten that part. And don't you ever threaten me again. Good night."

I stepped up on the stoop, turned my back to the door, and watched JB and Hannah retreat to their seventy-thousand-dollar car. Hannah had thrown Ned over for money. That had to be it. I hated JB for causing all this upheaval. Then my emotions immediately shifted to Ned; he'd put me in this crack and told me nothing about it. I wanted to sock him in the mouth and would without hesitation the next time I saw him.

Behind me, I sensed the door open a little more. Dad said, "You did the right thing, Son."

"What are you talking about?" I still had not turned around to face him. Hannah and JB started up; the headlights came on.

Dad said to my back, "They came to the door and asked for Beth."

"What'd you tell them?"

"I told them that Beth wasn't here."

The BMW moved off down the street.

"Is Beth still here?"

Dad said, "Well, hell yes, she is."

I spun around, found the door open with Dad standing there, his jaw clamped tight, his eyes fierce. He'd never, ever told anyone anything other than the truth. I mean *never*. My world shifted under my feet. My dad had told a bald-faced lie. Not only that but he could now face criminal prosecution for that lie.

CHAPTER THIRTY-SIX

I PUSHED MY way into the house, the light turned down low from one lamp next to the couch. I closed the door. Dad stood there in his stocking feet, still wearing his blue-gray postal uniform pants with a white sling-strap tee shirt, his dark-skinned arms and shoulders lean and muscled. He held a ball bat down by his leg. As a street cop, I would never want to go up against him—not someone with truth on his side. He hadn't changed to his pajamas and had been standing vigil all night. I said, "What's going on, Dad? You always told me never to lie. And now you just involved yourself in—"

His eyes went wide, and he raised his bat, pointed it at the wall in the direction of where JB and Hannah had stood out in the yard. "Those are bad people out there."

"Take it easy, Dad, what are you talking about?" I put my hand on his shoulder.

He took a deep breath and let it out. He nodded. "I'm sorry, Son, I'm just a little worked up." He turned and stepped over to the kitchen area and sat in a chair at the table. He got right up and paced the floor. "They've been sitting out there all night just waiting like a couple of vultures over a carcass. Makes me sick."

I sat next to him. "What's going on? Tell me."

He nodded again. His eyes stared into mine, but his mind wandered somewhere else as he must've pondered all that had happened and his role in it. I waited for him to tell it in his own time.

He said, "I don't remember ever lying like that to anyone, and it makes me sick that those people made me do it."

I said nothing.

His mind returned as his eyes came back into focus looking at me. "But tonight, Son, tonight I realize there is only one exception to that rule I've always lived by. The exception is when it involves the safety of children. If a child is at risk and it's the only way to protect them, then it's okay to lie your ass off."

I sat back in the chair a little stunned. Dad never talked like this. It was unusual for him to use words like "hell" or "ass."

"What happened? Tell me what happened."

He held up his hand. "Okay, just give me a minute." He paused and swallowed hard. "All right, all right, here it is. I come home from the office, everything's fine and it's a good day to be alive. I send Mrs. Espinosa home. I start making the kids their dinner. It's about five o'clock, still lots of light outside being summer and all. Maybe it's five thirty, I'm not sure. Anyway, Olivia and Beth are both up on the couch jumping and bouncing around having a good time laughing and giggling. I'm over here in the kitchen makin' them some macaroni and cheese with hot dogs when I hear Beth let out a little yelp."

Dad points to the couch. "I look over in time to see her fall to her stomach, roll off the couch, and run to the bedroom." He points down the hall with the ball bat. "She goes in and slams the door. I follow her to see if she's okay. Something bad's happened, Son, that's what I think. I just don't know what it could be." Dad turned to look at me. "I found her under the bed backed up as far as she could go in the corner, whimpering. I started talking to her, tryin' to find out what happened just as someone knocks at the front door. I'm still not figuring it out until I come back in here." He again points with the ball bat. "As I'm going to the door, I realize Beth had been up on the couch and could see out the front window."

He didn't have to say anything more. For me the entire situation fell into place. I took the ball bat from him and leaned it against the wall. "You opened the door and there was JB and Hannah asking about Beth."

"That's right, how'd you know?"

"That's when you told them Beth wasn't here?"

"That's right." He pointed to the bat. "I also told him to get the hell off my porch."

"We're going to be in trouble if they come back with a warrant and the Sheriff's Department."

"What about that child in there? She can't go back to those . . . those people?"

"Dad, if the child belongs to—"

"No, sir. No, I won't have it. The police come here to take that child, force her to go someplace she doesn't want to go, they're going to have to fight me. I swear to God, Bruno, that's the way it's gonna be."

"Dad—"

"No, sir. Not going to happen, not as long as I'm breathin'. Come here. Come with me." He spun and hurried out of the kitchen through the living room and into the hall. I caught up to him at his bedroom door. He eased it open. He lowered his voice to a whisper. "Took me the better part of an hour to talk her out from under that bed."

The low light from the hall illuminated the bedroom. Beth and Olivia slept on a daybed in Dad's room. They laid facing each other, each of their arms draped over the other, best friends even as they slept. With the heat of the summer, they only wore light tee shirts and panties. No blanket or sheet covered them.

Dad pointed and whispered. "Look, look at the bottom of her feet."

All the air went out of me. Oh, no. I didn't want to look. I'd worked the street long enough to know what I'd find. And each and every time I found a child, hurt, abused, or exploited, I had a difficult time containing my anger, my rage.

I took a deep breath, steeled myself, and got down on one knee for a closer look. Some sick bastard had whipped the bottom of her feet with an electric cord—or something similar. Scars crisscrossed the skin on the bottoms of both her feet. How had I missed this?

I'd been too busy, too caught up in my own life, and hadn't slowed down long enough to pay attention to a small child who stayed in my house. Me, the big bad sheriff's detective whose main job it was to be observant and to ferret out crime, pick out the victims and keep them safe. I'd failed.

How could anyone hurt a child like that? Anger replaced the sadness and grief for this child in our charge.

I couldn't tell Ned about this; he'd kill JB outright. Ned would walk right up, and without saying a word, shoot JB in the face.

It had to be JB. He was the ex-cop. He'd know the best place to . . . the least likely place an injury would be discovered. Which also placed this heinous crime smack square in the middle of premeditation. JB had thought about it before acting—before torturing a small, defenseless child.

Then my mind skipped. Was that the reason why Ned had come to our house to hide out? Did he know about the abuse and that was the reason he'd taken Beth from Hannah? Out in the front yard, before I'd seen the scars, I'd jumped to the conclusion that Ned simply wanted more time with his daughter and had been on the dodge from Hannah in a child custody dispute.

No, I knew Ned. If he knew someone laid a hand on Beth, that person would no longer be above ground but buried somewhere out in the arid desert, the body desiccated, mummified under the sand.

What a mess; I couldn't tell Ned, no way. I didn't know what to do. I needed sleep and time to figure this all out.

Dad whispered, "What are we going to do, Son?"

"I don't know, Dad. I really don't know."

CHAPTER THIRTY-SEVEN

I STAYED IN my clothes and tried to rest on top of my rumpled bed, the bed Chelsea and I messed up the night before, a time that now seemed like weeks ago. I couldn't sleep even though exhausted.

Dad stuck his head in my open bedroom door. "Bruno, that gal that was here this morning, she came back and left you a note. Said it was real important. With all that happened, I forgot about it. I'm sorry."

A note from Chelsea. I jumped up, flipped on the light, and grabbed it from his hand. My heart sank. The piece of folded paper with one staple had the name Ollie inscribed on it. Ollie Bell had left the note that would contain the address of her nephew and the names of his friends. I didn't bother to open it.

Dad said, "What do you want me to do if those two come back again asking for that poor child?" The pain and confusion in his tone ripped my heart out and made me angry all over again with JB. What I really wanted to do was hunt down JB and put the boot to him. Ned would do nothing less for me if someone even looked crossways at Olivia. I was a bad best friend.

"I don't know, Dad. I told you, let me think about it, okay?"

He nodded. "You know, if we both go to jail, what's going to happen to Olivia?"

"We're not going to jail." Though I wasn't so sure anymore. I walked back down the hall to the phone mounted on the wall in the kitchen and picked up the receiver. Dad stood close by. I hesitated over the call. Was it the right thing to do? I dialed Wicks' phone number as I checked my watch, one a.m. He wasn't going to be happy.

He answered on the first ring and said, "Wicks."

"Lieutenant, it's me."

"What's goin' on, Bruno?"

"I'm sorry to wake you."

"Can that shit. You wouldn't have called unless it was important. What's going on?"

"Ned's wife and JB came to my house tonight looking for their daughter, Beth."

Silence.

I said, "That's what you wanted me to talk to Ned about, right?"

"I'm sorry you got caught up in the middle of this, Bruno. What happened—did you give her the child?"

"I told them they had to talk to Ned about it."

"Ned wasn't there?"

"No, he's out on the surveillance with Coffman. I'm due to relieve them in three hours."

"It's best that Ned gives the kid back. I told Ned that, but you know how boneheaded he can be. The best thing you can do is stay out of it and give him your best counsel. You know how these things are. Child custody issues are nothing but a hotbed of emotions that make responsible people do crazy things. And it tends to ruin lives. It never ends well. I'm not telling you anything you don't already know. No one ever thinks clearly when their kids are involved."

"You're saying to stay out of it? They're staying at my house, Lieutenant."

Dad whispered, "Our house." To remind me that he, too, was wrapped up in all this emotional soup.

"Bruno, I know he's your friend, but you don't want to get pulled into this thing any more than you already are. You're going to have to kick him out. You're just enabling him. While he stays at your house, you're making it easier to hide his daughter."

"Yeah, that makes a lot of sense, it does, but it also puts Beth in the crossfire. What happens when Ned doesn't have any place to go with his daughter?"

"I know it's a tough situation. Right now, Ned's not making the right choices, and we have to help him make those choices."

"Lieutenant, there's something else."

I didn't know exactly how to word it, didn't know if I even wanted to put him on notice, and paused. Once I put him on notice it was like letting the genie out of the bottle; you could never put him back in.

Wicks said, "Boy, I know I don't want to hear this. Go ahead."

"There's strong evidence that JB and Hannah have physically abused Beth."

"Son of a bitch. Well, that changes everything. I have to make notifications. IA has to come into it now, and the kid's gotta go to Child Protective Services until we get this whole thing straightened out."

"Not CPS. Come on, Lieutenant, not Beth. Can't she stay here until everything gets sorted out?"

"I'm sorry, that's the way it has to be. We can't show any sort of bias. Make sure Beth's available first thing in the morning. I'll have them there to pick her up at nine. Bruno, you want to tell Ned?"

I gripped the phone and closed my eyes. "Yeah, that's on me. I'll handle it."

"Tell Ned it's okay for him to take a few days off. Maybe you should, too—stay with him so he doesn't do anything crazy."

"What about the case? This guy Gadd is using children to rob banks." Then I remembered that Gadd was also the Darkman. I hadn't told anyone, not even the lieutenant. I wouldn't let that genie out. No way did I want to come down off the investigation with Gadd still running around free, ruining young lives.

"Use your best judgment. Maybe it'll be better if Ned does work, keep his mind off it. I'll leave that up to you."

"Thanks, Lieutenant."

"Get some sleep. I'll check in with you tomorrow."

Numb and bewildered, I muttered into the dead phone, "Its already tomorrow." I hung up.

I stepped into the living room and paced back and forth, trying to imagine the look on Ned's face when I told him, the pain, the pure anguish. He'd blame me in part—how could he not? I'd called and told the lieutenant, got the large bureaucratic ball rolling that would bulldoze right over Ned and Beth. I did it before I even gave Ned a chance to do anything about it.

I checked my watch—a little less than three hours before I had to relieve Ned and Coffman. I didn't have to tell Ned for three more hours. Chicken. I was just putting it off.

But I couldn't sleep, not with that mess swarming around in my thoughts. I reached up to the top of the entertainment center in the living room, took down my gun, and strapped it on.

Dad had been watching me. "What are you going to do?"

"I can't sleep." I pulled the folded and stapled note from my pocket. "I told another friend I'd help her out. I guess I'll go and try to at least take care of this problem."

I opened the front door and stepped out. Dad behind me said, "Be careful out there."

"I will." I eased the front door closed leaving Dad with nothing more than a ball bat to ward off an insidious kind of evil I'd laid at his doorstep.

CHAPTER THIRTY-EIGHT

IN THE FRONT yard at the curb, I sat motionless in the FBI-issued Toyota waiting for inspiration in how to handle the mess involving Ned and his little girl with no inkling at all forthcoming. Sleep would help, but no way would sleep come, not with everything swirling round and round. Wicks may have been right. There might only be one real option: let the system take over. Plug everything in, stand back, and just let it go. But no way, under similar circumstances, would I want that to happen to Olivia.

I opened Ollie's note by tearing loose the staple. Enough ambient light from the street allowed me to see without turning on the overhead dome. The note read:

> Dat little shit Devon's layin his head on Willowbrook tween Compton an Roscrans, 11431, its a lime green crib with white trim. He's a big kid, over six foot and chubby wears his hair in a fade. Has one of dem Cadillac medallions around his neck ona long chain.
>
> I fount out what you woodnt tell me about dat asshole Gadd. I know what he's all about now, what he's up to. You doon have ta worry about him no mo. I'll take care a his sorry ass. You jus hep out my nepfew.

Luv ya lots

See ya soon lover

O

Another load of adrenaline dumped into my already overtaxed nervous system. No way could Ollie tangle with Gadd. He'd kill her without thinking twice about it. She'd never see it coming either. She had no idea the danger she'd put herself in just entering Gadd's orbit, let alone trying to put him down. She carried an ice pick in her purse for self-defense. Gadd would never let her get that close. And she didn't know how to operate on stealth mode, not with her bulk and all those damn bracelets.

I got out, went back in the house to call Ollie to tell her to stay the hell away from Gadd, insist on it. Take her to jail if I had to. I couldn't tell her about our surveillance that she'd walk right into even if she did try something that dumb. The scary part about it—I knew her well enough that I knew she would try it.

Dad stood in the living room and didn't ask any questions when I came back in.

I dialed. The phone rang and rang. I hung up trying to think it through. I turned to Dad. "You heard the conversation with my lieutenant?"

He nodded.

I said, "Tomorrow morning CPS will be here for Beth. Under the circumstances, it's the best thing for her. You understand that, right?"

"No."

"Dad, you think it's right that Ned's on the run with his little girl? Would you want that for Olivia? You and I would never put any child through that kind of thing—I mean going on the lam and ducking the law, hiding out with the children like a gang of fugitives. No, we have to trust in the system and let it do its work."

"You sure?"

"Yes, I'm sure."

He put his hand up on my shoulder. "All right then, I'll make sure everything goes smoothly."

"Thanks, Dad."

I went back outside and got in the car. Disturbed—nothing seemed to be working out right, but I started up and headed to Willowbrook. At least Ollie had given me something I could take care of, something I could make right. I'd take Devon D'Arcy by the ear, yank him off the couch he slept on, and shake some sense into him.

Ten minutes later I made my first pass of 11431 Willowbrook Avenue and spotted Ned sitting down the street in the dark in his Pathfinder watching the place.

What the hell?

Seeing Ned let the guilt slither back in, guilt so heavy it about smothered me. I had to tell him, get it over with.

I pulled around the corner and came up on the radio. "Ned, what are you doing at this 10-20?"

"Hey, partner, good hearing from you. Thought you were supposed to be sleeping. We followed the primary over here after he finished up at that other location."

Coffman jumped in, "Bruno, what the hell are you doing here?"

"I, ah . . . was . . . following another lead, and it happens to be right where you two landed."

"I told you to get some sleep. You're due to relieve us in a couple hours. You can't work on no sleep."

"Couldn't sleep, I'm good. Hey, Ned, meet me around the corner over here."

"Roger that."

I made the turn into an unknown side street perpendicular to Willowbrook, the street sign removed by the local hoodlums. They also knocked out the streetlights making it much darker and easier to blend into the shadows. Seconds later Ned came around the corner with his headlights already off and double-parked, his driver's window to my driver's window, the cars only inches apart. He looked in good humor. The job did that for him; he loved it. He tilted back a chocolate Yoo-hoo and took a bite of a pink snowball cupcake. He spoke around the marshmallow and coconut confection. "What lead are you following that brought you here?"

"Remember this morning, Ollie, and the problem with her nephew? Well, this is the address she gave me."

"No shit. That means this pad might be Gadd's main location, the place he operates from. Very nice. What's the matter? Something's wrong?"

I couldn't find the words to answer him.

He sat up and leaned out a little. "Is it Beth? Did something happen to Beth?"

He just tipped his hand that he knew for sure Hannah and JB were on the hunt for Beth.

"I found out what's going on," I said. "You should've told me. You played me, Ned, and I'm not happy about it."

"Did Hannah find Beth? Did Hannah get Beth?"

"No, relax. Dad covered for you, but you put him right in the middle of your mess and that's not right."

He eased back in his seat and shot me the trademark Ned smile that under normal circumstances might've softened me up a little.

"She didn't get Beth," he said. "That's good, real good. Bruno, anything you want, anything I have it's all yours. I owe you."

"You're on the dodge from the service of a court order. You don't have anything but what's in that duffel bag sitting in my living room?"

"Sorry about this whole thing. I should've told you, but you're Mr. Law Enforcement, and you would've gone all policy and law on me and called CPS. The last thing I want is to have Beth in a foster care home while the court tries to decide who's the best parent. You wouldn't want Olivia in foster care, would ya?"

I shook my head; no words would surface.

The knot in my stomach tightened. In a few hours, that's exactly what was going to happen. Beth would be taken into protective custody and become a ward of the state. Right at that moment I realized no matter how hard that would be on Beth, it was still the best thing for all concerned. It might be the only way to keep Ned out of trouble. If Ned went crazy over this child custody battle, what good would it do Beth? What good would it do anyone? I had to consider the long game and made my decision.

I needed to change the subject and asked, "How long have you and Hannah been separated?"

Ned looked away. The question about losing Hannah yet again hurt him a great deal. "Seventeen months, ten days, and thirteen hours, if you have to know."

"How long have you been on the dodge?"

"Just since I've been at your place, that's all."

"She's got papers that she's looking to serve you, but I think you already know that."

"You know this game," he said. "The judge always, always rules in favor of the mother. It's not fair, Bruno." He slugged his steering wheel. "Hannah's going to get custody, and I'm going to be left out of raising that wonderful little girl."

I didn't think that would happen, not with the scars on Beth's feet. The judge would seriously consider Ned for full custody. But not if Hannah dumped JB, then the threat would be gone. Round and round we go.

"Don't sweat it," I said. "Everything's cool for right now. I haven't had any sleep and it's too late to drive home. Can you stay right there and watch my back for a couple hours?"

"You got it, partner, and thanks for covering for me."

The guilt again rose up in my throat and threatened to choke me. By the time Ned made it home in the morning, it'd be all over and he'd hate me for life. I eased the seat back as far as it would go and pulled the green John Deere ball cap down over my eyes, knowing I wouldn't be able to sleep.

But in an instant, one as brief as a heartbeat, sleep jumped up, grabbed me by the throat, and pulled me down into a dark abyss.

CHAPTER THIRTY-NINE

HEAT FROM THE sun woke me. I yanked my .357 from under my leg and sat bolt upright in my car looking around, looking for a threat, a target.

"Hey, partner, that can't be good for the old ticker," Ned said, from his window. He handed me a tall cup of coffee in a Styrofoam cup from his vehicle still parked in the same place, and I brought my seat back up, put my gun back under my leg, and popped the lid of the coffee. The lukewarm brew, laden with cream and sugar, tasted wonderful. "Man, did I need this. Thanks . . . Hey, how did you get coffee when—"

"Gibbs came in to relieve me and Coffman. He ran this coffee over. He's set up where Coffman was and has the eye on the location. Coffman's gone home to get some sleep."

"Why didn't you wake me?"

"You looked like a walking cadaver. You needed the sleep."

"You're not kiddin' about that."

The neighborhood looked different in the light of day, not nearly as ominous. Most all of the houses sported gang graffiti and wrought-iron bars. None of the cars on the street would sell for more than a couple of hundred dollars, cracked windshields, faded paint, bald tires. A dog with mange stopped to sniff something in the street and kept on going.

I checked my watch, nine o'clock. CPS would be at the house taking custody of Beth. A coward, I didn't want to tell him. He could find out by driving home. I hated myself for it.

"Okay," I said, "I got this now. You can take off. Are you and Coffman still coming back in four hours?"

"I'm not leavin'. The banks open at nine—that's right about now. That asshole Gadd blew his whole wad at the card club. He's got to be hurtin' for some cash. I'm not gonna miss out on all the action by going home and sleeping through it, no way. You cover for me now. I'll sack out."

"You got it." I didn't mind the delay. Maybe with a little more time I could work up the nerve to tell him about last night.

Ned put his seat down and disappeared below the door's windowsill.

My conscience worked on me like a starving man on a rib bone. I couldn't let him stay, not without telling him. I had to tell him. "Hey, Ned?"

His head popped back up. "Yeah?"

Gibbs came up on the radio. "Hey, our primary is moving. He's got one poo-butt with him and they're getting in the Lincoln."

Ned readjusted his seat to the "up" position and started his car. "It's showtime."

My partner had called it right. Gadd didn't go on the move that early with the children to go play b-ball. Yet another reprieve, I couldn't tell Ned about Beth, not now. We needed him for the mobile surveillance. Sure, that was a good enough reason not to. He needed his head in the game.

We followed the Lincoln over to Alameda and straight up toward downtown LA. Gadd turned the same as he did the day before onto 101st Street, eastbound, and then made another hard right into the Jordan Downs housing projects. Gibbs and Ned automatically fell back. I followed them in. The black Lincoln circled around in the side streets almost as if looking for a tail, but his manner was too passive for it. The entire time, Gadd talked with the kid in the car using his hands to emphasise the lesson. The kid just continued to nod.

Gadd pulled up to the basketball courts. The kid jumped out. My heart dropped—he matched the description of Ollie's nephew, Devon D'Arcy. Tall, chubby, his hair cut in a fade, a Cadillac medallion swinging from a chain around his neck. I'd worked the street long enough to know just by the way D'Arcy carried himself, the way he interacted with his peers, that he was too far gone to recover from his downward spiral into juvenile delinquency. The street had claimed another one. I didn't know how I'd tell Ollie, but she probably already knew and just couldn't accept it.

D'Arcy, with a weighted-down pillowcase in hand, met the three other boys on the sidewalk next to a metallic blue Pontiac and a white nondescript minivan. The pillowcase looked like it carried guns. Gadd, in his Lincoln, zoomed off.

For a long moment I didn't know what to do, follow Gadd or continue the surveillance of the kids who were now armed. Then Gadd helped with the decision; he didn't go far. He drove down the street, pulled a U-turn, stopped, and watched D'Arcy talk to the other three boys. D'Arcy now busy passing on the plan that Gadd had outlined.

I scrunched down in the seat and picked up the radio mike. "All right, this is it. They met with three other primaries and two vehicles—a white minivan and a metallic blue Pontiac. In a minute, they're going to be heading out. Stand by, I'll call which exit they take when they leave the projects. You're going to have to pick them up. I'll have to stay in here until they're out or I'll burn it. Be advised, our main primary will be following behind at a distance in the Lincoln."

Gibbs and Ned both clicked their radios in acknowledgment. Even though kids were involved, I couldn't help but feel the excitement of the thrill of the chase.

D'Arcy talked some more and then reached into the bag and handed out three handguns. He did it right in the open without hesitation, as if totally immune to the law. The three victims, now would-be bank robbers, nodded to what D'Arcy said. All three looked scared to death. D'Arcy finished his instructions and stuck out his fist the same as in preparation to the start of a basketball game. The other three fist-bumped him. They got in the blue Pontiac, started the car, and took off. D'Arcy looked down the block to the Lincoln and gave Gadd the thumbs-up. D'Arcy got in the white minivan and took off following the Pontiac. Gadd waited a minute, started up, and followed the minivan.

Before that moment we didn't know that Gadd used an intermediary, D'Arcy, to further insulate himself from any crime. But now I'd witnessed his conspiracy as he set his caper in motion. For Gadd, P.C. 182 Conspiracy carried the same penalty as the crime. We could also hang on him the gun charges and contributing to the delinquency of a minor, multiple counts. Sure, we could put him away for all of those. But what I really wanted was to catch him with a gun in his hand and be able to pull a Ned, say to Gadd: "Peekaboo, asshole." And pull the trigger. The thought of doing it, dropping the hammer on Gadd, made the sweat break out on my forehead and run in my eyes. Or it could have been the horrible summer heat.

Out on Alameda northbound, the blue Pontiac in the lead, followed by the white minivan, then the black Lincoln and then three members of the violent crimes team, stretched out for half a mile intermingled among unsuspecting citizens.

I came up on the radio and asked dispatch to call Coffman at home and to tell him the surveillance was in progress. To tell him that it was going down. A few minutes later dispatch came back up. "Sam three has been notified. He'll be up on the surveillance in twenty minutes. We'll keep him advised of your location."

The conga line of cars wound its way up to the freeway and headed eastbound. They transitioned to the Pomona Freeway. When we crossed the Los Angeles County line, into San Bernardino County, per department policy, I notified dispatch and also told dispatch that we'd soon be out of radio range. Minutes later we got off at Central Avenue and headed south. I broadcast the location in the blind. We could no longer receive dispatch. I just hoped they could hear us.

The Pontiac, minivan, and Lincoln made a slow pass at Chino Merchants bank and continued on for a couple of blocks. Gadd pulled to the side of the curb on Central in a perfect position to watch the robbery go down. Ned came up on the radio. "I'm staying with the primary." He pulled over a block from Gadd. Ned wanted a piece of Gadd just like I did, only Ned didn't know the whole truth about Darkman.

The minivan and the Pontiac drove three more blocks, turned onto a side street, and pulled over. D'Arcy stuck his arm out the window of the van and pointed down to the asphalt street. This would be the rendezvous spot to dump the hot Pontiac and change into the white minivan that was not stolen, the van D'Arcy would be waiting in to casually drive away like Joe-citizen.

At that moment, I realized we didn't have near enough cops to take down all these players. We needed six to ten more cops to do it right.

Ned came up on the radio, thinking the same thing. "Bruno, how are we going to take these guys down without firing a shot?"

CHAPTER FORTY

I KEYED THE mike: "Ned, you're going to have to come off the primary and come up on the Pontiac."

"No way. We need to take down the primary at the scene to make the case stronger."

"Can't do it. This thing is going down right now. There's no time to call in backup. We have to focus on the 211. We can pick up the other two later."

Gibbs came up on the radio. "Bruno, the Pontiac just pulled in front of the bank. All three ran in the front door, guns drawn."

"Okay," I said. "We wait until they come out, then we box their car with all three of ours. Do what you have to do. Do not let them drive out of the box; do not let this thing go mobile. You copy, Ned?"

He clicked his mike. He wasn't happy about letting Gadd and D'Arcy get away. Neither was I.

I pulled into the parking lot of the bank just as all three black juveniles with guns in their hands ran from the front door, two carrying bags of money.

I gunned the Toyota right at them. To the right, Ned in his Pathfinder bounced over the curb at high speed, his vehicle aimed at the Pontiac. Gibbs came in from the left.

Two more seconds we'd have them boxed.

The last juvenile getting in the left rear of the Pontiac saw Ned barreling at them broadside, his engine wound wide open. The kid raised his gun and fired twice. The gun bucked in his hand. White gun smoke rose in the hot summer air. Ned's windshield spider-webbed in two places in the front driver's window. Someone in the Pontiac pulled the shooter inside.

Ned?

Had he been hit? Was Ned shot?

The Pontiac lunged forward just as Gibbs rammed the front of the car at low speed, crumpling a bit of the hood, stopping it dead. A half second later Ned braked hard laying down a patch of skid. White smoke roiled up from his back tires. He rammed the side of the Pontiac. The Pontiac slewed sideways, the rear end swung around and stopped short of crashing into the front door of the bank. I came up and bumped into the rear at the corner of the car. Ned and Gibbs tightened up, putting their cars metal to metal with the Pontiac so the car couldn't move at all in any direction. Gibbs was at the front and Ned on the passenger side. That left only one side open, the driver's side that opened to the front door of the bank.

I slid across the seat, jumped out, and ran the few steps to the front door, blocking their only escape route, my gun out and down at my side. I stood there exposed with no cover. I couldn't let them slip inside and take hostages.

All three kids in the car looked dazed and scared. Ned and Gibbs both had their guns out as they squatted behind their cars, yelling, "Sheriff's Department, put your hands up! Put your hands up!"

Their hands shot up, three pairs of them.

"Ned," I yelled. "Are you all right?"

"You got this?" he yelled back.

"Yeah."

He ran, got back into his Pathfinder, and smoked his tires backing up. He cranked the wheel, sliding the car around, and hit the gas. He drove over the curb and back into the street the same way he came in. He headed up Central, the last place we'd seen Gadd.

Two Chino police cars bounced into the bank's driveway. Gibbs held up his badge. "Sheriff's Department! We're deputies!"

The two cops jumped out with shotguns and covered the kids.

I held up my hand and yelled, "It's okay. They're just kids. They have their hands up. I'm going to take them out one at a time." I pointed to the kid in the front seat on my side. "Come on, son, slide out. Open your door and slide on out."

"Don't shoot me, mister. Please don't shoot me. I already dropped the gun."

"I won't shoot. Just get your ass out here."

He did. "Now lay down right there." He did. "Now you, driver, slide over, get out, and lay right there next to your buddy." He complied. I said to the third, "Come on, son, it's your turn. Come on out." He'd been the one to fire at Ned, and kid or no kid, I didn't like him for it. He could've killed Ned with his reckless behavior.

He didn't move. "I said get the hell out of the car. Now!"

His hands still up, he turned to look at me. Tears streamed down his face. Fear wouldn't let him move. "Ah, shit. Okay, okay," I said. "It's okay, kid." I put my gun away and held up both hands to show him. "See, everything is okay. No one's going to shoot you."

He still couldn't move.

I stepped in between the two on the ground and headed to the rear door of the Pontiac.

Gibbs yelled, "Bruno, don't."

I took another step.

Coffman appeared next to Gibbs with his own shotgun pointed at the kid in the car. "Bruno, stand down. That's an order."

I looked at Coffman and then back at the kid. He wasn't going to come out on his own, no chance.

I took the final step to the back door. "Hey, kid, I'm not going to hurt you. You understand? I'm just going to open the door." I hesitated. When he didn't move, I opened the door. The gun, an old .38 revolver, lay on the seat next to him. The inside of the car smelled of burnt gunpowder and shit. The kid must've crapped himself.

Coffman said, "Goddamnit, Bruno, back off. Get the hell outta the line of fire."

I ignored him and held up both hands to show the kid. "See, no gun. What's your name? Come on, tell me your name."

He just stared at me, his eyes and cheeks wet with tears.

One of the kids facedown on the concrete said, "Dat's Sammy. He a'ight, he just ascared."

I leaned down, put one knee on the seat, and slowly moved my hand toward him. If Sammy wanted the gun, he could grab it and shoot me before I could stop him.

I stopped, looked over the roof of the car, and called to Gibbs and Coffman and the two Chino coppers with shotguns, "Nobody fire. I got this. Sammy's just a little scared. He'll be all right. Right, Sammy? You just need a minute to get it together. Right? You guys, put your guns down. You're scaring my friend Sammy." No one moved. "Go on, put your guns down."

They complied. I looked back in. "That better, Sammy? You want to come out now? Come on, son." I held out my hand. "It's okay, take my hand."

He slowly reached out. I leaned all the way in and took his hand. "That's it. Come on out."

I got him all the way out and leaned him up against the car. All the others hurried around to our side of the car and handcuffed the two on the ground along with Sammy who I held against the car.

The kid that spoke for Sammy said, "Hey, whattaya doing? We're juvies. You can't take us in. We're juvies. Hey, hey, you gotta let us go. We gotta get home. We got a game this afternoon." He still believed in the propaganda Gadd and D'Arcy had fed him, that juveniles couldn't be held responsible for their crimes.

Coffman said, "Sorry, kid, you three little shitasses are headed for juvie hall."

"No. Wait. Wait, that's not right. You can't take me in. I've got a scholarship, a full ride."

The Chino PD officers took custody of the three child bank robbers, put them in their patrol cars, and called a tow for the Pontiac.

The threat, all the action, was over; the adrenaline bled off. I backed up to the closest wall and slid down to the ground, my hands shaking, my knees too weak to hold me up. On the other side of the glass doors, the employees and bank customers talked and pointed at the Pontiac and pointed at me. With a felony arrest and conviction, the kid would lose his scholarship. I wanted to choke Gadd, ring his neck.

Coffman came over and grunted as he sat next to me. He puffed on his cigar in silence. After a time, still not looking at me, he said, "Without doubt, that was the dumbest thing I've ever witnessed. And I was in the Marine Corps for twenty years. Believe me when I say, that's saying something."

"Yeah, I kinda got that from the way you barked at me."

"You know I'm going to have to make a report and tell the lieutenant all about it. Tell him the whole thing just the way it went down. That horrible, reckless disregard of your training and the violation of policy in front of fifteen, twenty witnesses. The way you jeopardized your safety like that after I gave you a direct order."

"Yeah, I know, I wouldn't expect anything less."

"The way I write it up—"

He didn't finish and instead looked at me with his bloodshot, old man's watery eyes.

"Yeah?" I said.

"You're gonna get the medal of valor out of it, that's for damn sure. Bruno, don't ever do that shit again. This old heart can't take it." He struggled to his feet and walked off leaving in his wake a trail of blue-gray cigar smoke.

CHAPTER FORTY-ONE

I FINALLY STRUGGLED to my feet just as Ned pulled up and parked in the middle of the parking lot away from the cluster of emergency vehicles that now dominated the area close to the bank; Chino PD, San Bernardino County Sheriff, and a fire truck had all responded due to the crashed vehicles. Ned got out and walked around his car, checking the damaged front end, mainly the bumper, contorted and drooping on one side. Coffman and Gibbs headed toward him. When Coffman pointed to something on Ned's head, he reached up to his right ear. His hand came back with blood, and I rushed toward him. I saw Gibbs' look of concern as he broke away and flagged down one of the Chino PD guys. I heard him yell, "Hey, call paramedics for my partner, he's injured!"

Now I really moved. "Ned, you okay?" I asked.

"Shit, yeah, I'm okay. It's just a scratch." He put his hand up to the side of his head and came back with more blood than before.

Coffman took the cigar out of his mouth and pointed to the spiderwebbed windshield, the bullet holes, and then back to Ned's head. "That's a gotdamn bullet graze. That's what that is. Ned, my boy, that little shitass missed killing you by an inch or less."

"Naw, it's probably just broken glass. Sorry. I lost him, Bruno. Gadd got on the freeway and floored it. I saw him get on, but I was

too far back. By the time I got on, he was in the wind. I got this
beast up to a hundred miles an hour, thought it was going to rattle
apart. I went at least twenty miles, never saw him. He must've got
off somewhere in between. That asshole's slippery."

"That's okay. Maybe you should sit down."

"I'm fine. Let's go round up Gadd and D'Arcy. Gadd deserves a
good ass kickin'. It really pisses me off that he got away when he was
the one who put all this in motion. He made us do this." Ned swung
his arm toward the smashed-up Pontiac still parked in front of the
bank, then touched his head and looked at his hand again, the blood
still wet and not yet tacky. Some started to run down his neck and
onto his shirt.

Coffman said, "You're gettin' checked out by the medics, and
that's an order."

"Sarge—"

Coffman took his cigar from his mouth and squinted in the
smoke. "Sarge, my achin' ass. No bullshit this time, Ned. You're
gonna get checked out if I have to hold you down myself."

Sirens from down the street echoed off the houses en route to our
location, further disrupting the quiet morning.

Coffman turned to Gibbs. "You write this mess up and walk it
through for arrests warrants on Gadd and D'Arcy. Bruno, get on
the phone and get a telephonic search warrant for the place on
Willowbrook. I don't want to dick around with this. I don't want to
give these two any time to think. I want to hit the Willowbrook
house by . . ." He looked at his watch. "It's almost noon now, so no
later than three. Let's shoot for three. Get on it."

Stunned, I checked my watch. How had the time slipped by that
quickly? Three o'clock for a search warrant and two arrest warrants.
Just three hours to write them and get them signed was a pipe dream
under any circumstances.

I moved over and peered into the driver's compartment of Ned's vehicle. For the two wild shots the kid threw, he did pretty damn well. Lucky shots. One impacted right where Ned's head should've been, dead center on the driver's side. The other went wide and low but still struck the windshield at the corner of the passenger side. With a car barreling right at me, I didn't know if I could've done any better.

I stood up on the doorsill and pointed to the windshield. "Not to sound like an uncaring fool, but, partner, how did that bullet miss you?"

Ned smiled. "Wasn't my turn, I guess. I ducked. Saw him throw down on my truck and scrunched down a little."

"Bruno," Coffman said. "What'd I say? Get your ass to a phone and get that telephonic search warrant started."

The paramedics pulled up and shut down their siren.

"I'm going with Ned to the hospital. I can use a phone there."

"No, I want—"

My glare cut him short. He knew that if it came to taking care of Ned or jumping into a telephonic, Coffman would lose no matter what kind of threats he threw my way.

The paramedics set down their gear and put on latex gloves. Ned made half an effort to shoo them away and then relented. One paramedic asked him questions as he filled in the information on his clipboard. The other daubed with a gauze pad at the laceration above Ned's ear.

I looked on. "Son of a bitch, Ned, you can't see this," I said. "Coffman's right—this cut looks more like a furrow. You're lucky to be alive."

"Cut the crap. It was a piece of shrapnel. The bullet fragmented when it went through the window. Check the gun. I bet you're gonna find it loaded with some round-nose, all-lead bullets circa

1966 or some shit like that. I'm good. Just bandage me up, we got police work to do."

The paramedic said, "You're going to need at least ten stitches."

"I don't have time to wait in any packed ER. We have to keep rolling on this case or we're gonna lose the momentum; we'll lose the other two responsible for this cluster fuck. Right, Bruno? Tell 'em, Bruno."

I said to the paramedic, "You don't see any sign of a concussion, do you?"

"Yeah, yeah," Ned said. "Of course they don't, because there isn't any."

"Listen," the paramedic said and hesitated. He looked at the bullet holes in the windshield and then at the smashed-up getaway vehicle in front of the bank. "We can run you over in the squad. My wife works today and she'll get you moved right up to the head of the line. An hour, tops."

Ned offered him his hand. "I'm in for that, thanks."

The paramedics packed up their gear, and Ned followed them over to their squad as he held a blood-soaked pad to his head.

Chino PD crime scene techs worked the scene like four busy little ants, taking photos, fingerprints, and measurements. I didn't say a thing to them, got in my damaged car, backed up, and pulled away. They all yelled, "Hey! Hey!" One ran a short way after me before giving up.

CHAPTER FORTY-TWO

THE PARAMEDIC, TRUE to his word, got Ned in the back door and into a closed-door trauma room. I stayed with him and settled into in a chair by the wall. He sat on the exam table and flirted with the pretty nurse as she prepped him for the sutures, shaved the side of his head around the laceration, and sterilized it with Betadine. I got up and whispered in his ear, "Hey, partner, this is the paramedic's wife, remember? So, knock it off."

She heard me and blushed. Ned said, "Oh right, sorry, really, ah, you have to excuse me, I've been shot in the head." He shrugged, pointed to the laceration, and gave her the classic Ned smile, his eyes bright and mischievous.

The nurse prepped the tray and said, "The doctor will be right in to put in the staples."

"Staples?" Ned said. "Staples? Really?"

The post-adrenaline symptoms started to ease up on me. I wanted to avoid talking with Ned. I still needed to tell him about Beth and used every excuse to avoid doing so. I went back to my chair and picked up the phone mounted on the wall. I dialed the narco desk clerk at headquarters, the one assigned specifically to the violent crimes team. I quickly dictated the affidavit and then the search warrant. Since I had witnessed the crime—the bank robbery—and I'd seen the same suspects from that crime go into the location on

11431 Willowbrook, I only needed three long paragraphs for the affidavit, one of the easiest search warrants I'd ever completed. Next I dialed the on-call judge, gave him the circumstances verbally as he read the faxed copy the clerk had sent him. The judge signed the warrant and faxed it to the hospital ER. From start to finish, the warrant in my hand took thirty-two minutes.

I thanked the judge as Chelsea came in the door to the trauma room. My heart gave a little skip. I wanted to go up and hug her and couldn't, not in public; that'd be unprofessional.

She wore a fake smile. I tried to look behind her as she entered to see if she'd brought along ol' Jim Turner. She said, "Ah, Bruno, can I talk to you for a minute outside?"

I hesitated and said to Ned, "You going to be okay?"

"What's the matter with you?" He again pointed to his head. "This is all about nothin'. I've been hurt worse playing basketball." He pointed at me and smiled big. He lowered his voice. "But you, my friend, better take a cold shower. I can see the way you're looking at her." He shook his hand and said, "Va va voom."

I tried to keep from smiling and couldn't. I checked to see that Chelsea made it out the first door, and in a harsh whisper said, "I told you nothing's going on, so knock it off."

I went out and caught up with her, my heart beating faster in her presence. I needed to apologize. I should've called her. The doctor passed me with a staple gun in hand on his way to attend to Ned. Chelsea continued on through the emergency entrance doors to the outside. She turned and crossed her arms on her chest, the fake smile gone, replaced with anger.

"Uh-oh," I said.

"First, let me congratulate you and your team for the fine job you did capturing those three kids." She said it in a way I couldn't miss the sarcasm.

"What do you mean? No one got hurt."

She took a step closer. "Why, then, are we standing outside a hospital ER?"

"We—"

"You missed the primary suspect in this whole thing and managed to smash up three of our cars. Anyone could've grabbed the secondary suspects. Third-rate security guards could've done that."

Now we were third-rate security guards. I fought down the rising anger.

She said, "We wanted Gadd with his fingers caught in the cookie jar. That was your whole purpose for the inception of your team, and you blew it. You crashed three cars and got your partner shot."

"Hey, ease up off me, would ya? You have absolutely no room to talk smack about what happened out there in front of that bank. You set my team up to fail because your agency didn't want the liability of taking on juveniles robbing banks."

Her mouth dropped open as if surprised we'd figured out the FBI's motivation.

I said, "That was a grade-A screw-over and you know it."

She regained some control. "You missed the main player. You missed Gadd."

"No we didn't. We're getting arrest warrants right now, and here's the search warrant for his pad."

Her anger fled. She grabbed the warrant from my hand. "You're kidding me. You got enough for an arrest warrant on Gadd?"

"That's right, we got Gadd slam-dunk on conspiracy to commit bank robbery and about ten other crimes. He's going away for a long time."

I should've also told her about Gadd being the Darkman but held my tongue; no one needed to know that. No one.

I really didn't need her jumping my case, not with the pressure from the two secrets that involved Beth and the Darkman, piling on, smothering me, giving me a magnitude-eight headache.

"Bruno, you really got enough to make it stick in court?"

"Deadbang, no problem, he'll get twenty years guaranteed."

"That's wonderful. I didn't think . . . I mean this is really great. Do you need any help taking Gadd down? I can assign a full FBI robbery team if—"

"No, I think we got it." I shouldn't have answered so quickly. Pride got in the way. We did need help. We could use four or five more bodies for the takedown and search warrant service.

The ER doors whooshed open, and Ned charged out, the staples on the shaved side of his head glinting in the sunlight. He didn't slow and came right up to me. He pulled back and slugged me in the mouth. I saw it coming and didn't flinch. The heavy guilt made me want it. Made me need it.

The blow lit up the afternoon in bright yellow and orange lights, made the air turn thick and the ambient sound warble. I stumbled back, spitting blood, more scared of the eternal guilt than the inflicted pain.

Ned yelled, "You asshole, you're supposed to be my friend."

"I am your friend. I swear I am. It was for the best for everyone."

Ned moved in again to hit me. "You're a judge now, a judge on what's best for my daughter?"

I didn't raise my hands to defend myself. He slugged me in the head again and again.

Chelsea grabbed him from behind. "Stop it. Stop it right now."

He shrugged her off, shoved her away. "Let me go."

I ran at him and shoved him. "Don't you touch her."

He said to me, "Then fight me. Raise your hands and fight me like a man, you sniveling little coward."

His words bore down into my soul and made me sick, words that would stay with me forevermore.

The ER doors swung open again, and Coffman hurried out. "That's enough, Ned. Stand down. That's an order." To me, he said,

"I'm sorry, Bruno, I thought you already told him. I thought he already knew."

Coffman must've talked with Wicks—and Wicks told him about Ned's status with Beth.

I wiped blood from my split lip with the back of my hand as the air turned back to thin and tasteless. "No, it's okay. I deserve every bit of this and more."

"Damn straight you do," Ned said. "How could you do this to Beth?"

Chelsea said, "What's going on? What's happened to Beth?"

Coffman waved her off and stepped in between Ned and me, facing her up close. He said, "I'm sorry, this is personal."

Gibbs chose that moment to pull around to the back of the hospital in his car.

Coffman said, "Per the lieutenant, Ned, you're to take some days off. Bruno, you, too."

Ned stared me down. "Like hell I will. There's nothing I can do now for Beth. CPS will never tell me where they're keeping her. I got nothing to do now but wait on a court date. That could be days, thanks to you, Bruno. I won't see Beth for days. So I'm working. I'm going after Gadd."

I should've stepped in right then, told him about the scars on Beth's feet, how it'd change everything in his favor, but I couldn't. He'd take off after JB, and no one in this world would keep him from killing him.

"Suit yourself," Coffman said.

I broke Ned's stare and looked at Coffman in stunned awe—stunned at the inappropriateness of the wrong call, allowing Ned to work in his emotional state.

Coffman said, "Don't give me that look, Bruno. Ned wants to work, he works. Come on, let's go grapple up this asshole Gadd, finish this screwed-up case so we can all move on." The last part he threw at Chelsea with a scowl.

I walked away. Chelsea grabbed my wrist. "Bruno, wait."

I jerked my hand from hers and glared at her. The full weight of her words from moments ago had just started to sink in. She didn't care one whit about me, about her and me. All she cared about was closing a difficult case and making her stats look good for her upward mobility.

"Wait, let's talk. Please come back and talk to me."

I kept going, raised my hand over my head, and gave her a last wave. If I would have turned and looked at her, her eyes, her mouth, her . . . I would've caved. I would've crawled back and let her stomp on my emotional vulnerability, let her grind it into the ground.

And maybe I would've liked it.

CHAPTER FORTY-THREE

TINA MITCHELL, CALLED Tiny Tina by the deputies at Lynwood station, responded to our request for a marked sheriff's unit with a uniform. She'd go in on the search warrant entry for visibility's sake. We met in the Compton Court parking lot at three o'clock, about a mile from the location we intended to hit, 11431 Willowbrook. All four of our cars sat in a row, the trunks open. No one said a word as we donned our body armor, our Sam Brown belts, and green nylon windbreakers with *Sheriff* in bold yellow letters across the back. Except Ned; he preferred the cooler green mesh vest. I would, too, but couldn't afford those kinds of extras, not with all the money I put away for Olivia's college fund. She'd need college to escape the heavy gravitational pull of the ghetto. Thinking about Olivia helped keep my mind off the terrible words Ned had spoken.

Tina stood by and watched, a new deputy just off probation and eager to please, eager to get into the action, and a warrant going after a violent criminal smelled of heavy action. "Hey, why's everyone so quiet?" She couldn't stand still and moved from one trunk to another, hanging a little longer at Ned's. "What's going on? You guys are never this quiet. You're always baggin' on each other." She stood five feet four with a waist so narrow all her gear on her Sam Brown looked jammed together in a bunch. She wore her sun-bleached blond haircut in a bob and had intense green eyes and a small mouth. She had a thing for Ned and, try as she might, couldn't quite keep it hidden.

No one answered her; they continued snapping on keepers and checking the loads of both revolvers. One trunk after another slammed closed.

Tina's expression turned serious. "Hey, Ned, what happened to the side of your head? Oh, my God. Are you okay?"

Ned closed and locked the diamond plate aluminum equipment box in the back of the Pathfinder. "I'm fine, kid, it's just a scratch. Don't worry your pretty little head."

"Doesn't look like just a scratch. Are you sure you shouldn't be off IOD?"

"I'm sure." He walked away from her and over to Coffman's car where everyone else congregated. "What's the lineup, Sarge?" he asked.

"This is a heavy caper with a heavy dude. You and Bruno have worked together the most, so you two go in number one and number two. Mitchell, you're third, take in a gauge to bat cleanup if it goes down bad. Watch your field of fire. Gibbs, you take a shotgun to the back of the house. Holler if you get a runner. I'll be out front on the ram. I'll take the door—then, Bruno, you're first. Ned, you come in right on his ass. Bruno, you know the routine, second guy in is at risk, you cover Ned. Take out the threat if there is one. Stay tight, cover and move and clear those rooms fast."

"You don't need to tell me how to do my job," Ned said.

Gibbs said, "I get entry next time; I'm tired of covering the back." Gibbs never complained. Everyone was on edge over the disharmony in our team. The disharmony I'd caused.

Coffman said, "We don't need all these cars. Double up. Ned and Bruno, take Ned's car. Gibbs, you jump in with Mitchell." Coffman turned and faced Ned. "Listen, I know there's some shit going on between you two, and I don't want it bleeding over into my operation. You understand?"

Ned didn't answer and went to the driver's side of his car.

I hesitated as Coffman looked at me. I said, "It'll be okay."

Coffman said, "It damn well better be. I'm counting on you. Let's hit it."

I got in Ned's car with a thousand words swimming around in my head, words that had to be said, words too hot and emotional to come out in the scant few moments on the drive over. Maybe in a few hours after Ned cooled out a little. Sure, in a few hours after everything with Gadd was settled and we stood in the parking lot of some grocery store drinking a victory beer.

Ned drove angry, his eyes to the front. He jerked the wheel this way and that as we maneuvered through the streets headed to 11431 Willowbrook. He kept his head slightly tilted to the side to see around the spiderweb in the windshield from the bullet he'd dodged. The damaged front bumper rattled and banged. I had to say something, anything. I needed him to say something to me. I said, "Did you see Coffman, how he looked like an old man too frail to be—"

Ned's head pivoted toward me, his eyes cold. "Enough with your shit about Coffman. He's the best man we got. I think your time on this team has come to an end. When this investigation is over, I think you should transfer out."

I looked away from him and out the window. "After this is over, if that's what you still think, you got it, partner. I'm gone."

"Don't call me partner."

I looked back at him. "Get your head out of your ass—we're going on-scene."

"You don't need to worry about me," he said.

Thick plywood sheets covered the front windows on an all-green house with white trim, the plywood covered in murals of gang graffiti, the white paint chipped and peeling. A three-foot, trampled-over chain-link fence without a gate separated the sidewalk from the all-dirt front yard. Three desiccated wood steps led up to the narrow wooden porch.

All three of our cars zoomed up to the front. We bailed out, Gibbs going to the side headed for the back, toting a shotgun port arms. He immediately came up against a tall fence he'd have to overcome.

Coffman took a couple of seconds longer than the rest of us, lugging the heavy door ram.

I mounted the wood porch alongside Ned, leaving no room for Tiny Tina. She stayed on the ground. The shotgun looked too big in her small hands, her eyes wider than normal as she covered the door from below us.

Coffman ran up in between Ned and me. His breath came hard from the exertion of carrying the ram. He swung it back. I started to move with the ram to get inside right away. We'd already lost a second and a half, but still carried the initiative, barely.

The ram came forward and struck the door in the right place right by the knob. Only without enough oomph behind it. Coffman lacked body weight, the muscle needed for the job.

The ram bounced back. The door remained locked.

We'd just lost the element of surprise. I shoved Coffman out of the way, went up on my left foot, and booted the door with everything I had.

The door banged open. I fell to the side, my balance gone from the rebound. Ned moved quickly through the opening, the window of death. He took my position. I was supposed to be first in. But it didn't matter, the failed entry changed the entire dynamic. I recovered and came in right behind him, right on his ass.

I caught a glimpse of one suspect, and maybe a second, a shadow of the second.

Devon D'Arcy, six feet, two hundred and fifty pounds of him, stood at the entrance to the kitchen, backlit by the only light in the house that emanated from the kitchen. The living room was dark without any light except from the now-open front door. He'd heard the first thump of the ram. The moment we'd lost the initiative. He stood ready, his gun raised.

Ned fired on the run just as D'Arcy fired.

The round thumped into Ned's body armor, high to the right chest. The impact spun him around to face me, his expression blank, without any emotion.

D'Arcy fired a second time.

Ned's head jerked forward. A small red hole appeared beside Ned's nose, an exit wound. The light in his eyes winked out. He wilted to the floor.

CHAPTER FORTY-FOUR

"NED! NED!"

I went to my knees next to him.

The shotgun bellowed in Tiny Tina's hands. The recoil knocked her backward. The shotgun's pattern, nine .32 cal lead pellets, hit D'Arcy low, at the knees. He crumpled to the floor wailing in pain.

Coffman stood between Tiny Tina and me and Ned. He fired his handgun. Bang. Bang. Bang. His rounds struck the back wall behind where D'Arcy used to be a half-second before. I shoved Coffman's leg. "He's down. The suspect's down. Call for med aid. Ned's hit. Call for med aid."

Gun smoke filled the room, thick and white and acrid.

I got underneath Ned and gently cradled his head.

Coffman took a step closer. His gun fell and hung in his hand by his leg. His eyes focused on Ned, his mouth agape.

"Tina," I yelled, "cuff D'Arcy and then call for med aid."

She came out of her trance and leapt into action. "How's Ned?" she asked as she threw the shotgun to the floor, drew her handgun, and moved toward D'Arcy. "Is he okay? How bad is Ned, Bruno? Talk to me."

"Watch your ass, watch what you're doing. There's another one. I saw another one."

Ned lay inert in my arms, his eyes wide open staring at the grimy ceiling in a little shitbox of a house in the middle of the ghetto. His mouth sagged open and his tongue lolled in the back of his throat. The exit wound beside his nose wasn't bleeding.

I didn't want it to be true.

It couldn't be true.

Hot tears streamed down my face. I couldn't answer Tina about Ned's condition. I didn't think I'd ever be able to talk again as the darkness of the world tried to close in and snuff out everything else. I fought off the shock that threatened to shut down my body.

Tiny Tina made it over to D'Arcy, kicked the gun further away into the kitchen. She fell with both knees onto D'Arcy's back and holstered her gun. In his agony, D'Arcy floundered on the floor like a harpooned whale, smearing blood in big swaths on the filthy linoleum. She got him cuffed and came away with bloodied hands.

Gibbs rushed in and froze at the sight of the deadly tableau on the floor before him. "Ah shit. Ah shit. Bruno, I'll get med aid responding. I'll get med aid."

"Who's out back? Did you see anyone come out the back?"

"No, but there was a fence; I had trouble with it. I wasn't set up before I heard the front door go down. Someone could've got out."

He turned and fled. Coffman stood frozen in the same place. From the floor with Ned's head cradled in my lap, I reached up and pried Coffman's revolver from his hands. In his condition he didn't need a gun, shouldn't have one.

The loss of his weapon must've triggered some deep-seated primal instinct drilled into him from his Marine Corps days. His head turned; his eyes finally left Ned as he looked at me. "Is he . . ."

I still couldn't speak; the lump in my throat had grown too large. Coffman let out a roar of grief. He picked up Tina's discarded shotgun from the floor and ran toward the prostate D'Arcy.

I struggled to get out from underneath Ned. I placed his head gently on the floor as I yelled, "Tina. Tina, stop him. Stop him."

Tina stepped in front of Coffman and raised her bloodied hands. Coffman knocked her aside. He raised the shotgun and brought the butt down on D'Arcy's head. I tackled Coffman as he raised it to strike downward on D'Arcy a second time. We fell and rolled into the kitchen. Coffman lacked meat on his bones. Something cracked inside him when we hit the floor, ribs maybe. His muscles went slack underneath me as his body moved in racking sobs. He grabbed ahold of me and held on. I let him. I needed the consoling, too.

In the other room, Tina had moved over to Ned. "My God, Bruno! Bruno! Ned's . . . Ned's . . ."

I no longer had the luxury of grief. I needed to take control of the scene or give myself in to shock. I struggled to my feet and left Coffman on the floor to weep alone. "Tina, clear the rest of the house. Do it right now and watch yourself. I saw someone else."

She didn't move and didn't look like she could if she wanted to as she knelt next to my best friend. I picked up her shotgun and Coffman's handgun. I went through the rest of the house. Lucky for us Gadd hadn't been lying in wait along with D'Arcy, or we'd have all been dead. If there had been a second man, he was gone. Ollie's nephew D'Arcy would never get out of prison. Gadd had pumped enough propaganda into D'Arcy that he'd pulled the trigger on Ned.

Gibbs rushed back in. "How's he doin'? How's Ned doin', Bruno?"

I couldn't answer and just looked at Gibbs. He caught the eye-to-eye communication. "Son of a bitch." He moved to the wall and kicked holes in it. "Son of a bitch. Son of a bitch."

Sirens reached out to us inside the stifling house, hundreds of them. Gibbs had put out code 999, "An officer down." With a call of an officer down, cops from miles around responded, and not just from the Sheriff's Department but from every nearby agency. Deputies half-dressed in the locker room grabbed their guns, left their lockers open, and ran to the parking lot to flag down a ride; cops left their food uneaten in restaurants; everyone within earshot of the radio call ran to help. That's the way it always went when a brother went down.

11431 Willowbrook would quickly turn into a writhing beast of cops with guns out, looking to make right a terrible wrong with no way to vent their anguish and grief. If I didn't take immediate control, they would trample and ruin the crime scene.

I gently took Tina by the shoulders and lifted her to her feet. "Go to your trunk and get out the roll of crime scene tape. Tape off this entire house and the street. Don't let anyone in. You understand? No one."

She nodded, her face wet with tears.

"Gibbs? Gibbs, you help her." He, too, nodded and moved with heavy feet out the front door.

Coffman sidestepped D'Arcy and came into the living room. He'd composed himself and looked ashen but back in control. "Bruno, get med aid in here for this asshole." He kicked at D'Arcy's leg.

Coffman took off his green nylon raid jacket and eased it over Ned's face.

Something I should've done.

CHAPTER FORTY-FIVE

I STOOD OVER Ned at a complete loss as to what to do next. All ambition and motivation fled as I stared down at him. His one arm peeked out from under Coffman's green raid jacket. The sleeve of Ned's tee shirt was scrunched up, revealing a portion of the team's tattoo, the "F" in "BMF."

Coffman took hold of my arm and shook me. "Bruno? Bruno? Pull your head out of your ass and get out front. I want you to take control of the scene. Can you do that for me, son?"

I looked at him, then over at D'Arcy on the floor half in the kitchen, half in the living room. Coffman read my mind and said, "I'm okay now, I'm not going to do anything to that punk. I'm okay. I'm good. Go on, get out there and supervise."

I nodded and tried to pull myself away from where I stood, tried to pull myself away from my dead friend on the floor. I couldn't believe it. It wasn't real. Coffman took hold of my arm and tugged me along.

Once outside, the bright light and the heat of the day reminded me life moved on, nothing could stop it, not even a tragedy of historic proportions. Coffman took his revolver from my hand and put it back in his holster.

More and more cop cars continued to arrive, their brakes smoking and smelling of asbestos. The sea of cop cars already spread clear back to the intersection. Gibbs and Tiny Tina stood, one on the sidewalk and one in the street, the flat of their hands up as they yelled to keep all the uniforms back. I walked up and recognized in the mob four deputies from Lynwood station. Grief hung over me like a dark cloud, making it difficult to speak. The dry summer air didn't help. I pointed. "You four, come here." Tina let them through.

I placed them on the sidewalk in front of the house. "No one goes in under any circumstances." They nodded with somber expressions, just happy to be doing something. I went back to the group. "Anybody else want something to do?" All of them in earshot yelled versions of "Hell, yes."

"One suspect might've slipped out. I need this neighborhood locked down, five blocks in either direction until we can organize a door-to-door search." The front of the herd of uniforms turned and ran to their cars. The others moved up. "The rest of you that are left," I said, "I need this street cleared for paramedics and the ambulance so we can get the suspect out of here."

Nobody moved to get the cars cleared from the street. I understood how they felt. "Come on, let's move. Act professional, get these cars out of the way, now."

Some of them started to make their way back to their units. Not to cooperate but more to get away from the emotional pain.

I yelled, "Someone get on the radio and put out code four so we can stop all these cars from showing up. It's all over. It's done. There's nothing anybody can . . ." I couldn't finish.

Paramedics arrived and could only make it to within half a block of 11431 Willowbrook. They left their siren on, pulled up onto the center meridian and drove the rest of the way on the dead grass in between the hundred-year-old pepper trees, and parked. They pulled out boxes of gear and the gurney and wheeled up to the front of the house. I said, "Follow me," and took them inside.

D'Arcy no longer moaned and writhed on the floor. He now lay on his side handcuffed behind his back in a puddle of his own blood. The side of his face swelled red and purple from where Coffman butt-stroked him with the shotgun. He saw the paramedics. "'Bout time you all got your asses in here. Git on over here and help me. These fools 'bout killed me. I thought dey was here to jack me. I was defending myself. You hear? You're witnesses. I thought dey came here to jack me."

The paramedics ignored him and set their gear down next to my friend. They pulled away Coffman's green raid jacket.

Ned's dead eyes stared right at me. I grabbed my stomach and turned to the side and threw up until I dry-heaved.

D'Arcy yelled, "Hey. Hey, you assholes, git your asses over here and hep me. I'm the victim here. Dey shot me for no reason. Din one of 'm hit me over the head with the shotgun. You believe dat? After I was already handcuffed. Dat's poolease brutality for sure. I'm gonna own dem for it. You wait and see if I don't."

The paramedics cut off Ned's vest. They took off his body armor and cut off his shirt. They put on EKG leads and ran a tape that showed a flatline. They wanted to be sure. They replaced the green jacket covering him and moved their gear over to D'Arcy.

Coffman, with a strange expression, walked past Ned without looking down and went outside. I'd seen that look before, years ago, the night in the ER room when he'd come in half-dressed and asked me how many we'd lost, a flashback to a time long ago on a South Pacific island.

I followed.

Coffman walked out to the sidewalk and up to Tiny Tina who was still holding the line. He took her by the arm and started across the street, weaving in and around the cars.

On the sidewalk, I yelled at Gibbs above the din. "Go inside, you got custody from now on. D'Arcy's your responsibility." Gibbs nodded and hurried past me. He was a good man. I went after Coffman and Tina.

I found them standing alone next to the back doors of the ambulance. I stopped by a large tree out of their view and listened.

Tina said, "I don't know, Sarge. I don't know if I can do it."

"Listen, Ned Kiefer is lying in there dead, and that little shitass is going to get away with it. The law won't do anything to him. He'll get twenty-five years, and when he turns twenty-one, juvie hall will kick him out. He'll do six years for killin' Ned. Six years, Mitchell, think about it. Ned's one of ours. We take care of our own. Now, you're small, and a girl, and you can get away with it easy, trust me on this. Hand me your gun."

Tina stared up at her sergeant, her mentor, drew her handgun, and handed it to him. He unloaded it and handed it back to her. "Put this empty gun back in your holster." She did. He handed her back the six bullets. "Now be sure to reload it afterward, you understand? You ride in the ambulance with D'Arcy and let him grab your duty gun, put your hip right up where he can see it, put it right in his face. He'll go for it, I promise you. I know the type. Then you take him out with your backup gun. You have a backup, right?"

She nodded.

He said, "Good. Give him all five shots right up close, you understand? Aim for his head point blank, you understand?"

She looked scared to death at the prospect of committing murder in the name of some malignant, misplaced sense of honor.

The paramedics came out of the house wheeling D'Arcy on the gurney. The mob of cops in the street went silent, their eyes filled with anger and hate. Gibbs stayed right alongside. When they passed me, I fell in with them. The paramedics slid the gurney with D'Arcy into the back of the ambulance.

Coffman said, "That's okay, Gibbs, Mitchell here is going to ride in the ambulance to the hospital with the suspect."

With her blank stare, Tina looked like a zombie. I stepped up and into the back of the ambulance.

"Bruno?" Coffman said. "What are you doing? I said Mitchell's gonna take this ride."

"She can't," I said. "She was the one who shot him. That's a major conflict, and she also has to stay here to be interviewed by the shooting team. I'll take this."

"No!" Coffman said. He looked bewildered and didn't have a good answer for my logic. Tina caught my eye with an expression of relief as she nodded to me.

I got in. I didn't want to go. I didn't know how I would be able to handle being in the same enclosed space as D'Arcy, but I needed to make sure he got to county hospital safely. That's what the law dictated. D'Arcy deserved his due process. Ned's words echoed back at me, the title he'd hung on me, *Mr. Law Enforcement*. And now, in the quiet calm of grief, I realized I would never live down the fact that Ned died while angry at me, believing I'd betrayed him.

CHAPTER FORTY-SIX

I DIDN'T GET home until after dark. Booking D'Arcy into LCMC—Los Angeles County Medical Center—took hours. Homicide finally arrived to interview him as I walked out of the jail ward. One of the homicide detectives said to my back as I kept going and didn't slow down, "Hey, you Bruno Johnson? We need to talk to you. Hold up." I didn't care if I talked to anyone else, didn't think I could for at least a couple of weeks. I ignored him.

The deputy assigned to give me a ride home sensed my mood and didn't say a word the entire trip. He made the turn onto Nord. Cars filled both sides of my street; many more double parked, leaving only a one-way path for two-way traffic to negotiate through. In my front yard a hundred people or more milled about a fifty-five-gallon drum burning bright with orange and yellow and red flames leaping five feet in the air. Inky black smoke rose into the dark moonless night. Someone used oil to burn in the drum along with the busted-up wooden pallet protruding out the top of the can. More pallets stood tall next to it. A drumfire, what the hell? With the kind of oppressive heat the two-year drought flung upon us day after day—those people in my yard didn't have brain one. People who'd come to pay their respects, grieving brother officers who gathered together to be with others of their own kind.

Some still wore uniform pants and boots with an off-duty holster. Others wore Levi's and tee shirts with Sam Brown belts. All drank from red plastic cups, beer drawn from two kegs up by the house. At either end of the yard on the sidewalk, a deputy stood with a shotgun cradled in one arm, security, a statement to the type of neighborhood and to let everyone know now was not the time to mess around.

Ned didn't have a house; he'd been staying at mine. That's why they all came to Nord.

Everyone went silent when the black-and-white pulled up to let me off. The front door stood open. More people filled the house. Dad stepped out onto the naked stoop. I made my way through the crowd; some of the people I knew, a lot I didn't. When I passed by, all of them reached out and put a hand on my shoulder or back and mumbled a weak-assed apology. No amount of sorry would help. Nothing would help.

Shadows from the fire danced around, creating a strobe in their faces and reflected in their eyes, deepening the overall sadness. A path in the crowd opened up to reveal Lieutenant Robby Wicks and Sergeant Coffman standing together sharing a pint bottle of Jack.

I approached them, all eyes on me now. A vast emptiness filled my insides. Wicks offered the pint to me. I waved it off. Neither one said anything. Though, I knew exactly what Wicks would say. In a few days after the sharp edge of loss simmered to a bearable heat, he'd take me aside and say, "When you chase violence, sometimes it turns and bites back." An adage he carried around his back pocket that he thought soothed all ills. In his life maybe.

I spoke first. "I just came home to get my car. Would you have these guys clear cars away from mine so I can get out? I just want to talk to my dad, kiss my daughter, then I'm going back out."

Coffman said, "Just where the hell you think you're going tonight?"

"After Gadd."

Coffman looked to Wicks, waiting for him to tell me no. Wicks held my eyes and said nothing. He tilted back the pint and took on two large gulps. Coffman looked pale, washed out, like a cut rose left out in the sun. He said, "What the hell, Bruno? We've got the whole damn department out looking for that asshole. What do you think you're going to do that they can't? And you're a direct participant in what happened. You're emotionally involved. No way. Department regs says no chance."

"What am I going to do? I'm going to find him and—and take him down." In the yard behind me stood too many witnesses to say what I really intended to do to Gadd.

"No you're not," Coffman said. "You're off for two weeks. That's an order." This time he didn't look at Wicks for approval.

Had the ram that Coffman wielded against the door at 11431 Willowbrook not bounced off, Ned and I would've been through the window of death in time to brace D'Arcy before he raised the gun. And Ned would still be alive. Even Tiny Tina could've taken that flimsy door with the ram, taken it down in one whack.

I lowered my voice and said to Coffman, "Time for you to retire, old man." Words I knew I'd regret later on. As I passed by him heading to the porch, he took the dead cigar from his mouth and grabbed my arm. The wet smack of the cigar slapped up against my skin. He got right up in my face, angry, his breath hot and musty with tobacco. "Don't you dare talk to me like that. You're nothing but a wet-nosed punk, and you will do what I order you to do. You will take the time off." He lowered his voice. "That thing at Merchants Bank could go a different way. I could tell the truth, put in my report that I ordered you to stand down and you went against a direct order. And, son, that's a terminating offense."

I lowered my voice even further, moved in closer almost up to his ear, and whispered, "I heard what you said to Tina Mitchell at the back of the ambulance. Who do you think she'll back if it comes down to it? Put your papers in, old man, you're through."

Coffman staggered back, his tan face going even paler in the firelight, his mouth sagging open. In the shadowy light, he looked cadaverous.

Wicks screwed the cap onto the Jack and tossed it over the top of the crowd of grieving deputies. Someone caught it, pulled it down out of the air. Wicks said to me, "I'm going with you. Just let me get a shotgun and some extra magazines. I'll meet you by my car in five."

I looked back at Coffman as he eased down into a sitting position in the grass. I felt bad for having taken him off at the knees, but God damn I loved Ned. And if Coffman stuck around, he'd only get someone else hurt or killed. Even so, the sorrow I felt for Coffman didn't penetrate that vast emptiness inside me. Only one thing would: putting a bullet in Gadd. I'd give him all six.

CHAPTER FORTY-SEVEN

I MOUNTED THE steps. People inside moved out of the way to let me enter. Dad stood in the kitchen, holding Olivia. I went to him, took her out of his arms, and buried my face in a hug. She smelled great, baby powder and little girl. She patted the side of my head with her tiny soft hand. "You ungry, Pop Pop? Is the monster ungry?" She wanted to play our game. I pulled her back and looked at her; the innocence and the truth she spoke took my breath away. "Yes, baby, Pop Pop is ungry." I handed her back to Dad.

He took her. "I'm sorry about what happened to Ned, Son. That's just awful. I am so sorry." He reached out and put a warm hand on my arm. I turned away so I wouldn't break down right there and cry—cry for days and days.

"Yes, it is. I have to go out."

"When you comin' back?"

I looked around at all the folks in our house, neighbors, friends, but mostly cops, who silently looked on. I needed more than anything to be alone, and these folks violated that solitude. I looked back at Dad. "I'll be back when the job's done."

"You sure you shouldn't have some rest first? You look terrible and on the verge of collapse."

"No."

"You be careful then."

I didn't expect that from him. I expected him to try and convince me to stay home with my daughter where I belonged. Insist upon it.

Then I remembered my promise to Ned. "Dad, where's Beth?"

He looked away from me for just a second, before looking back. "This morning a deputy knocked on the door. He had a court order in his hand. I didn't know what to do. I thought you said Child Protective Services was coming and they did, but not until later, about an hour later. They showed up too late. But before that I didn't know what to do about the deputy standing in our living room with a piece of paper signed by a judge. I'm sorry, Son, I think they gave that poor child back to her mother."

"It's not your fault, you understand? You did the right thing. I'll take care of it." I turned and headed back out.

On the stoop, I hesitated. Off to the left and down the street at the corner, a silver BMW bumped the front tires over the curb and rolled slowly down the sidewalk headed to our house. The deputy with the shotgun stepped aside to let it pass. The BMW came right into the yard and stopped by the fifty-five-gallon drum with the ebbing fire. The crowd filled in back around the car. Shadows flickered and danced off the tinted windows. Everyone stayed silent, waiting to see what would happen next.

I'd never seen such pure, unmitigated arrogance in the way JB just drove into my yard, the yard of the house where Ned had been staying. I fought down the rage. JB had been the catalyst of Ned's anger at me. He'd stolen Hannah away with money, turned her head away from Ned, broke them up as a couple.

The passenger door opened and out stepped Hannah, her eyes and face puffy from crying. She wore a plain white hundred-dollar tee shirt tucked into denim pants with black cowboy boots. Her wavy blond hair fell loose about her shoulders.

She stood by the open car door looking up at me, her blue eyes pleading to end her pain, her grief. She wouldn't get that from me. I didn't have it to offer. She didn't move. "Bruno?"

I took the three steps down the stoop to the ground. She launched right at me. I took her in my arms and hugged her. Hugged her like I never hugged anyone before. She hugged back.

She finally whispered into my neck. "I'm sorry. This is all my fault, isn't it? Isn't it?"

I didn't answer, couldn't.

"Tell me, Bruno." Her voice a whisper, barely audible. "Did he . . . did he die because of me? Was his mind somewhere it shouldn't have been? Did he hesitate? Was it me, Bruno?"

Her words made me flash back for the thousandth time to the entry into that house, and in my mind's eye, I witnessed again the flash and noise from Ned firing his gun.

He'd fired first.

I realized right then, Ned had fired first. He'd missed. Ned never missed.

A part of me wanted to tell her the truth, but at that moment whom would the truth benefit? It could only cause more grief and pain and solve nothing.

I pulled her away to look into her eyes. "No, it was just a bad set of circumstances that all came together at the same time."

She sobbed and gulped. "Are you sure?"

I nodded. "But there is something you should know."

I took her back into the hug and whispered. The crowd didn't need to hear our personal business.

"Hannah . . . Hannah." She nodded, waiting for me to tell her. "Ned asked me to look after Beth, to make sure—"

Hannah tried to pull away. "What? Wha—"

I held on and wouldn't let her pull back.

"Listen to me. Just listen. Beth has been abused."

Hannah let out a little scream and fought until I let her go. "What the hell are you talking about?" She stood with the firelight dancing on her blond hair, her fists clenched.

"JB used a cord and whipped the bottom of her feet."

Her eyes went wide and her mouth dropped open. On the other side of the BMW, the driver's door opened. JB had heard what I'd said through Hannah's open passenger door. His head popped up over the roof of the car.

"No!" Hannah yelled. "That's not true. I don't believe you." She hurried the few steps back to the BMW and flung open the back door. Beth was sleeping in a car seat, her head cocked to one side. Hannah, in her rush, yanked off Beth's little shoes and woke Beth, who let out a yelp. Hannah's back went stiff as she screeched, "Oh my God. Oh my God." She pulled out of the car and looked at JB, who now walked around, taking off his black leather designer jacket. He tossed it on the trunk deck of his car. He wore a red silk shirt open in a vee at the top, revealing his chest hair and a thick gold chain around his neck. His black denim pants covered most of his rattlesnake-skin cowboy boots.

"What have you done?" Hannah yelled. "What have you done to my baby?"

"Of course, that isn't true, babe. It's a lie. Think about it. Beth has been with Ned and—"

I went at him. He would not disparage Ned's name, especially with a false accusation. Coffman and Gibbs grabbed me, tried to hold me back and couldn't. Several more deputies jumped on and stopped the ass-kicking JB so richly deserved.

Hannah came over to JB. "Did you hit my baby?"

"No. He's lying. Honey, who are you going to believe?"

She looked at me. "Bruno?"

I relaxed, and so did the grip from all the guys restraining me. "Hannah, have I ever lied to you?"

She gulped hard and slowly shook her head, no.

"Now," I said. "Has this piece of shit ever lied to you? The injuries on Beth's feet are scarred. Ned couldn't have done it."

She spun on JB. "You son of a bitch." She went at him, clawing and slapping and kicking.

JB put his hand on her face and shoved her down. He turned and faced me and the group of men holding me. "You've meddled in my life once too often. Let him go." He started rolling up his sleeves.

Coffman yelled, "Get the hell outta here, Johnny. You got two minutes or I'll tell these boys to take you down and book you for felony child abuse. See how you'll like that in prison as an ex-cop and a child abuser. They'll eat your lunch the minute you get there."

"You got no evidence. Let him go. This has been a long time coming."

Wicks shoved his way through the crowd and into the circle that had opened up around us. The fire in the barrel had started to die down even more as no one paid attention to it. Now someone stoked it with pieces of broken wood pallet. Darkness crept in fighting back the orange from the shortened flames licking at the emptiness contained in the evening. Even in the low light, anyone could see JB had spent his time in the gym working out since his medical retirement from the Sheriff's Department. He'd put on twenty-five pounds of muscle. He'd be hard to take. Not that I cared.

Off to the right, the crowd of deputies surged to reveal an apparition. Ned stood there with a bullet hole under his eye. "Partner, you're gonna need a BFR, a big fuckin' rock, like the kind we used on ol' Willis Simpkins." He shot me that smile of his. Fatigue and grief made strange bedfellows. I rubbed my eyes and he disappeared.

Wicks said, "Let Bruno go."

Coffman said, "No."

Wicks said, "On my responsibility, let him go. You boys back off and give them some room. JB's been needing his ass kicked for a long time now."

JB scoffed at Wicks. "You so sure Bruno can kick my ass?"

"Bruno?" Dad stood just inside the front door with his head sticking out, holding Olivia on the other side so she couldn't see the foolish folly of her pop.

The group of men let me go. I looked at JB and said, "Dad, please go back inside. I know you don't—"

"Bruno!"

I turned to look at Dad. His arm came out the door in a blur. The ball bat flew through air. I caught it. Dad said, "Just do it right, Son. No one hurts a helpless child. No one."

His words stunned me.

JB said, "Go ahead, use the bat—it won't do you any good."

I threw the bat to the side. "I won't need a bat." I suddenly found a place to vent my anger and grief, a violent place of quiet calm.

We moved toward each other, fists raised.

CHAPTER FORTY-EIGHT

THE FIRELIGHT ROSE, brightened as the new fuel found the heat in the drum. When he unbuttoned his red silk shirt and shrugged out of it, JB's shoulder muscles looked more like brown softballs protruding from his slingshot tee shirt. His eye sockets flickered in and out of shadow. The crowd yelled and surged, slopping the cheap beer out of their red plastic cups. The air filled with a cloud of dirt that carried the scent of wet hops, wood smoke, and burnt oil.

I came straight in. Fists up, too hungry for him for me to think strategy and foot position as Dad had taught me. I swung and caught air. JB scoffed, "Hah," and easily sidestepped out of the way. He swung. His answering fist caught me behind the ear. The night's darkness lit up with a thousand specks of light brighter than the sun. I pivoted on my feet as he followed in and caught me on the jaw. The thousand specks flickered just that quickly and went out. For a second everything turned black. Then the world came back on. Energy left my knees, and I wilted to the ground. He came in quick and kicked me in the side. I went over onto hands in the dirt, gasping.

Wicks stepped in and shoved JB away mid-kick when he came at me for another. "Not while he's down. Step back. Get back, you asshole." He shoved JB again, then came over and tried to help me to my feet. With his mouth close to my ear, his breath sweet with Jack

Daniels, he said, "You want me to call it? I'm going to call it. You're in no condition—" I shoved him away and turned to face JB.

JB grinned, the orange firelight dancing on his overly tanned face. "I hoped you weren't going to be this easy. I'm havin' too much fun for it to end so soon."

Like a fool I came in again, instead of letting him come at me and circling like I should've. I let out a yell so filled with grief it came up from the bottoms of my feet and sounded alien even to me. I swung a long sweeping roundhouse. JB giggled like a little girl, stepped inside the swing, and caught me in the ribs with a sledgehammer blow that knocked the wind out of me. I continued on into the crowd of deputies, who propped me up and offered their support—"You can do it. Don't let him on the inside like that. Come on, kick his ass," and other useless suggestions. I'd been up for two days without food or sleep and could hardly see straight, let alone fight someone of JB's size and experience.

Wicks stepped in front of me as I tried to reengage JB. With one hand on my shoulder, he tried to put a roll of quarters in my hand. I let them drop to the ground. His words came out urgent. "Don't be a fool, he's going to mop the dirt with you. Go for his knee. He went out on a medical for his knee. Kick his knee out from under him."

I shoved Wicks and got clear of him. The way I felt, I welcomed the pain. I preferred the physical pain over the gut-wrenching grief of losing my best friend. Ned.

Ned.

I went at JB again just like the first two attempts, only this time I focused on my footing. When he sidestepped like before and chuckled, I stopped short and rabbit-punched him in the throat. Caught him solid. The crowd cheered.

His eyes went large. Both hands flew to his throat as he made a noise of a steam engine going up a steep grade. I circled behind him, came in, and gave him a shot to the kidneys. And then a second one in the same place that sent him to his knees. He'd be pissing blood for a week, and each time he'd see pink in the bowl he'd remember this.

Dizziness suddenly shook my world and took over all else. It tilted the ground this way and that. I staggered to keep my balance. JB fell back, sat on his butt, still gasping and holding his throat. He sat back further on his butt, his legs going straight out in front of him like a disheartened kid on the playground. I continued to stagger backward and sat on the porch steps, my head and eyes and ribs throbbing from the blows I'd taken. Fatigue had me by the throat, had me on the ropes with all the emotions of the day piling on.

I blinked several times to right the world. JB suddenly turned into the little girl trapped under her father's station wagon in the parking lot of the Mayfair Market. She—I mean—JB keened just as the little girl had while she clawed at the tire. I shook my head and the world shifted back into high gear. The keening had really come from Hannah, who, off to the side, cuddled and soothed little Beth. She held her the same way Dad had held the girl from under the station wagon with one arm under her legs as he tried to hand her off to me.

I looked into the crowd one more time searching for Ned, hoping he'd reappear so I could tell him how sorry I was about what happened. He didn't show. Of course he wouldn't. I leaned over and put my cheek on the coolness of the wooden step, closed my eyes, and tried to conjure Ned's smile. I really needed to see that smile.

CHAPTER FORTY-NINE

I woke in a bedroom, one unfamiliar and strange. I didn't really care. My face throbbed along with my ribs. Ned yelling "Go get 'em, partner, you can take 'em. Kick their asses" echoed in my head and made me smile. Ned was really something else.

Then reality set in. The warrant service from hours before on Willowbrook played on the big screen of my mind, the sudden violence, the smell of gun smoke, the way it all ended so abruptly with Ned on the floor, his eyes looking off into the vastness of the big nowhere.

In the dark, I swung my legs over the edge of the bed and sat with my head in my hands. Chelsea. I needed to see Chelsea, to hold her in my arms and never let her go. I needed to call her. I stood on wobbly legs. That's when I realized the room belonged to me. A place where I'd spent my childhood. A place where I'd returned after I'd become a father. I shook myself trying to scare off the last remnants of bone-racking fatigue. I opened the door to more darkness and a flickering light at the end of the hall. Everyone had cleared out. I walked into the living room. Dad sat on the couch watching television with Olivia asleep on his lap. He didn't say anything and just followed me with his eyes. I went to the front door and opened it to emptiness. I turned to look at him. I asked, "What's going on? The yard, it's all cleaned up. The drumfire is out. The drum is gone. What happened?"

"Son, it's eight thirty at night. You slept the whole day through. You really needed it. You were dead on your feet."

I sat down on the couch next to him trying to reconcile this stunning information. That brief interlude of slumber had only felt like a twenty-minute nap, and when I woke I'd found I'd entered the twilight zone.

He gently transferred Olivia to me. *Wait*, I wanted to say, *I need to call Chelsea.*

"Here, take her," he said. "I'll fix you some supper. You have to be hungry." Olivia didn't stir.

The warmth of my daughter, the soft, gentle movement each time she took a breath, her innocent expression, all helped fight off the ugliness of the previous day, kept it at bay. It also served to distract me from Chelsea.

Olivia was growing bigger by the day, by the minute. I wanted to slow her childhood, enjoy her more, but I could never seem to find the time. Time was slipping through my fingers no matter how hard I tried to grasp it.

Dad tinkered in the kitchen. "Folks came by and left a ton of food. The fridge is full. How about some fried chicken and a warmed-up waffle?"

"I'm really not hungry, Dad. Thanks, though."

He stuck his head from around the kitchen. "You're going to eat something if I have to hold you down."

I nodded. He went back to tinkering. He said, "Chelsea came by, stayed most of the day waiting for you to wake up. She brought a couple of pizzas. You want pizza instead?"

"She did? She waited for me to wake up?" Just the thought of her sitting on the same couch, waiting, let a warmth ease through me.

"That's what I just said. You got wax in your ears? Now which one, pizza or—"

"No, chicken's fine." I relaxed some. My mind started to catch up, allowing in the responsibility I'd been shirking. "Did Wicks call? Did they find Gadd?"

Dad stuck his head out of the kitchen again. "He called twice, and I'm sorry, Son, he wanted me to wake you, and I refused. You can go ahead and be mad at me, but you were bad off last night and—"

I waved my free hand. "It's okay. What did he say about Gadd?"

Dad shrugged. "Didn't ask him and he didn't offer." He disappeared again, then came the sound of the oven door opening and closing. "Be ready in twenty minutes."

I eased Olivia down onto the couch, moved her hair out of her face, and kissed her forehead. I went to the phone and paged Chelsea, then dialed Wicks' direct number to his desk. He picked up on the first ring. Not a good sign. If there had been even a whiff of Gadd out on the street, Wicks would've been right there following the trail, looking to make a counter entry on the balance sheet, a little blood and bone.

I said, "Talk to me."

"He's in the wind, Bruno. Bad news. Word is he took off. Headed down to Mexico until things cool off."

Instinct told me Mexico was a woof cookie tossed simply to keep me out of it.

"Where in Mexico?"

He paused a second too long. "We're working on that."

"Bullshit. I'm coming down there." I hung up.

Dad came over and stood close. "I know I can't stop you from doing this, but you're going to eat something first or you're going to have to fight me to get out that door."

I moved around him, angry that after all that had happened, Wicks would lie to me. I opened the refrigerator. Casseroles and fast food packed the shelves. The sight of it all caused my stomach to growl and agree with Dad about eating first. I didn't want to wait twenty minutes for the chicken. I pulled out a pizza box, took it over to the table, and sat down. Pineapple and ham, really? Fruit didn't belong on a pizza. What was Chelsea thinking? I pulled out two slices, knocked off the little yellow wedges of sweet fruit, and started to eat, my mouth wet with anticipation. After two bites I scarfed down the rest, a lot hungrier than I thought.

Dad sat at the table and watched and waited while I finished the two slices. "I know you don't need any more problems."

I stopped chewing on the second slice.

He said, "Ah, maybe we should talk about it later."

I shook my head. "No, I'm good, tell me now."

"Olivia was upset all day; she missed her friend Beth. They're like sisters now, you know."

I let the half-eaten slices of pizza drop back onto the box. I'd forgotten all about Beth. I wiped my hands on a napkin. "I promised Ned I'd take care of Beth."

"I think you did your part last night. Now Hannah knows what kind of man she's been involved with. Before he left last night, your boss said that today he'd be sure a warrant was issued for JB."

I smiled and immediately regretted it, bad Karma. I picked up the pizza again and started to eat. Now I didn't need to worry too much about Beth until after I dealt with Gadd. Later, I'd have a talk with the social worker assigned to the case, make sure CPS kept me advised so I could continue to keep tabs on her. Make sure Beth knew I was a part of her life. Maybe start a college fund for her.

"When do you think the funeral will be?" Dad asked.

With the heavy emotions lurking just below the surface, the overwhelming grief needed the least excuse to return and smother everything else. The room dimmed a bit, nothing more than an illusion caught up in an emotionally overheated mind. The abrupt finality of what had happened dropped yesterday's event deep into the horror category and a recurring nightmare not easily diminished. By sleeping the day away, I'd missed all the daylight needed to help clear away some of the depression. Now it seemed as if the world would remain in a perpetual state of darkness.

I picked up another two slices, knocked off the pineapple, took a large bite, and spoke around the food. "It's a homicide. They . . . they won't release Ned for at least a week, probably even two." I dropped the pizza for the last time and shoved the box away, my appetite gone for good over the thought of some unfeeling doctor taking a high-speed saw to my friend. I fought back tears and had to swallow hard several times.

A knock sounded at the door.

I got up, thankful for the distraction. I opened the door and found Chelsea, her eyes brimming with tears. She stepped in and hugged me, her head buried in my chest. Her shoulders shook as she sobbed. "I'm so sorry, Bruno." I let my chin rest on her hair and took in her scent. I loved her so and at that moment needed her more than anything else.

Except Olivia.

I didn't know what to say and could only hug her back. Finally, she looked up and her voice came out husky as she asked, "What are you going to do on your two weeks off? I hope you want some company. I already got it cleared with my boss. I was thinking we could go to the Grand Cayman Islands, huh? What do you say, some fun in the sun in the Caribbean? We don't ever have to come back. Just you and me, white sand beaches and piña coladas forever."

"I'm not taking two weeks off."

She grabbed ahold of my wrists and took a step back. "What?" She stepped out of my hug. Her next words came out with an edge. "Bruno, you are not going after Gadd."

I didn't answer.

"Bruno?"

I said nothing.

She stepped around me and spoke to Dad. "Xander, you're not going to let him go after Gadd, are you?"

"I don't think there's anyone in this world who could stop him. We're talking about Ned here, Chelsea."

"No, Bruno. Nothing good will come of it. You'll just get yourself in trouble. Think about Olivia. Come on, Bruno, this isn't the smart move."

I shook my head. "How many kids do you think Gadd has corrupted? How many good people has he killed?" I stopped short of saying that the FBI could've shown some balls and taken Gadd off the board a long time ago had they not wanted to keep their pristine reputation untarnished. And then none of this would have happened. "Do you think I want to bring my daughter up in a world with a killer like Gadd walking around? Even on the dodge, he'll be hurting people, because that's what he does."

"Don't." She pointed a finger at me. "You're a good street cop, I'll give you that, but don't think for a minute we won't get him without your help. Right now, every cop and federal agent in the state is looking for him. He'll fall in a matter of hours, you just wait and see."

"Like you did with the Bogart Bandit and Handsome Bandit? Took your agency two years."

"That's not fair."

"I'm not going to wait for anything or anyone. In fact, I've waited too long."

"Fine, then I'm going with you." She stepped around me. "I've got to use your phone to tell the task force you and I are coming up on this."

"Chels, I don't think that's a good idea."

She stopped. "What, using your phone? Why?" Her confused expression shifted, and she came back and put a finger in my face. "No. No, you are not going without me."

I said nothing.

She thought about it some more and finally caught on to my meaning. "Don't do this, Bruno, don't take this curbside."

If there had ever been a case for curbside justice, this was it. Ned wouldn't get fair representation in our judicial system, and that left it to me. I wasn't sure I could do it. I'd never done it before, but I intended to try.

I lowered my voice. "Four years ago, Gadd killed an entire family. Put a mother and her two sons down on their knees and shot them in the back of the head."

Dad, still sitting at the kitchen table, said, "Oh, dear Lord, you're talking about the Humphreys, aren't you, down in Compton?"

CHAPTER FIFTY

I WASN'T SURPRISED Dad knew about the triple murder of the Humphrey family, especially after he'd been the one to break the Bogart Bandit case. Ned had been right when he said it took a mailman to know what was happening on the street.

"What do you know about it, Dad?"

He shrugged. "What everyone knows, I guess."

Chelsea stepped closer to Dad. "What are you two talking about?"

Dad shrugged. "A while back, a woman—a mother and her two sons—were shot to death not far from here down in Compton." He turned to me. "I heard the woman had a tryst with a man and she ended up pregnant. She threatened to take him to court for child support, and he snuck over late one night. He wanted to keep her quiet. She'd never told anyone the man's name. They never caught him."

"And he killed the woman and her two boys to keep from paying child support?" Chelsea asked, stunned.

Dad shrugged. "That's what I heard."

I didn't bring up the part about the woman being Scab's sister, another great reason why Gadd told the woman never to tell anyone his name.

Chelsea rounded on me. "And just how do you know it's Leroy Gadd who did this?"

"I was there that night with Ned. We chased Willis Simpkins on foot. We got separated. While I was looking for Ned and Simpkins, I came across Gadd in the alley leaving the back of the house where the three victims were later found. I didn't know they were dead inside, not at the time." I turned to Dad. "Or that the woman had been pregnant. Compton PD never told me that part. They gave me the report on the Darkman case but withheld the autopsy. I didn't know Gadd's name at the time and just recently figured it out."

"And how did you do that?" Chelsea asked.

"It's in the surveillance notes. While we followed Gadd on the bank robbery, I sat next to him in a bar. If it's true that she was pregnant, that makes it a quadruple murder that he'll never answer for." I looked at Chelsea. "And we'll never make him on killing Ned either, even though he's responsible, the same as if he pulled the trigger. He wound up those kids like little toy soldiers and sent them out to do the dirty."

She pointed a finger at me. "I'm still going with you, and when we take him, he gets a chance to surrender. You understand, Bruno? That's the way it's going to be."

I stared her down and said nothing.

"Bruno?"

The phone rang and saved me from having to tell her the truth about my blood-filled intent that no one could talk me out of—not even Chelsea.

I took the receiver off the wall. "Hello?"

I hoped it was Wicks so he could tell me they'd just come up on Gadd with a possible location and for me to saddle up. Instead, I got Ollie Bell.

"Asshole."

I recognized her with that one word. "Ollie, I'm sorry about what happened." But not as much as I should've been; her nephew D'Arcy had been the one to pull the trigger on Ned.

Her voice came over the phone lower, almost a whisper. "Mister, you doon sound all dat sorry. Meet me right now. Meet at Lucy's in ten minutes. Come alone." She hung up.

I put the receiver on the hook. She wanted to meet so she could shove the ice pick between my ribs and scramble my heart. I couldn't help thinking maybe I deserved it.

Chelsea asked, "Who's Ollie?"

"An informant. She wants to talk."

"Does she know where to find Gadd?"

"No. It's about something else."

"Then she can wait."

"No."

"Then I'm going with you."

"Fine, but we're taking two cars. She said come alone."

"Fine, I'll run cover then. Where we going?"

"Lucy's. It's a—"

"I know Lucy's. Bruno, don't you dare try and lose me."

"Wouldn't think of it."

"Be careful, Son."

"I will, Dad." I hugged him. "I'll be home soon."

*   *   *

I made one pass on Long Beach Boulevard and clocked Ollie's turquoise Cadillac Eldorado parked at the curb right in front of Lucy's. The sodium vapor streetlights changed all the colors and gave them a yellowish tint. The usual foot traffic patrolled the streets, the disenfranchised, the coke freaks and hookers, all the good folks now all in for the night behind locked doors. I turned around and came back and parked behind the Caddy. Chelsea pulled over on Century and Barlow where she'd be able to see most of the restaurant, the important part, the windows of the patio area. Chelsea turned off her headlights. I got out and looked down the street at her maroon Crown Victoria. Her window came down, and she let her arm hang out, a signal that she had my back.

Ollie Bell sat inside the enclosed patio on one of the picnic table benches that swayed a little under the weight. She didn't smile. I never knew Ollie when she didn't smile, and that night she looked like someone else entirely, someone I didn't know. Anger didn't suit her.

She wore a shiny purple mumu-like dress—more of a gown really, with gold fringe and a beautiful and intricate multicolored dragon embroidered on the back. It wasn't in her to roll incognito. She took up half the picnic bench. I came over and sat next to her in easy range of the pick if she wanted to use it.

We sat there, not moving.

She spoke first. "I trusted you."

"And Ned was my best friend."

Her whole body started to quiver as she silently cried. "My sister, she won't even talk to me. I tolt her I'd take care of dis. She believed me. I believed in you."

"I'm sorry."

"Sorry doesn't get it, cowboy, not for somthin' like dis. I took that young'un to Dinneeland twice when he was no more 'n a tot. Bought him dat cute little hat with the ears and some blue cotton candy. The way he smiled dat day, damn. Now he gone. In prison for life."

"I know."

"Do you?"

"Yes, I do. I promise you I do. And I wish every conscious second I could go back to the time just before we took down that door. I'd change things. I swear I would."

She shook her big head. "No. No, sir. You're just like all the rest of dem asshole cops. I tought you were different. You're not."

I reached over and put my hand on her arm. She didn't flinch. The anger in her eyes liked to burn right through me. I didn't look away. Slowly, she leaned over as her eyes softened. She put her head on my shoulder. I put my arm around her. She put her big arm around me and pulled me in tight. We sat that way until a Hispanic girl dressed in Lucy's garb came out to the patio with an orange plastic tray holding three orders of taquitos along with two paper trays piled high with guacamole and a supersized cup of Coca Cola.

She let go of me and went at the taquitos as if she hadn't eaten in days. She spoke around the food. "You hungry? Go ahead and order yourself some. Dis is all mine, though." She smiled, her face still wet with tears. Comfort food obviously took the edge off her grief.

"No, that's okay."

She stopped. "What? I'm not good enough to eat wit'?"

"You know that's not true. I just had some pizza with pineapple."

She wrinkled her nose. "Pineapple doon belong on no pizza. Meat and cheese, dat's all."

"Ollie, you know where Gadd is layin' his head?"

She took another taquito, scooped up a large gob of guac, and put it in her mouth, then nodded in the affirmative.

My heart raced. Of course she knew. This was Ollie. "You know where I can find Gadd? Really?" I wanted him more than I'd ever wanted anything in my life. I fought to stay calm.

She chewed and shook her head this time. She swallowed. "No, I know where *I* kin find his sorry ass, and after I get done with this little snack I'm goin' after him. I'm gonna pop a cap in his ass, you just wait and see if I don't. Then you kin come take me ta jail, I don't care. I'm gonna do it."

"Ollie—"

She froze. Her eyes turned fierce. I held up my hands in surrender. She didn't trust me anymore, and maybe it was something she thought she just had to do. That's the way it was for me, and I liked her a little less for her not giving me the information on the man responsible for Ned. I'd just have to follow her.

My pager went off. I checked it: Dad's number along with a "911." With all that had happened recently, I needed to call Dad right away. "I'm sorry, I have to go. Can we talk about this before you do something you're going to regret? Please, Ollie?"

She waved her big arm. "Get on wit' ya. No way are you gonna talk me outta dis. Go on now. I'll call after it's done so you kin come pick up the body."

I stood. She stopped and watched me. I shot my hand out, grabbed a taquito, and dodged her as she swung at me chuckling. "You really somethin' else, Bruno Johnson."

I didn't want the taquito but couldn't toss it to the ground to waste it either. I shoved the whole thing in my mouth as I ran to a pay phone a short way down Long Beach Boulevard. I dialed while I watched Chelsea's car. Her window came down, but she leaned back in the darkness so I couldn't see her.

Dad picked up on the first ring.

"Dad, it's me."

"It's awful, Son. It's just awful."

"What? What's going on?"

"Here, talk to her."

"Who?"

CHAPTER FIFTY-ONE

HANNAH CAME ON the phone, breathless, sobbing. "Bruno! He's got her. He's got my baby. You have to do something. Please you have to help me."

"Who's got Beth?"

But I knew.

"JB."

"Call the police."

"I did. They won't do a thing. He's got a court order. His family has a judge in their pocket. They have too much money."

She'd wanted the bigger life JB's money had to offer, and now it was working against her.

Dad came on the phone. "This isn't right, Son. That man, he's done harm to that little girl. How can the court give that child back to him? It's not right."

"Dad, put Hannah back on."

He handed the phone back to Hannah. I said, "I thought JB went to jail for what he did to Beth."

"That's right, but he bailed out. I'm scared, Bruno. JB's angry, angrier than I've ever seen him. He's going to take it out on Beth, hurt her for what I've done. And the police won't do a thing about it until it's already happened. Please, please you have to help."

"He's got the law on his side."

Dad must've had his ear next to Hannah's. His faraway voice came over the phone. "Son, if you won't do something about it, I'm gonna take my ball bat and teach that man how the cow eats the cabbage."

I closed my eyes tight. To take any kind of action in this instance would go against what the law prescribed. But I promised Ned I'd take care of Beth. My body went totally calm, the answer obvious, the decision made. I stood up straight. "Hannah, where is he right now?"

"He's at their family's house in Downey. Do you know it? It's the one where he threw his retirement party."

I hadn't attended but I knew it. "Yes. Listen, I promise you I will take care of this. Put my dad back on."

"Yes, Son."

"I'm on my way to take care of this, you understand? I don't want you getting involved."

"What are you going to do? You don't want to ruin your career. This guy's got the law on his side, Bruno. If you do anything, he can have your job."

"It's okay, I'm just going to talk to him, use a little reason and logic."

"That won't work with this guy. You saw what he was like last night. Let me take a bat to him. It won't matter if they put me in jail. I can't lose my job over it, and that way it won't ruin your career."

"Dad, I said I'd take care of it. Promise me you won't leave the house."

Silence.

"Dad?"

"Yeah, I promise, I won't leave the house."

"I'm on my way to handle this. Tell Hannah she'll have Beth back within the hour. You got that? Stay right there."

"Fine, I won't move."

"Thanks, Dad. See you soon."

I hung up, dropped another quarter, and dialed Wicks' desk. He picked up. "Talk to me."

"It's me. I need a surveillance team right now."

His tone changed to urgent. "Bruno, whatta you got? I'll run the op myself. Just tell me what you need."

"You know Lucy's on Long Beach."

"Yes, of course I do."

"Ollie Bell is there right now, and as soon as she finishes eating, she's going to drive to where Gadd is staying. She's driving an old turquoise Caddy; it's parked out front at the curb."

He pulled the phone away from his mouth and yelled, "Gibbs, you and three others, in your cars in the parking lot, now."

Back on the phone, he said, "Bruno, why are you telling me this? How come you're not handling it yourself with some gun smoke therapy?"

"Something else more important has come up."

He paused. "Don't do it, Bruno. There's only one thing that would pull you off this asshole Gadd, and JB's not worth it. Let the law handle it. The law works slow in a case like this, but it does work."

This coming from a man who gunned bad guys for a living—took out animals who preyed on victims who couldn't defend themselves. Took them off the board without due process.

"I'm telling you as a friend, let this go."

"JB bailed out and got Beth back with a court order."

Another pause. "I'm sorry, I didn't know." He lowered his voice to a whisper. "Just make sure there aren't any witnesses. If they don't have pictures, they don't have shit."

"I'm only going to talk to him. Use logic and—"

"Bruno, it's me you're talking to."

I said nothing.

"Go with God, my friend. I'll take care of Gadd for you. We're twenty minutes out. *We will* be there though—you don't worry about that." He hung up.

I ran across the street and got in the passenger side of Chelsea's car.

"What's going on? Who did you call?"

"Dad. JB took Beth. I have to go get her. I need to ask a big favor."

Her eyes narrowed. "Bruno, I'm sorry about Beth, I am. But right now, honestly, I think you're about to play me and I don't like it."

"No, this is the truth. That second call was to Wicks; he's coming with a full team. He'll be here in twenty minutes. See that Caddy? In a few minutes my informant is going to leave here and go to where Gadd is hiding out."

"So you want me to stay with the car until they get here while you go take care of Beth?"

"That's right."

She looked into my eyes, then reached and gripped my hand. "All right."

I leaned over and kissed her. She put a hand at the back of my head and pulled me into the kiss. The world started to fall away before I realized it. I wanted to stay there. Instead I broke away, huffing, and looked her in the eyes. "Two weeks? The Grand Caymans, huh?"

"Yes."

"Can we talk about it later?"

"Damn straight we can. Now get out of here and take care of Ned's kid."

I squeezed her hand. "Thanks."

I got out of Chelsea's car, ran back across the street, and got into my truck.

CHAPTER FIFTY-TWO

I caught Imperial, a direct route from Lucy's into Downey. As I drove, I thought of what I'd say to a man like JB. He wasn't into logical debate, nor one to be deterred from his self-righteous goal, or the way Dad would put it, "Don't try and take a bone from the mouth of a vicious dog. You'll get bit for sure."

This time, though, that bone happened to be an innocent and vulnerable little girl who didn't know any better and by nature would only try to please no matter what the abuse. The story Ned told of the little five-year-old boy who put Band-Aids on his dead father returned and added fuel to my anger. Then the question, how to handle the vicious dog, and in JB's case, a vicious and rabid dog? Only one way came to mind. I was about to get bit.

I stopped for a red signal at Atlantic Avenue and waited, the anxiety rising with each second. What would I do? What could I do?

On the sidewalk up ahead, just this side of Duncan Avenue, there lay a crumpled and abandoned kid's Stingray bike, run over by a car. The signal changed; I hesitated. There really wasn't time. To hell with it. I pulled to the curb by the bike, and got out. The chain hung loose with one link broken. I untangled it and wrapped the cold steel around my fist. Rabid dogs responded well to chains. The irony that the weapon came from a child's bike wasn't lost on me.

I got in and took off. I wanted to get it over with. I just hoped JB hadn't hurt Beth any more than he already had.

I drove faster.

A couple minutes later I made a left onto Garfield, and all of a sudden slowed and pulled to the side. My mind had started to wander after making the decision to physically take on JB, to make him believe that Beth going with me would be the wisest choice he'd ever make.

Dad's words from the phone conversation finally had time to settle in and process. He'd given in far too easily for someone so stubborn. Until that moment I hadn't heard it in his words. Had I really been listening, his tone would've given him away. He'd promised to stay home, said it several times. And I'd missed it.

I whipped the truck around, the tires screeching. I slammed the gearshift into first and burned rubber. No way would I get there in time.

Dad would've had Hannah call JB and coax him to come over, coached her to tell him she wanted to make up and to come pick her up. Tell him how much she loved him. Oh, and be sure to bring Beth because she missed her so.

I punched the steering wheel and pushed the truck faster, blowing through red signals once the other cars cleared the intersections.

Dad had protected Noble and me from gang members while we grew up. I always thought of Dad as the strongest, most capable man in the entire world. Until I became a cop and saw the kind of violence that broke men like him with the flick of a finger. Three pounds of pressure on a trigger was all it took.

I turned down Nord. JB's Silver BMW was parked the wrong way at the curb in front of our house. I skidded up and stopped, laying down a white cloud of burnt rubber.

The only illumination for the front yard came from the naked bulb over the front door. JB, the ball bat in his hand, pulled back to hit Dad again and stopped. Dad lay on the ground at JB's feet. Dad had his arm up to fend off the spun aluminum that had rained down pain and damaged flesh and bone. Dad wore his blue-gray postal pants and a slingshot tee shirt, spotted with his blood from injuries to his head and face.

JB looked up and smiled. I turned cold inside. I grabbed the bike chain off the seat and wrapped it around my hand as I got out. JB stepped away from Dad and brought the bat back over his shoulder, ready for the home run ball to be pitched. I roared and charged. I came straight in. He swung. I stutter-stepped, leaned all the way back, and barely kept my balance. The bat whisked by, inches from my face. I recovered just as he brought the bat to his shoulder for another try.

I stepped in close so he couldn't use it. With the chain wrapped around my fist, I hit him square in the face. He dropped with a grunt and floundered on the ground, his legs kicking in spasms. I jumped on top of him and hit him again.

And again.

I didn't know how many times I'd hit him when someone put a hand on my shoulder. "Bruno, don't. No more, he's had enough. You're going to kill him."

I came out of my blind rage and looked over my shoulder. Dad stood on shaky knees, his face a bumpy mess like a swarm of giant bumblebees had attacked him. He put his hand back on his obviously broken arm and gently propped it up. His expression, what there was of it, looked peaceful and calm. How could that be after what had just happened?

Sirens. Lots of them.

"Bruno?" Dad said.

"Are you okay?" I asked.

"Of course I am. I've been hurt worse from old man Levine's Rottweiler over on Western Avenue." His bloated lips made his words come out a bit slurred.

"You're a rotten liar, Dad. Come over here and sit down."

Hannah appeared, took my wrist, and unwound the bike chain from my hand. She took two steps back and tossed it up onto the roof. It clattered and slid but stopped before it came down. She'd been married to Ned long enough to know the rules of the game.

Two black-and-white patrol cars slid to the curb. Four uniform deputies from Lynwood station jumped out. I didn't know them personally but recognized one from the wake the night before.

I held up my badge. "This man attacked my father."

One of the deputies jumped on JB, flipped him over, and started to cuff him. His partner said, "No problem, he won't be bothering you anymore, Detective Johnson."

"Thank you. You might want to wait and have med aide take a look at him first."

"He can wait. We'll take him straight to LCMC downtown."

"That's a long way. St. Francis or MLK are closer."

"Naw, it'll give him time to think about what he's done and give us a chance to talk to him. Make sure he understands."

"Understands?"

"Yeah, that as long as you and your father live in our area, he better not drive within ten miles of this reporting district."

"Thank you. Really, thanks. Can you call med aide for my father?"

"It's on the way. The new guy here is going to take the paper on this." The deputy helped his partner drag the moaning JB to the patrol car and shove him in the back seat. They got in and took off.

Just like that, it was over.

The fresh-faced rookie stepped up with his notebook open. His training officer said, "Put that away. I already know what happened here. I'll write it up. We got this, Bruno." He turned to his trainee. "Call for an 1185 for that BMW, tow it, and list it as 'driver arrested.'"

"Thanks again." I didn't know how to fully describe my gratitude.

They turned and walked to the street just as the fire department and ambulance pulled up.

I looked around. "Where's Beth?"

Hannah said, "In the house with Olivia. They didn't see any of this. I made sure of it. I'm real sorry you got hurt, Xander. I never meant—"

"Stop it," he said. "I told you I'm not hurt."

He looked like he'd been run over by a truck and spit out the back. It made me want to climb in the back of that patrol car and take that bike chain to JB all over again.

The paramedics came in close, set their gear down next to Dad, and went to work. One of them came over and took my wrist; that's when I realized blood was dripping down to the tips of my fingers and to the ground. I'd cut the web of my hand with the bike chain wrapped around it.

I stood there as he cleaned and bandaged my hand. I watched Dad try not to flinch in pain when they splinted his broken arm and placed it into a sling.

In my rage I had not realized, not stopped long enough to think, that to take JB on at his home would have put me in the jackpot. Not to mention that his house was in another jurisdiction, that cops who didn't know the score would have been handling it. I'd have been in jail for sure pending an assault with a deadly weapon charge, or worse. Dad knew that and knew if he took on JB in front of our home, even if Dad lost the fight, JB would lose more. I said to Dad, "I still have a lot to learn from you, old man."

He smiled. "I'm not old. Not yet. And I was about to take him if you hadn't shown up and interfered."

CHAPTER FIFTY-THREE

I STAYED WITH Dad in the ER, drove him home, got him comfortable on the couch with the TV controller, and checked on Hannah. She had a handle on our two little girls, who both seemed unaffected by everything that had happened and were already asleep. Hannah and Beth would stay with us for a few days to help out with Dad. Hannah would take my bed and I'd take the couch. The same place where Ned had slept.

Three hours had passed, making it two o'clock in the morning. Oddly, my pager remained silent. Not a good sign. They should've had Gadd all grappled up by now, or the way Coffman would've put it, "On a slab." But if the takedown had gone to guns, they would still be busy with the interviews with the shooting team. Telling me about it would drop way down their priority list. I was worried that I had not heard from Chelsea. She could take care of herself—I'd seen her in action. But Gadd wasn't your normal violent criminal. I'd never come across a sociopath so devoid of empathy that he'd wind up young boys like tin soldiers and send them into harm's way. I pushed out the image of Chelsea lying in the gutter somewhere, hurt and alone.

And the fact that I'd been the one to put her on Gadd.

I decided to drive to the violent crimes office. Pulling into the defunct grocery store, I saw the parking lot filled with far too many cars. Something was not right.

When I walked in, I saw thirty or forty cops milling around, waiting for something to break. Drinking coffee, eating cold tacos and stale donuts. All looked haggard and tired from too many hours in the saddle without a break. Gibbs hurried over, took me by the arm, and tried to hurry me out of the office. "I don't think it's a good idea for you to be here right now. Wicks is on a tirade. Come on. Come back in the morning after he cools off."

Too late.

Wicks saw me through the windows of his office. He jumped up from his desk. I shrugged out of Gibbs' grasp. The door to Wicks' office slammed open. "Johnson, get your black ass in here."

Gibbs whispered, "Don't say I didn't try to warn you." He quickly moved away as if I were nuclear waste.

I entered Wicks' office. He slammed the door and moved around to the other side of his desk. I had no idea what had made him so angry.

I pulled a chair around to sit.

"No one said take a seat." He remained standing and stared me down.

I asked, "What happened with Ollie? Did she take you to Gadd?" A rhetorical question to get him talking.

He said nothing and fumed, his lips a straight line, his eyes narrowed. I didn't like displeasing him. I respected him too much.

"The Caddy wasn't there," he said.

"What about Chelsea?" I was more worried about Chelsea.

"You mean Agent Miller? Never saw her, never heard from her."

"What? Are you sure?" Something had to have happened to her. She should've called. I double-checked my pager. She hadn't tried to get ahold of me. I went to his phone on his desk and paged her.

"Oh, feel free to use my phone, Deputy."

I punched in Wicks' desk number for her to return the call and hung up. I watched the phone, waiting for it to ring.

"We jumped out for nothing," he said. "I mobilized an entire team for nothing."

I looked from the phone to him. "That can't be what's got your back up. You know how those things go. What's going on?"

"Coffman put in his papers. No two weeks' notice. No nothing. Gone, just like that." He snapped his fingers. "Took vacation time with all this shit going on. He's never taken a vacation in all the time I've known him. This isn't like him. I wanna know what you said to him."

It felt like someone let all the air out of me. I sat down. I'd thought I wanted Coffman gone, but now that he was, a vast emptiness opened inside me. The man had been an icon, a mentor at Lynwood station when I was learning how to be a deputy.

"Mister, no one gave you permission to sit."

I didn't get up. "You talked to Coffman, then?"

"Of course I talked to Coffman. I told you we're a team here. He didn't want to tell me what happened, but I pumped a pint of Chivas Regal into him, and he spilled it, told me you twisted his arm. I want to know what you said to him."

I shook off the sad emptiness as my ire started to rise. I stood. "It was time for that old man to retire."

Wicks slapped his desk. "That's not for you to decide, buddy boy. We're a team here and I'm the one who runs this team, not you. Now I've lost a good man, one I'll never be able to replace, not one with his experience. Not one I could trust like I could trust him. You don't find that kind of loyalty every day. I thought I had that kind of loyalty with you and look what that got me. You've violated that trust."

"Did he tell you what happened?"

"He did, and I can't say I wouldn't have done the same thing. There weren't any witnesses in that house. I probably would've done more than butt-stroke that prick. He shot and killed Ned, Bruno. And don't give me any shit about D'Arcy being handcuffed."

I said nothing and stared at him.

He said, "What? What? Tell me."

I continued to stare.

His expression softened. "Ah, shit. Am I missing something here? I'm missing something, aren't I?"

"That's not for me to say. But maybe you should have another talk with him before you jump down my throat."

"Tell me."

"No, it's not my place. He needed to go." I went for the door, opened it.

He said, "You're going to tell me, maybe not today or even to-morrow, but you're going to tell me."

"Don't think so." I left, walked over to my desk, and sat down with all the detectives in the room staring at me. I picked up the phone and again paged Chelsea.

Come on, Chels, call me back. Go to a phone and call me back.

I watched the second hand of the clock on the wall sweep around three times. The phone didn't ring. I paged Ollie and waited some more. I stood and made eye contact with Gibbs. "Where are the op notes on Gadd?"

He brought over a thick four-inch binder and set it on my desk. "Good luck with it. We've checked every possible lead, had forty, fifty eyes on it. As of right now, we got nothing. We're waiting for something to break, anything at all." He sat in the desk chair facing me. Ned's desk. I stared at him until he squirmed a little and finally got up and moved.

I sat down and opened the binder.

An hour later Ollie and Chelsea still had not called. Why hadn't Chelsea called? I couldn't think of any reason why she'd not answered the page other than the obvious. That she was hurt and couldn't.

I'd scanned the entire binder, twice. Gibbs had been right; they'd checked every possible lead and then some inconsequential, long, long shots as swell. I closed it, sat back, closed my eyes, tried to relax, tried to think about all that had happened since we first came up on Gadd. And just like that the answer bubbled to the surface.

My eyes shot open.

I grabbed the binder and flipped it to the table of contents. It couldn't be that easy. It just couldn't. I ran my finger down to the list of addresses already checked by the detectives and checked it again. I looked up and found Gibbs and half the detectives looking at me. Wicks had caught on to something happening and came out of his office. "What? Whatta you have, Bruno?"

I moved around my desk over to the "out" tray on Ned's desk and quickly thumbed through all his reports, those recently typed and waiting for Ned to approve and pass along for approval and filing. But that was never going to happen, not by him. I found what I was looking for—typed notes on the bank robbery surveillance, the ones with children on the crews. I moved my finger down until I found the two addresses I wanted.

I ran for the door.

Wicks followed. "Son of a bitch, Bruno, wait up. Gibbs, grab your shit, gear up. Gear up, you guys, let's roll."

CHAPTER FIFTY-FOUR

IN A CHAOTIC situation, like the death of a beloved detective, the small things tend to fall through the cracks. And in some cases, the big things. Coffman putting in his papers and leaving the team contributed to the error. Compounded by the fact that Ned had been the case agent on the bank robbery investigation involving Gadd. Some of the fault also fell to me. I couldn't see through the grief to jump right into the chase or I'd have spotted the error sooner. At least I hoped I would've.

I drove my truck as fast as I could. The headlights from a string of undercover cop cars followed along, oblivious to traffic infractions and even misdemeanors trying to keep up. Wicks stayed on my ass close enough that I could see his face strobe in his windshield when the streetlights passed. He came up on the radio. "Bruno, where we going?"

I couldn't answer, too busy shifting and clutching and steering and dodging the scant civilians out late who drove into my path. We made it to Lilac in Cerritos in record time. The apartment where Gadd picked up his girlfriend, the one he took to the card club in Gardenia. The girlfriend who Gadd shoved out of the car and left in the street when Ned pulled over and picked her up. All that information was in his surveillance notes in his "out" tray no one thought to check. Reading the notes, I remembered the name of Gadd's girl-friend: Emma Wells.

I shut off my headlights when I turned down the street. Too many cars from the folks who lived in the cul-de-sac left nowhere to park. I skidded to a stop in the middle of the street right next to Ollie's Caddy. I got out and headed for the apartment, scared to death at what I'd find.

"Bruno?" Wicks grabbed a hold of my arm and said in a harsh whisper, "What is this? What are we doing here?"

Gibbs ran up carrying a shotgun along with ten other detectives, all of them anxious to get in the action to take down a cop killer.

I said, "It's Gadd's girlfriend's place. We followed him here on the bank robbery surveillance. That's the Caddy I briefed you on earlier."

Wicks didn't complain about the error that they'd missed; he just pointed. "You five take the back. Watch your crossfire. The rest come to the front and just flow in behind me and Bruno." He took out his Colt .45. "Let's go."

Gibbs said, "I'm not sitting this one out on the perimeter. I'm going in with you two."

Wicks looked at him for a second. "Okay. On entries Bruno always goes right, and I go left, you bat cleanup with that gauge and go right. Watch where you point that thing."

Gibbs nodded, his expression solemn.

"The rest of you hold at the front door until we need you."

We ran to the apartment. The designated five detectives split off to cover the back.

The apartments looked more like single-story upscale town houses with common walls. The entrance to each had a long concrete walk to a front door, shielded by shrubs and low pony walls stuccoed to match the apartments. The configuration, the funnel effect, made the approach dangerous. Someone with an automatic weapon could kill us all.

I drew my service revolver, moving down the walkway. Wicks whispered, "Remember, if he's good for one, give him all six. Give him all six for Ned, Bruno. And if you can't, then step out of my way and put your fingers in your ears."

I just hoped Gadd had a gun in his hand, or at least something small and dark and unrecognizable. I could do it if it came down to it—if he had something in his hand. I knew I could. I came to the door, one reinforced with a wrought-iron screen.

"Shit," Wicks said in a harsh whisper. "Someone go back and get a Halligan tool."

I tried the door. "Open. It's open." I swung it out and entered.

I stopped dead. .

Wicks bumped into me.

In the living room, not moving on the floor, Ollie lay splayed out facedown. The handle of an ice pick protruded from the center of her back. Blood spread outward from the pick, changing the purple splendor of her silken gown to dark black.

Wicks shoved me out of the way and yelled, "Go. Go. Don't stand there, Bruno, move. Move your ass. Move. Move."

I snapped out of it and did my job. I moved through the luxurious apartment, checking the rooms.

I found Emma Wells in the master bedroom. She sat naked on the king-sized bed, her back against the headboard, her eyelids tented. Her face was bloated with blue, the rest of her body smooth and colored in the purest alabaster. Except the scabs on her knees and hands from when Gadd shoved her out of his car. The red tip of her tongue protruded from the corner of her mouth almost like a small animal checking to see if it was all right to come out.

She'd been throttled. Blue finger marks encircled her neck.

In the master bathroom, the floor was littered with old bandages covered in both dried and wet blood. An open box of Kotex sat on the sink alongside an open roll of medical tape. Gadd had been hit during the entry to the Willowbrook house. The shadow I'd thought I'd seen had been Gadd, after all. Ned hadn't missed. Good for Ned. Good for goddamn Ned.

But that begged a question: Who, then, shot Ned—Gadd or D'Arcy? Didn't matter. Not anymore. Not to me.

I came back into the living room and reholstered.

Wicks said, "Gibbs, notify Downey PD and then our homicide. This is theirs. The rest of you guys, get out—this is a crime scene." He turned to me. "We just missed him, Bruno. Tell me how we got here?"

Gibbs answered. "We followed Gadd here on the surveillance and—" He cut himself off as he realized he'd screwed up by not remembering it earlier, getting there sooner and maybe saving some lives. Wicks lit into him.

Wicks' words bounced off with little effect as I knelt beside Ollie. She'd been a great friend. A few years back we'd gone into a dope house on a ruse to take it down. We entered a "birdcage," one of the most deadly situations you could encounter while working narcotics. She'd kept her cool or we'd have been killed. Since then she'd fed me top-drawer information on violent criminals in the ghetto. We were a good team and did good work together.

The ice pick handle looked incongruent and grotesque. Gadd had planted it right in the center of the brightly colored embroidered dragon. He'd slain the dragon. I intended to do the same to him. No question now, he'd never make it to trial.

I stood with a strength I'd never felt before.

Wicks came in close. "I've seen that look," he said. "What are you going to do? Where you going?"

I didn't answer, just turned and walked from the apartment. I knew where to find Gadd and didn't want to take anyone with me. No witnesses. No prisoners.

Wicks followed me out. "Bruno, I'm going with you."

I stopped and looked at him.

He caught the gist. He patted my shoulder. "Okay, partner, I guess I owe you this one. My student's finally ready to go out on his own. Watch your back, my friend. And call me as soon as the smoke clears, you understand? I'm your first call."

CHAPTER FIFTY-FIVE

I CAME OUT into the yard and yelled for the loitering deputies to move their cars. I got in my truck without saying anything else and headed for Avalon and 213th in the city of Carson. I watched my rearview mirror as I hit Imperial Highway to see if anyone followed. The chances of Gadd being at the 213th Street address were pretty good. With all the heat the cops put on him, he needed a place where no one knew him, a place he could lay his head without the risk of someone he knew ratting him out. If I hurried, I might even save the woman he'd met and picked up at the Harbor Town Pub, the place where I sat at the bar and had a beer with him.

The place where I first recognized him as the Darkman. I should've clocked him over the head then and there, dragged him out into the sunlight, put the boot to him. If I had, Ned would still be alive.

In the late hour, not many cars remained on the street. I drove fast. In the rearview, a set of headlights popped up behind me and quickly closed. Shit. I pushed down on the pedal. Moments later I came to a red signal and had to slow, intending to run it once the intersection cleared. I braked harder as a new red Ford van came southbound to my right. Instead of slowing when the driver saw me traversing the intersection against the red, he sped up. I stood on the brake.

Too late.

The red van came on too fast. At the last second, it veered into the front of my truck. I braced, gripping the steering wheel. The impact slammed me into the door, where I banged my head too hard. Everything slowed.

Four men dressed all in black with balaclavas jumped out of the van's sliding door, MP5 machine guns up and pointed at me.

What the hell?

They opened the driver's door, dragged me out, and shoved me facedown onto the asphalt. One put his knee in my back and zip-tied my hands. I shook off the crash and found my voice. "I'm an LA County Sheriff's deputy. What's going on? What are you doing?" I didn't know what else to say. One of the men pulled a black sack over my head. They picked me up and carried me to the van, tossed me on the cargo floor, and slid the door shut. We rode in silence for ten minutes. The men's agitated state, their hard breathing, started to slow as they calmed.

I tried to visualize each turn the van made, tried to visualize the streets and quickly lost track, hopelessly lost.

After ten minutes they bumped into a driveway, drove a little farther, then stopped. The side door slid open. Hands pulled me out. They wouldn't let me get to my feet and dragged me along to keep me off balance. We entered a room. A door closed behind us. They sat me in a chair. I stayed like that for several minutes. The door finally opened and closed again. Even through the black hood, the strong scent of Old Spice assaulted my sense of smell. I relaxed and said, "Special Agent in Charge Joshua Whitney, can we please dispense with these theatrics?"

Someone pulled the hood off. I blinked and blinked while my eyes adjusted. Two men stood in the room. One was Joshua Whitney, with his thinning hair and eczema in the shape of Cuba that snaked across his scalp in red with white flakes. The other one, Jim Turner, stood to the side, his arms crossed. I didn't know which one I despised more.

They both wore nice suits, not the normal attire for a kidnapping. Turner took two steps closer, leaned over, and got in my face. "Where is Agent Miller, Deputy Johnson?"

"Agent Mil . . . Chelsea? You mean Chelsea? I don't know. I'm worried about her, too. She's your agent. Why are you asking me about her?"

"Answer the question."

"I don't know. I've paged several times, and she's never called me back. I—"

Jim Turner slugged me in the stomach. All the air went out of my lungs, and I fought to keep from throwing up.

Whitney said, "That's enough of that. Do it again and you'll find yourself in front of a board of inquiry."

"He's lying," Turner said. "He knows where she is."

Whitney pulled up another chair and sat close, his knee touching mine, a classic interrogation tactic. "I'm sorry about Special Agent Turner hitting you. If you'd like to file a formal complaint, I will handle it personally after we get through this other part."

"What is this, a really screwed-up version of the FBI's good cop/ bad cop? Cut me loose and I won't say anything. But you keep me bound up much longer and you're going to find your asses in prison for kidnap and torture. I haven't done anything wrong, nothing to deserve this type of treatment."

Turner said, "You weren't kidnapped. You're being detained pending arrest."

"What? Are you two smoking crack? I haven't—"

Whitney said, "Cut him loose. I'm done with all of this. It's not working anyway. Cut him loose."

"With all due respect, sir, I don't think that's a good idea."

"Do it. I don't think he knows where she is. And now I don't think he's a part of it either."

"You can tell just like that?"

"I said cut him loose. This was a stupid move, and I should never have gone along with it."

Turner stepped behind the chair, opened a knife, and cut the zip ties. I rubbed my wrists and noticed they'd taken my duty weapon. "My gun, I want it back."

Whitney nodded. Turner shook his head, pulled it from the waistband at the small of his back. He opened the cylinder, kicked out the bullets, closed it, and handed it to me. He kept the bullets. I took the gun, extended my hand, and waited. He hesitated and then gave me the ammunition. I reloaded and holstered. "I'm just as worried about her as you are."

"When's the last time you saw her?" Whitney asked.

"Out in front of Lucy's on Long Beach Boulevard about four hours ago."

Whitney looked up at Turner.

"What?" I asked.

Whitney said, "That's when we lost her."

"What are you talking about? Are you following Chelsea? Why? What did you mean by you didn't think I was involved? Involved in what?"

Turner said, "That's on a need-to-know basis, and, friend, you don't have a need to know."

I looked at Whitney. "You two buffoons crashed into my truck, tied me up, and brought me to this sleazebag motel." I looked around at the broken-down and scarred furniture, the tired and worn carpeting. "Now you're saying I don't have a need to know?" I shifted my gaze to Turner. "And for the record, I'm not your friend."

Whitney stood, turned his back, and moved a couple steps away in the small motel room. He put his hands on his hips and took a deep breath. "We made a mistake and then compounded it." He couldn't face me while admitting guilt. He continued, "It's time to contain this as best we can. I'm afraid we're all going to be in trouble on this one." He turned. "I'm going to trust you and tell you what's going on."

"Tell me what? What did you two do?"

Turner said, "Not all of it. Don't tell him all of it."

"Shut up." Whitney turned back to me. "It's not what we've done. It's what Chelsea's done."

"She hasn't done a damn thing wrong. The only thing she did was save my life two years ago by ramming her car through the wall. And you guys crucified her for it. Sent her to Bismarck on a midnight transfer when she should've been given a medal."

Whitney stepped back and sat in the chair. "I don't disagree with you, Deputy Johnson, but we've lost her and we need to find her as fast as we can, so I'm going to trust you."

Turner said, "I'm telling you, don't do this, sir."

Whitney shook his head. "I said, shut up."

I asked, "What is it you think Chelsea's done?"

CHAPTER FIFTY-SIX

WHITNEY IGNORED MY question and asked, "What did she tell you about what happened in North Dakota?"

Turner, more contemptuous now, said, "We know about you and Chelsea, so don't try and pretend she didn't tell you during your pillow talk."

Whitney scowled at him.

I directed my answer to Whitney, ignoring Turner or I'd lose it and end up pistol-whipping him. I thought about doing it anyway. He couldn't report it, not after what he had just done to me. "She told me an agent by the name of Mac got sideways with an informant that he used on a dope deal. Mac was supposed to pay this informant—I think his name was Beals—a million-dollar commission on a ten-million-dollar asset forfeiture. This Mac held back 200k. So when the informant got his 1099, he saw the discrepancy and called to blow the whistle on Mac. How am I doing?"

"You have a good memory, Deputy," Whitney said. "Keep going."

"Is that all correct? Is that the way it happened?"

"Keep going."

She'd been emotional when she'd told me, her face resting on my chest as she cried warm tears that wet my skin. I didn't tell them that part. They didn't have a need to know. "She said she took the call as the Officer of the Day and went to alert Mac of the impending disaster. Her thinking was that if Mac gave the money back before anyone discovered the crime, he might at least avoid some jail time. Anyway, she told him and left. He was really drunk. When she got down to the car, she realized she'd made a mistake and went back, but it was too late. Mac had shot himself. She felt terrible about what happened and blamed herself." I swallowed hard, afraid of what Whitney would say next and cringed a little when he spoke.

"You have everything correct except the numbers—they're reversed. Agent MacDonald paid the informant two hundred thousand and skimmed the other eight hundred for himself."

I let that sink in and tried to make it work. "That can't be all of it. Give me the rest," I said, as my jaw tightened.

Turner interjected. "The money's missing. And she's in violation now for telling you. She signed a nondisclosure agreement regarding our internal investigation into the matter."

"If the money is missing," I said, "it doesn't mean a thing. Mac was a Special Agent for the FBI. He'd know how and where to hide it, how to launder it." I ignored the part about the nondisclosure agreement; that wasn't a criminal violation. She could deal with a black mark in her file, but not prison.

Whitney stared at me, his eyes old and bleary.

"Come on," I said. "You can't possibly think she took the money? You know her. She's very good at her job. One of the best I've seen and . . . she . . . she saved my life. Put her whole career at risk doing it. Does that sound like a thief with a skewed moral compass? No, sir." I shook my head. "You're wrong about her. Did you pull her in and ask her? I'm sure she can clear it all up if you'd just give her a chance and ask her."

"I know how you must feel," Whitney said. "But here's the rest of it. Under the circumstances, the Bureau decided to transfer her out for the betterment of the Bureau and everyone involved."

"She told me that, too, said they tossed her a bone to keep her quiet. The fact that you gave her a nondisclosure backs that up. She said the press never found out about it."

Whitney held up his hand. "Wait, just listen to me. We jumped the gun transferring her. The forensics came back on the shooting of MacDonald."

I jumped up and paced. "No. No. No. She didn't shoot MacDonald. For sure you got that part all wrong."

"Please sit. I never said she shot MacDonald."

I paced a few more times and then sat.

Whitney spoke, calm and controlled. "The TOD—the time of death—does not match her statement as far as how it went down. She said she heard the shot and went right back in and found him with no time lapse in between."

"How long?" I asked, too loud and with contempt.

"Close to four hours."

I leaned over and put my face in my hands. Twenty minutes, thirty minutes, even an hour and a half could be within the margin of error for the TOD, but four hours? That gave her plenty of time to hide—

I suddenly sat back in the chair, my mouth sagging open.

"What?" Whitney asked. "You just thought of something important. What is it?"

"Nothing. Nothing at all. I'm just trying to rectify every part of this in my mind."

But that was a lie. I'd just remembered what she'd said not hours earlier: "We don't ever have to come back. Just you and me, white sand beaches and piña coladas forever." She wanted to go to the

Grand Caymans, a place well known for keeping offshore money hidden from the US Government.

Whitney said, "The cause of death was also in question. The angle of the entry wound wasn't normal for most suicides. A very low percentage for them, anyway." He shrugged. "Which doesn't make a big difference, not in and of itself."

I didn't know what to say.

I swallowed hard. "Okay. Then I'm still missing something here. Why am I here if you know all of this?" My mind came up to speed just as I said it and I answered the question myself in a whisper. "She's working Bank Robbery. You think that if she were already dirty in Dakota . . . that . . . that she's taken this opportunity to seize money to . . . to keep recovered bank money from robberies. That's why you were following her. Oh my God, that's why you asked to have our team folded in with yours. But . . . but that still doesn't make any sense; you didn't bring me into it to watch her. So there wouldn't be any reason to . . ." I looked at Whitney for him to help in my confusion.

He waited for me to work it out all on my own. Only I couldn't. The answer floated in the back of my brain, refusing to come forward. Refusing to believe the truth.

Whitney whispered, "Sergeant Ned Kiefer from your Internal Affairs was a plant, and now he's dead."

CHAPTER FIFTY-SEVEN

Sergeant?

Ned? Ned was a sergeant?

"Ned was a sergeant with Internal Affairs? What are you talking about? You mean Ned was—"

Turner leaned against the dresser with his arms crossed. "As it turns out, Ned Kiefer was a poor choice. He had too many personal problems that got in the way of doing his job."

"I don't believe you. He would've told me. He would've told—" Then I remembered my first undercover assignment, the number one rule: "Tell no one."

I'd violated that rule and it almost killed me. When I made that terrible mistake, Chelsea had come to my rescue and saved me. Now with the Gadd investigation I'd again been thrust into a similar situation. Only this time I was one of the people on the inside who didn't know the game and wasn't told the rules. Ned had not violated the first rule, he'd not told his best friend what was going on. The consummate professional. The sadness that he didn't trust me took hold and dragged me down further.

Had it contributed to his death? If he had told me, would it have made a difference? Would things have changed going through that door?

After my mind put all the pieces together, I looked at Whitney. "There's only one reason you'd put an undercover on the team. You thought Chelsea was somehow linked to the bank robbers. Is that right? Am I right?" I raised my voice. "You think she's aligned herself with that asshole, Gadd? You're out of your ever lovin' mind."

Whitney didn't verbally answer; he didn't have to. I read it in his eyes. I shot a hand out and grabbed a handful of his dress shirt and tie. "So that means . . . that means, because Chelsea and I were involved on a personal level, you didn't know whether or not I had agreed to come into her little game. Is that it? That's it, isn't it? That's why it was appropriate to use our department's Internal Affairs division. Right?"

Turner tried to intervene and grabbed onto me. Whitney held up his hand and stopped him. Turner let go.

I let go of Whitney. I said, "No, that's not enough to prove a thing. You have to have more. You have to have something that implicates her with Gadd. It can't just be supposition, or circumstantial. You have to have something solid. What is it? Wait. Let me guess, you're up on her phone and you have conversation. Right? Is that it?"

Turner looked at Whitney and said, "This bonehead is too smart for his own good."

"What is it? What do you have? What did she say?"

Whitney stood and straightened his tie. "We didn't have enough for the tap."

"So a pin register then?" I said. "You trapped and traced all of the phone numbers she used coming in and going out. So what? So she called Gadd's phone number. That doesn't mean a damn thing. Anybody could've answered. You don't know for sure. For all you know, she could have an informant inside his crew."

Turner said, "According to our policy, she would have had to notify her supervisor if she did and also have an informant file with a registered number. She made no such notification and there isn't a file or number."

"That's a policy violation. That doesn't rise to the level of a criminal conspiracy that would get a judge to agree to a pin register."

Whitney said nothing.

I said, "That ain't shit. That could mean anything and you know it."

Whitney shook his head. "Don't be a fool. You're looking at this as someone emotionally involved and not thinking objectively. Look at the totality of the circumstances."

"There's not enough. There's not."

Whitney said to Turner, "Show him."

I looked at Turner. "Yeah, show me." But I really didn't want to see what they had. I loved her too much. I'd lost Ned. Now they wanted me to think I'd lost Chelsea, too.

Turner went over to the scarred bureau, reached into a black nylon field case, and pulled out a manila file folder. He came over and handed it to me. My hands quivered as I opened the file to 8"x10" black-and-white photos.

Turner said, "Don't feel too bad, she's made fools out of all of us as well."

From a distance, the photo depicted a large black man with his back to the camera, who could or could not have been the Darkman. He leaned into a maroon Crown Victoria handing over a package, a folded paper bag in the size and shape that could've been a stack of US currency. I recognized the location—the parking lot of Roscoe's Chicken and Waffles.

I also recognized Chelsea as the driver of the Crown Vic.

My stomach turned sick. How could she do it?

I thumbed through the other photos looking for one that confirmed the guy as the Darkman and didn't find it. "Who's the dude?"

Turner jumped forward, pointed his finger, and raised his voice. "That's Gadd and you damn well know it. That happened right after one of the bank jobs four weeks ago, before you came into this thing. Before we put your team on him."

"Before you put Ned on her, you mean." I closed the file and handed it back. "I can't confirm that it's Gadd, not by those. Whoever took these really screwed up and ought to be fired."

Turner yelled, "I took them. It was the best I could get. It was almost like the dude knew someone was on him."

"If you were involved, I bet he did."

He let the file drop and clenched his fists.

Whitney yelled, "Stop it, the both of you!"

He came over to me. "This thing has gone off the rails. We're asking you nice to help us get it back on track."

"Not only no, but hell no." I headed for the door.

Whitney said, "Where are you going?"

"You want me to wear a wire to trap Chelsea. I won't do it. Make your case any way you want, but not with me. I'm going to prove you two assholes are wrong."

"It wouldn't be prudent to do that alone, Deputy Johnson. Let us go with you."

At the motel room door, I looked back at them. "Not a chance, pal." I stepped back over to the file on the floor and grabbed one of the photos with Chelsea and Gadd. I folded it twice into a square and stuck it in my back pocket. I slammed the door on my way out and took off running.

And kept running.

After fifteen minutes of weaving in and out for five blocks, I got my bearings. They'd driven me into the city of Compton off of Rosecrans. I found a pay phone and paged Chelsea once more but this time with a "911. 911. 911."

I stepped back into the shadows and waited, watching the street. No way did I want members from the Sheriff's Department or the FBI following along.

I checked my watch. Checked it again. At eleven minutes the pay phone rang. I stepped back into the halo of illumination cast by the streetlight, visibly vulnerable for far too long, and jerked up the phone. "Chelsea?"

"Bruno, where are you?"

"What happened? You were supposed to follow Ollie. Never mind, come pick me up. I'll be at the corner of Spring and Elm in Compton. Hurry." I hung up so she couldn't object. I stepped back into the shadows one more time and watched. They would have at least tried to follow me from the motel. I know I would've. I turned and jumped the fence heading south through the yards, crossing more streets. The black-and-white photos of Chelsea with Gadd wouldn't leave me alone and scraped on my soul like fingernails on a chalkboard. Not Gadd, Jesus, not with Gadd.

I cut over to Spring Street, traveled west through the alley and back into the yards. Without a helicopter, they wouldn't know that I'd left the shadows by the phone, if they'd even been with me up to that point. I zigzagged a few more times until I came out onto Elm just as a white Toyota Celica pulled up and shut off its lights. I tried to peer in through the tinted glass. The driver's window came down. I put my hand on my gun butt.

"Bruno, quit messing around and get in."

Chelsea.

I ran around and got in. She took off.

CHAPTER FIFTY-EIGHT

AFTER TWO LONG blocks, she pulled over and stopped. She leaned over for a kiss. I wanted that kiss and put everything else aside, closed my eyes and kissed her like I'd never kissed her before. Kissed her like it would be the last. I wound my fingers in her hair and pulled her in.

She tasted of warm, wet peppermint. And for a second, the briefest of moments, I didn't care if she did do what they accused her of, I'd still follow her to the dark side of the moon.

She chuffed when we broke, but she held on to my head looking into my eyes. "Well, hello, cowboy, where have you been all of my life?"

After all that had happened, holding her felt like holding a live grenade and not being able to let go.

Her eyes were alive, ready to handle anything that came along. Ready to drive a car through a wall to get to me. I didn't see any deception, or any form of the evil Whitney and his flunky had described. They were out of their minds.

"Come on," I said, "let's go."

"All right. But why are you out here on foot? Where's your car? Is Gadd around here someplace?"

"Let's move. But don't go up to Rosecrans; stay down here in the side streets. Keep heading west."

She took off again driving fifty in a twenty-five. "What's going on, Bruno?"

I said, "Tell me what happened with Ollie."

Chelsea took her eyes from the road and looked at me. "I'm not sure I like your tone. What's going on?"

"Tell me your side of the story."

She yanked the steering wheel, took us over to the curb, and stopped with her foot on the brake. "Talk to me. My side of the story? What are you trying to say?"

"Ollie's dead. Gadd stabbed her in the back with an ice pick."

To give suspects information during an interrogation, to expose your hand, was taboo, but this was Chelsea, not a suspect.

"Ah, Bruno, I'm so sorry." She reached over and gripped my hand. "I know how much you liked her."

"What happened?" I asked.

Chelsea pulled away from me. "I lost her. Ollie took off before Wicks and his team came up on her. I tried to follow her, but she knew what she was doing. She did counter surveillance. Right at the end I said screw it and didn't care if she saw me. And she still lost me. I tried. I really did. I guess I should've tried harder. I'm so sorry."

"Why didn't you answer all those pages I sent you?"

"What's with the third degree? What's eating at you?"

I said nothing.

"Okay," she said. "I was trying to find her, and by the time I found a phone to call you back, you were already gone. What is this, an interrogation? Do you think I did something wrong?"

"No, I don't."

She hesitated a long time staring at me, searching for the truth in my expression.

"Let's go," I said.

"Where to?"

"To get Gadd."

She smiled. "You know where he is?"

I waved my hand. "Go on, head to 213th Street and Avalon in Carson."

She took off as my mind went back over her responses, her reactions to the information I'd given her. Maybe Whitney was right, maybe I was too close to look at this thing objectively.

She didn't know the way and asked several times for directions. Otherwise, neither of us spoke.

In the dead of night, three o'clock in the morning, nothing moved in the predawn silence.

"Right there. Pull up and stop right there."

She did, stopping under the deep shadow of a huge tree. She shut off the headlights. "Which one is it?"

I pointed. "That one right there, first floor, third from this end. We should call in for backup."

"Why? You and I can handle Gadd. What's with you? Come on, let's go get this son of a bitch." She got out and eased her door closed so it clicked shut. I waited and watched her. She bent down, looked in through the driver's window, and waved for me to follow.

I got out and eased my door closed. I came around to her side and stopped.

She pulled her gun. "Well, come on, big man, what are we waiting for?"

I reached in my back pocket and took out the folded photo of her and Gadd and held it out, just a white folded square.

"What's that?" The light in her smile went out.

And then I knew for sure.

I tried to hand it to her. She wouldn't take it. Her eyes turned sad, her shoulders sagged, her voice barely a whisper. "How much do they know?"

I let the folded photo drop to the ground and shook my head. "All of it."

"Bruno, you don't know what it was like working in that hellhole. All that boring, mundane bullshit, day after day. I couldn't take it. I was a rising star out here and working big cases, interesting cases. Cases that mattered, that made a difference. Then they go and banish me for no good reason. I didn't deserve that. You know what happened, you were there. Do you think I deserved that?" She spoke waving her gun around for emphasis, forgetting her gun safety training. Why not? She'd forgotten the meaning of integrity and honor and truth.

I said nothing and stared at her. Who was this person I was so attracted to? How could I have been so wrong about her? But I hadn't been wrong. The system ground her up and spit her out. It could do it to anyone. At that moment the system had me torn in three different directions. Even so, I could still see the correct path.

She read my thoughts. She pointed her gun toward the apartment. "They don't have shit on me if Gadd can't testify. You understand me, Bruno? We can fix this right here and now. Then we can take a long-deserved vacation."

I said nothing. A large hole opened up in my chest and grew larger by the second, making it harder to breathe.

"Bruno, Gadd killed Ned."

The sadness in me shifted to anger. "Don't you dare bring his name into this." She'd tried to tarnish his good name, use it as a distraction, an excuse for what she'd done. No way did she know who pulled the trigger, D'Arcy or Gadd. But Gadd had been responsible for the whole mess so it didn't matter.

She was about to say something else and shut her mouth. Then she said, "Bruno, please? Please, you owe me."

I froze. All the air left me. I wanted to wilt to the ground. I did owe her. No truer statement had ever been uttered to me. I owed her my life.

I'd been teetering on the fence about what to do with her until she said that. I reached out and took her left hand, pulled her into me, and hugged her, my face buried in her hair. She started to cry. Her whole body shook. She tried to pull away. I held on tight.

"Bruno"—her voice was muffled against my chest—"Come with me. Please, I'm begging you."

I swallowed the large lump that was growing in my throat. "I don't think I could take the cold where you're going."

"I'm not going to prison. I won't go." Her body convulsed as she sobbed. "Bruno?" With her right hand she stuck her gun in my ribs hard enough to hurt.

I closed my eyes and thought of Olivia.

"Bruno?" she said a little louder.

I held on tight and said, "Run. That's all you got left. Run." I let her go.

She took a step back, wiped tears from her cheeks and nose. "Okay. Okay. But you have to promise me you won't be the one to come after me. I couldn't take it if you showed up one day and—"

"Chelsea, run."

She nodded, holstered her gun. She got in her car, started it up, and took off without turning on the headlights.

I watched her go until she turned a corner at the first block. Once she was out of sight, I questioned whether I'd made the right choice.

I drew my gun and went after Gadd.

CHAPTER FIFTY-NINE

THE SEMI-DERELICT APARTMENT complex, the Catalina Arms, looked one step away from condemnation. At least a third of the windows sported plywood with gang graffiti. Some of the doors stood ajar, those apartments dark and vacant, a perfect hidey-hole for a slimy crook of Gadd's ilk. The woman from the Harbor Town bar Gadd picked up and brought back there had looked better heeled than having been reduced to living in a hovel like the Catalina. Splotches in the sea-green stucco made the building look diseased.

A sliver of dim yellow light peeked out from the crack in the curtains of number 17. I didn't dare stick my nose up to the window to see inside for fear of getting it shot off. I carefully put my hand on the doorknob and turned. It wasn't locked. I pushed the door open an inch and stopped just before it cracked open to the light inside. I stepped back out of the "window of death," my gun up and pointed. With my foot I slowly eased the door open, holding my breath, waiting for the gunfire.

I smelled burnt gunpowder.

The door continued to open more and more, exposing the small living room a little at a time: a large chair, an end table, a love seat, and a long-necked lamp with a cheap shade, the only light for the entire apartment. Too little light that cast too many shadows. On the floor next to the lamp lay a .380 automatic pistol with the slide locked open, which meant it was empty.

With the door open at the halfway point, I froze. Over on the couch sat Leroy Gadd. I'd recognize him anywhere. He looked right at me, his eyes tented, half-open. He wore pants and a sling-shot tee shirt. A bloody Kotex taped to his shoulder wept blood down his chest.

He held a blue-steel .38 pistol in his hand, loose, about to drop to the floor. I'd waited too many years for this. Since that night I'd seen him in the dark alley, I'd dreamt and hoped that I'd catch him with a gun in his hand. And here he sat, my dream come true.

I pointed my gun and stepped inside. "Sheriff's Department. Sheriff's Department. Drop it. Drop it now, Gadd."

His hand didn't move. A grin crept across his ugly face, exposing bloody white teeth.

"I give up, Deputy Dog. Call me an ambulance. I need to get ta hospital. I'm bad hurt." He coughed; a little blood rolled out of the corner of his mouth. "That dumb fat bitch went and stabbed me with an ice pick when I wasn't lookin'."

I moved in closer, my total focus on him and that gun. If it moved an inch, I'd gun him. *Just move it an inch. Come on, move it.*

Wicks' voice rose up in my ear. "You pussy, shoot. Shoot. There aren't any witnesses. This is the man who killed your best friend, Ned. Bruno, shoot him. He's got a gun in his hand. Shoot. Give him a little bit of that blood and bone."

"Hey, I know you," Gadd said. "Where do I know you from?"

"I said drop the gun. Do it now."

He let it slip from his fingers and plop on the floor. My breath caught. He'd gone and done it. I couldn't shoot him, not now. No matter how much I wanted to, I just couldn't do it in cold blood.

"It ain't loaded anyway. Crazy old peckerwood came at me with a gun that wasn't loaded. You believe that shit? I don't. Seems to me like he wanted to die."

"Put your hands up."

"Take it easy, my brother, I said I give up. Get your black ass over ta that phone on the wall and call me an ambulance. Big man, you ain't gonna shoot me, I kin see it in your eyes. You ain't got the balls for it. Now call me that ambulance." He put his hand to his side, then pulled it away to show a slime of wet blood. "Bitch stuck me good."

I moved over, went down on one knee, and recovered the .38 revolver, one with a worn black rubber grip. I took my eyes off Gadd for a quick second and looked at the gun in my hand. I thought I recognized it but couldn't place where, not right at that moment anyway. I popped open the cylinder. Empty just like he said. Not even any empty shells. Then it locked in my brain. I'd held that same gun and it wasn't all that long ago. It was ... it was in the house where Ned had been shot and killed.

I jumped back, my head whipping around.

Over by the large chair, and half-concealed by the love seat, lay a body facedown.

"Nooo. You son of a bitch, nooo." I took the two long steps over to Sergeant Coffman. I eased him over onto his back. His arm flopped over, exposing his faded Marine Corps tattoo.

Tears filled my eyes and I choked on the lump that rose up in my throat. "Why did you come here all alone, old man? Why?"

Multiple bullet holes covered the front of his shirt without much blood. His mouth hung open. His eyes stared back at me as if trying to impart the obvious truth.

"Tolt ya," Gadd said, "that crazy ol' bastard came at me with a gun with no bullets in it. It's still self-defense, loaded or not. I know that much. You cain't hang that one on me, no sir, you cain't."

I screamed, turned, and ran to the couch. I put my knee in his chest and pistol-whipped him again and again.

He tried to put his hands up to fend me off, but he was too weak. "Hey, hey, nigga, stop. Stop."

I pulled back and stuck my gun in his mouth. "Shut up. You hear me? Shut up or I swear to God I'll pull this trigger."

We were both breathing hard. He didn't move. The moment hung long and fat. The rage gradually subsided. I pulled my gun out of his mouth. He stared at me with crazed eyes filled with fear. He knew how close I'd come to pulling the trigger.

I didn't know what to do. I was torn. I needed to call it in, have dispatch send a couple of patrol cars to take over the scene.

But now Gadd had shot my patrol sergeant. Killed him just like he did Ned. At what point did justice step in and right those wrongs?

Gadd saw my weakness as it consumed me. I couldn't shoot him in cold blood, or I already would have. That terrible, ugly grin worked its way across his face. He raised his hand and flipped me off.

I nodded. "Oh, is that right?"

He grinned and said nothing. I went to the phone on the wall and dialed.

* * *

Less than an hour later I stood next to Coffman's truck in the rear parking lot of the defunct Sears on Long Beach Boulevard in Lynwood as two sets of headlights pulled in and panned across me. I held up my empty hands. The headlights approached to within twenty feet and stopped. I picked up the tails of my shirt to expose my waistband and slowly turned all the way around.

The four doors on both cars opened at the same time. The headlights kept me from seeing them. I walked closer.

"Stop," the voice said.

I held up my arm to shield my eyes. "Turn off the lights."

The lights went off. Shadows danced in my vision as my eyes adjusted.

Out of the four gang members, three held guns on me. The leader said, "Baldy here says you're a cop. He recognizes you. Says you beat his ass over some rock."

"If I beat his ass it was because he had it coming. Ask him if that isn't true."

"So, you are a cop?"

"That's right. Are you Scab?"

"Depends, is this some kinda weird setup? You trying to entrap me?"

"No."

"Prove it."

I turned to walk back to the truck.

"Hold it."

I froze, held up my hands. "You're just going to have to trust me." My eyes adjusted to the dark. I continued to the truck and reached for the tarp.

"Hold it." I froze again.

"Baldy, check it."

One of them moved over and looked in the truck bed. "He's got some mayate in here all taped up."

Scab came over and peered in. "Who is it?"

"It's the guy who killed your sister and your two nephews four years ago." In the truck bed, Gadd tried to scream through the duct tape. It came out more of a moan.

Scab's eyes narrowed and turned hard. He said, "How do you know he did it?"

"Because that night four years ago I saw him come out into the alley from behind your sister's house. I've been looking for him ever since."

His mouth shifted to a straight line and his jaw muscle knotted. "You swear ta God this ain't some kinda trick?"

"You have my word. Ask Baldy if my word on the street is good."

Baldy nodded.

Scab asked, "Why are you doing this? What do you want? You want the hundred thou I put out on the street for this puto? Is that it?"

"I want nothing in return."

He stepped forward and offered his hand. "Then I will owe you a great debt."

I took his hand and shook. He nodded to his men. They jumped in the back of the truck, lifted Gadd out, moaning and struggling, and dragged him over to their cars. The whole time Scab stared at me. Once loaded, they mounted their cars and drove off into the coming dawn.

CHAPTER SIXTY

THREE DAYS LATER, on the way to Ned's funeral, I steered the black-and-white patrol car in the wrong direction. I headed south deeper into the ghetto rather than east into Downey to the church and cemetery where they would lay my friend to rest. I'd allowed plenty of time to get there. I wore my best class-A uniform, the creases razor sharp, the leather on my Sam Brown and shoes polished to a bright sheen. The star on my chest gleamed and winked when it caught the light.

Clouds filled the sky, and for the first time in two years the dry air smelled of ozone. Off in the distance the summer storm let loose with a peal of thunder.

The swelling in my face had started to go down, but there still remained a faint throb that matched my heartbeat. A constant reminder of the fight with JB in my front yard and of what had happened at 11431 Willowbrook and also on Avalon Avenue.

I pulled to the curb and parked in front of the shop. I got out and looked around. Somehow this place where I'd grown up, South Central Los Angeles, looked different now. I opened the glass door painted over in black and, as I entered, immediately started unbuttoning my uniform shirt. Jacko Marx, the shop owner, a skinny guy with a ponytail and pierced ear and acne-cratered face, locked the door behind me. I'd called ahead, told him I didn't want anyone else present, that this was deeply personal. He'd said he understood.

He went over to the chair mounted in the floor and stood ready. I carefully took my uniform shirt off, put it on a hanger, and hung it on the coat tree. Without a word, I sat down in the chair in front of Jacko.

He said, "You sure about this?"

"I'm sure."

"Plain, no frills? Right? That's what you want?"

"Yes," I said. "All I want are the letters 'BMF.'"

AUTHOR'S NOTE

One of the most emotional times in my career had nothing to do with the death and mayhem I witnessed while working the street. All the murder victims, the abused children, the carnage left in the wake of car accidents, all of these life-changing incidents that created unwanted memories and nightmares for everyone involved, their lives ruined forever. No, the most emotional incident in my career came in the form of a phone call late one night, a phone call from a good friend who told me "Ned" had been killed during the service of a search warrant. Shot by a fifteen-year-old kid, a rock coke dealer. Ned was struck in the vest by the first bullet, which spun him around; he took the second bullet to the back of the head. I don't mention Ned's real name in this Author's Note, because I in no way want to exploit his death.

Even though I was not present with Ned when he died, the phone call was devastating.

In writing this novel, I continually heard Ned's voice, his words filling in the scene all on their own. Each morning when I sit down to write, I first go back twenty pages and edit forward before I start anew. Several times during the writing of this novel, I started back on those twenty pages and found Ned's real name in the place of

Ned. In writing the day before, I'd been so engrossed in the character of Ned, I'd inadvertently replaced the name.

In the Bruno Johnson novels, Bruno never swears. He does one time in this book when he refers to how much he loved Ned.

In real life, I attended Ned's funeral. Thousands of cops came from all over the nation to pay their respects. Many more times the number of people that filled the packed church stood outside in a group shoulder to shoulder, silent, their heads bowed.

Ned's untimely and senseless death happened early in my career, and later on, even though other fellow cops—some I knew, most I didn't—died in the line of duty, I never again attended another cop's funeral.

By far the most difficult chapter I have ever written was the one where Ned, dies.

Ned used to make me laugh like no one else.

* * *

During my tenure on an FBI-sponsored violent crimes team, we did go after a husband-wife team who corrupted young boys, fed them propaganda, and cajoled them into robbing banks. In one incident, my team witnessed one of these bank robberies committed by kids, teens. We took them down by pulling our cars in on three sides of their car, boxing them in. Afterward, while we had them sitting handcuffed on the curb, I spoke with one of these newly minted delinquents. He had a full-ride scholarship to a big college for basketball. He asked me when we would be letting him go because he had to get home for a game. The felony conviction ruined his chances of escaping his life in the ghetto.

* * *

My favorite brother, Van, followed me into law enforcement and followed a very similar career path. While working on a violent crimes team, his team tracked a murderer into an adjoining state, Arizona. The suspect spooked before my brother's team could close the net around him. The armed and dangerous suspect fled. He would have escaped had Van not used bold and unflinching initiative. He rammed the suspect's car broadside with his truck. The moment before Van's truck slammed into the side of the suspect's car, the suspect fired one shot, trying to kill my brother. This bullet, fired out of hate, pierced the windshield, narrowly missing Van. For his valiant efforts, the Sheriff's Department awarded him the Medal of Valor.